BREAKTHROUGH

BREAKTHROUGH

Trevor Stubbs

The Listening People
15 Cleeve Grove
Keynsham,
Bristol, BS31 2HF

Email: TLPpress@yahoo.com
Web: www.thelisteningpeople.co.uk

ISBN 978-1-915288-13-4
British Library Cataloguing in Publication Data.
A catalogue record for this book is available from the British Library.

For my aunt, Valerie Stead, who spent her life supporting young people near and far through her long service to the Guide movement, and the large family God had given her to care for.

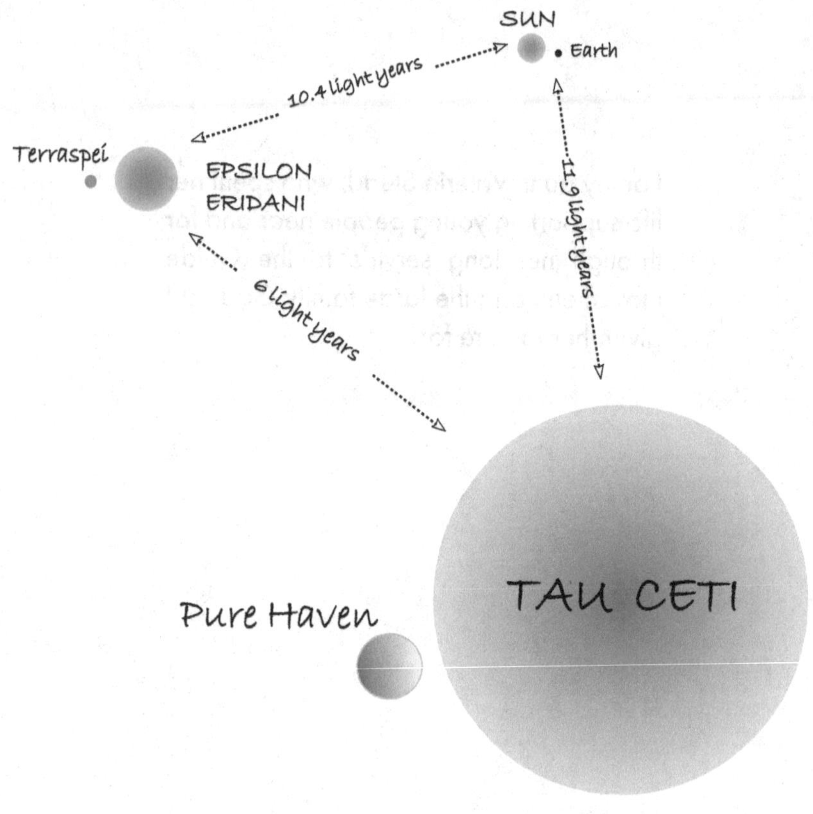

The human homelands
in 2330

Who's Who

On Pure Haven:

Jonah Williams. Husband of Dorcas and father of Raph, Charity and Luke.

Dorcas Williams. Wife of Jonah and mother of Raph, Charity and Luke.

Raphael (Raph) Williams (17 Earth years). Son of Jonah and Dorcas and brother to Charity and Luke.

Charity Suzanna Williams (16 EY). Daughter of Jonah and Dorcas.

Luke Williams (12). Son of Jonah and Dorcas.

Zac (17). Friend of Raph and Nathan.

Nathan Rogerson (21). Charity's betrothed.

Leah Donaldson (16). Charity's friend and classmate.

Betty Jenkins (16). Charity's friend and classmate.

On Terraspei:

Danny Thatcher (Grandpops) (94 EY). Grandfather of Mary Fisher and Great-grandparent to her children. Widower of Natasha.

Peter Fisher. Husband of Mary and father of Elle, Squirt, Tammy and Benny. A master builder.

Mary Fisher. Wife of Peter and mother of Elle, Squirt, Tammy and Benny.

Elle Fisher (16 EY). Daughter of Peter and Mary, sister of Squirt, Tammy and Benny.

Squirt Fisher (12 EY). Son of Peter and Mary, brother of Elle, Tammy and Benny.

Tammy Fisher (8 EY). Daughter of Peter and Mary, sister of Elle,

Squirt and Benny.

Benny Fisher (6 EY). Son of Peter and Mary, brother of Elle, Squirt and Tammy.

Anna (16 EY). Elle's friend and classmate.

Mrs Bannister. Elle and Anna's childcare teacher.

Mrs. Patel. Elle and Anna's science teacher.

On Earth:

Dean Brooks. Husband of Rose and father of Sam and Min.

Rose Brooks. Wife of Dean and mother of Sam and Min.

Sam Brooks (16) Son of Dean and Rose and brother of Min.

Min Brooks (14). Sister of Sam.

Tom Schulz (16). Sam's online friend living in Warwick, Australia.

Amy Huck (16). Sam's classmate and friend.

Tanya Payne (16). Sam's science partner at Stanton Wick.

Mr. Gilbert. Headteacher of Stanton Wick.

Miss Brankhurst. Science teacher at Stanton Wick.

On Space-Village Talbot:

Dave McPherson. Husband of Faith and father of Joseph and Beth.

Faith McPherson. Wife of Dave and mother of Joseph and Beth.

Joseph McPherson (16). Son of Dave and Faith and brother of Beth.

Beth McPherson (12). Daughter of Faith and Dave. Sister of Joseph.

Fran Davies (16). Joseph's friend and classmate.

Commander Pritchard. Senior commander of Space-Village Talbot.

Matt. The chief of communications aboard Space-Village Talbot.

Izzy. Comms technician.

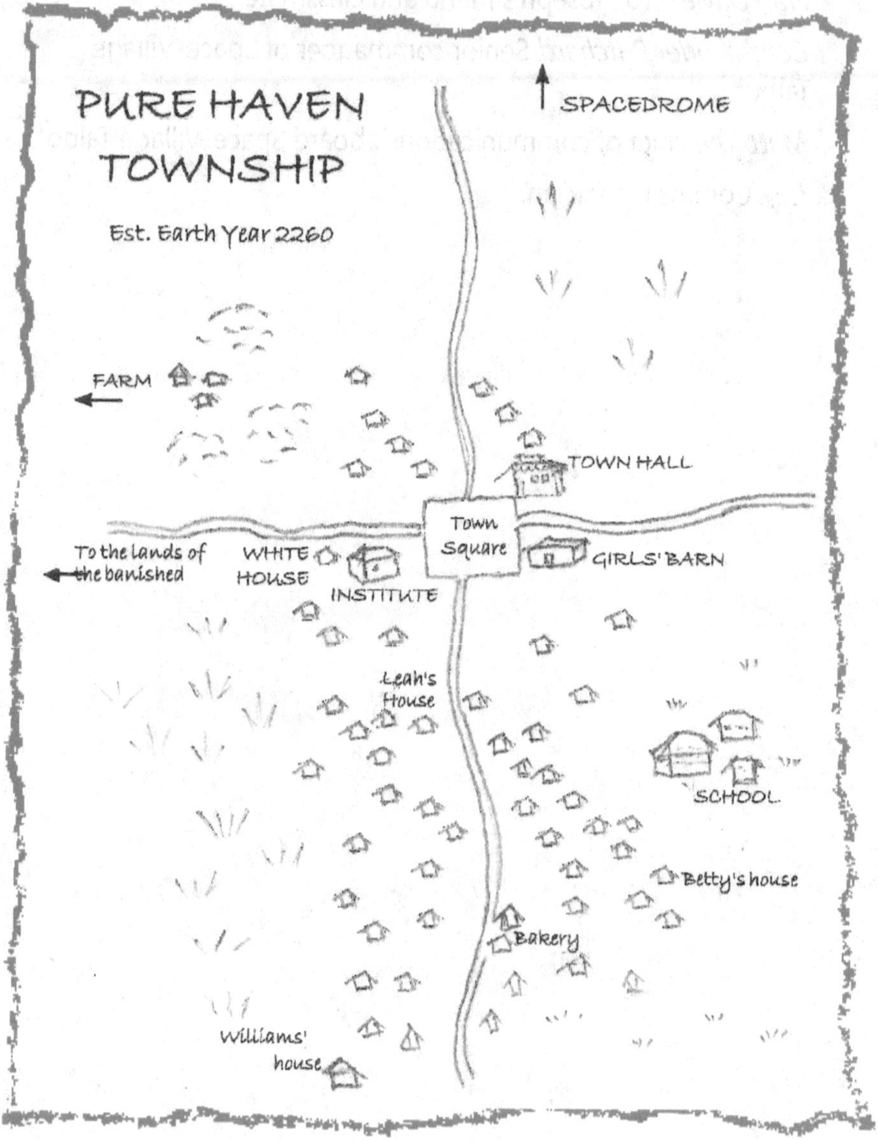

PURE HAVEN TOWNSHIP
Est. Earth Year 2260
SPACEDROME
FARM
TOWN HALL
Town Square
To the lands of the banished
WHITE HOUSE
INSTITUTE
GIRLS' BARN
Leah's House
SCHOOL
Betty's house
Bakery
Williams' house

1

Pure Haven. Earth date: 2330

Charity Williams looked up at the new sign outside her school. It read, 'Pure Haven School'. She thought the name was lame and lacked imagination. "And, anyway," she told herself, "it's a lie. Our planet is not a haven, and it's certainly not pure... Well, the human inhabitants aren't."

The remarkable thing about the planet 'Tau Ceti m' was that it circled its sun almost exactly once every two Earth years with a day of twenty-two hours and twenty minutes. This fact made it possible for the inhabitants arriving on space-villages to keep to the rhythms of their earthly ancestry. At 1.2 times the size of Earth, 'm' was almost perfect. Tilted on its axis, the temperate zones enjoyed seasons where carbon-based life had advanced to provide a covering of green vegetation, although animal life was limited to minibeasts and creatures that lived in the seas and lakes. The planet had not yet spawned or hosted any intelligent beings – not until the first arrivals from Earth some sixty years before. These migrants had dubbed the planet 'Pure Haven'.

Sixteen-year-old Charity was a product of the fourth generation of human settlers. Although the colony got by, it hadn't grown as had been planned. Recently, there had been an unexplained spate of child mortality, as if the children just lacked the will to live. But these setbacks had not dimmed the Ruling Council's determination to keep to their interpretation of strict traditional values.

Charity sat upright at her family dinner table. At first glance, there was nothing about her that might merit her mother's description of

1

her as deep, dark and dangerous. Like all the girls her age on Pure Haven, she was primly dressed in a plain undyed shift on top of a dull-brown shirt. Her long straw-coloured hair beneath an off-white headscarf tumbled midway down her back.

Her parents' conversation was about yet another untimely death of a child who had never thrived. This wasn't a conversation that the three Williams children were expected to contribute to. But Charity was sixteen, and it just came out.

"I think one of the reasons why so many children die is that they aren't getting the right kind of food," she said. "Perhaps we need a wider variety of foodstuffs. We rely too heavily on so few crops."

Teenage brains can issue impulsive remarks that have not gone through the conscious control of the prefrontal cortex. As soon as it was out, Charity wondered why she had said it. She shouldn't have spoken.

"And what would you know about it, young lady?" said her father, crossly.

Her prefrontal cortex was still too slow. "Just seems, like, a bit obvious." Oops. *Your big mouth, Charry. Now I'm for it.*

"Are you suggesting you know more about it than the Department of Agriculture?"

The youngest, twelve-year-old Luke, smiled from ear to ear. He liked it when Charry got into trouble. It was fun watching her squirm.

"No, Dad. But the job of the people in that department is to make the crops we already have produce more. Maybe we need some fresh ideas."

Her father bristled. "When your opinion is required, it will be asked for."

Charity's heart burnt. Her brain screamed, *"Which for me, being female, will never be."* But those words stayed unspoken – the self-preservation part of her brain was at last kicking in and replaced the retort with the required simple demure expression but she saw her mother begin to cry and knew she had no way back. The situation had gone beyond an apology – even submissive body language was too late.

Mr Williams pronounced the punishment. "Go to your room and reflect on your behaviour. Leave the rest of your dinner... I will decide if you can be allowed breakfast."

Charity didn't argue; there was no point. She got up from her chair and slowly walked to the door.

"And leave your phone here. I'll not have you communicating your insubordination with your friends. If this gets out, it will be to our shame."

Charity fished out her phone and put it on the table. She hoped that her father couldn't read the surging turmoil in her head. *I hate you! I hate...* no, that wasn't really true. His problem was he was a man – he couldn't help it. It was required of him; this was how Pure Haven worked.

As she climbed the stairs, she heard her mother say, softly, "Don't be hard on her; she just–"

"Not you, too. Eat your dinner."

Charity's isolation didn't last long. There was a quiet tap on her door. She knew her elder brother would come. Raphael was two years her senior and definitely her favourite male person on the planet. She opened the door, and Raph tiptoed across the room.

"Don't tell me. I opened my mouth too wide... again."

"Yes... and no," he grinned. "Dad is unfair. What you said made perfect sense. He should listen."

"To a sixteen-year-old girl. Don't be ridiculous."

"All I know is that you're cleverer than I am... Look, Charry, I need you to help me with my maths homework."

"It's all in the books," she said, sullenly. She knew he was saying this to be kind. But he often got her to help him.

"Yeah. But where and how do I apply it?"

She sighed. He was a caring brother, and she was grateful. "What's the question?"

"How far away is our planet from Terraspei?"

"That's not difficult. *They* are supposed to be founded on the principles of equality. In the way they live, I would say, like half a universe."

"I know. But this is not a way-of-life question but a simple maths one."

"Six light-years. We all know that."

"But how? I have to show how we know."

"Raph. I'm your younger sister, and all the maths and science I know is self-taught, mostly from your books."

"I know. But where does the Sun come in?"

"The Sun? As in Earth's star? Why?"

"The teacher says we are allowed to know how far we are from the Sun. And how far Terraspei is from the Sun. It's slightly nearer – 10.4 light-years."

"Oh. So it's very basic. You should have been doing this, like, long before you were my age."

"Yeah. So the teacher says. I still don't get it."

Charity gave in. "Have you got a scrap of paper?" Paper was valuable on Haven. The paper mill had taken decades to get going; the quality was poor and the quantity strictly rationed, but her brother went to his room and came back with a bit with an unused corner.

Charity drew a triangle with two sides roughly the same length but one slightly longer than the other and the third side shorter. She marked the most pointed angle with an S, the one at the other end of the longer side with a T and the third angle with an E.

"S is the sun, T is us, Tau Ceti, and E is Epsilon Eridani, Terraspei's star. So you want to know T-E. Right?"

Raph nodded. "It's six light-years. We all know that. But I'm to prove it... and I'm not to do any drawing. It has to be just maths."

"OK. What are we allowed to know?"

Raph indicated the side S-T. "This is 10.4 light-years."

"And we're 11.9 light-years away. Good. What else do we know?"

"Nothing."

"Think again. Where's Epsilon Eridani and the Sun?"

Raph drew back the curtains. There wasn't a cloud in the sky that night and light pollution from the colony was almost zero.

Charity came to the window and they gazed at the stunning starscape.

"It's amazing, isn't it?" Charity's heart glowed at the freedom the universe seemed to promise. If she could, she would get up there.

Earth's star and Terraspei's were two of the brightest stars in the sky – everyone knew where to find them.

"I often look at Epsilon Eridani and wonder whether our great-grandparents came to the right new world," mused Raph.

"They didn't. We'd be much better off on Terraspei. But, as in everything, we didn't get to choose... We need to find the angle between the Sun and Ep from here. You could try and pretend to measure it tonight. But you already know the answer, so you can work backwards."

"It's 61.6 degrees."

"You already know that? Well done."

"The teacher told us. I didn't think it mattered."

"Of course it matters. Angles matter as much as the length of the sides. He's made it really easy for you."

"If you say so."

Charity went through the workings with him, patiently.

"You taught yourself this? You've never done anything like this in class?"

"Of course not. Girls are too busy sewing and cooking. Like I said, it's all in your books."

"I wish my teacher was more like you."

"That's nice, but don't tell Dad or anyone you lend your books to me."

"Why would I do that?"

"Just be careful."

"Like you have been this evening with your big mouth?"

She exhaled. "Like I'm going to be in future."

Later that evening, Charity was busying herself on her slate, rehearsing some trigonometrical calculations and positioning herself on Terraspei when her mum appeared. The rest of the family were in the living room, thinking that she had merely gone to the toilet. Even she had to sneak time with her daughter at times like these.

"Charry, can I come in?"

"Of course, Mum."

When she was inside, she shut the door.

"Do you remember what I have called you since you were seven?"

"Other than Charry?"

"My description of your character."

Charity smiled. "Yeah. Deep, dark and dangerous."

"Yes. Can your old mum share a bit of wisdom?"

Charity nodded. "You're not old."

"I feel it sometimes. It's just... you need to work on the dangerous bit."

"The wicked bit?"

"No. You're a good person. You're not dark like that. I wouldn't want this world to change you. Deep is good. You have to become a bit... less transparent."

"You mean 'be mysterious'."

"Precisely. That's how we women survive and even prosper, sometimes." Her mother gave her a hug. "Just hang on in there, girl." She tiptoed away, shutting the bathroom door noisily, as she passed.

Alone again and hungry, Charity sighed. Her mother was right, but was she going to have to wait all her life like *she* had with no hint of things changing for women and girls? *Hang on in there? For what? Nothing has changed in three generations. If there's a revolution about to happen, there is no sign of it. The only way I'm going to escape this planet before I die is through books or stowing away on a space-village... Or I could get banished into the wilderness by the Ruling Council. No one who is banished is ever seen again; no one knows what happens to them. At least, they don't have to put up with the rules they force on us in this town. But I know that would upset my family, and Dad would lose all his status, and probably his job.*

2

"**M**orning, Grandpops!" Elle called through her great-grandfather's door. She was already full of life at the prospect of a new day. She was going to the disability centre with her friend Anna, who was about to be fitted with a new running blade. Sports-mad Anna had been a rare victim of an accident in a careful but not completely risk-averse community. Her new blade was appealing but she was not given to excitement like Elle; most people weren't. That's why they nicknamed her Bubbles.

Grandpops – he rarely got his own name, Danny, anymore – opened his eyes. The morning light of Epsilon Eridani streamed into his bedroom, and it reminded him of the day he had said goodbye to Earth. That day, he had woken to see the Sun rising through the trees on the edge of a spacedrome in the south of England. Despite everything, he had slept more than he had expected to in a less-than-luxurious room on the base. The day before, he had taken leave of his family for the last time. His mother, predictably, had been in tears, and his dad tried hard not to convey his sadness. Sister Joyce had also been upset but in her it had shown itself as anger. How could he abandon his family and set off on a one-way mission into outer space? But Danny had bought into the dream, a vision that had now become a reality in 2258 – the beginning of a new stage in the evolution of humankind. They were about to colonise a new planet.

Like many of his time, Danny believed humanity had to explore and expand to survive – Earth was too small for them. They had narrowly avoided bringing an end to everything through self-imposed climate change. The industrial revolution of the 18th and 19th centuries had begun to release the fossilised carbon. For a while, they had been ignorant of the damage they were causing, but the generations of the late 20th and 21st centuries were not so innocent. While their scientists were screaming and the poles were melting, the short-term profiteers of the world focused on new ways to exploit the planet. They shut their ears and eyes to the damage they were causing. The only thing in their favour was that no one had been quite mad enough to push the nuclear destruct button. But when the major coastal cities of the developed world began suffering catastrophic flooding, leaving swaths of uninhabitable wastelands where there had once been bustling metropolises, drowning their financial empires, not even the money-makers could ignore the problem.

Now in the 23rd century, the powers-that-be adopted the vision of sending humanity into outer space. There might not be much chance for Earth but there may be hope in new worlds. Tribalism had not gone away, however – humanity was just as flawed as it had always been. One faction wanted a fresh moral start. Just like the Puritans setting off for America from Plymouth, England, in 1620 on the *Mayflower*, a select group were aiming to establish a new 'purer' kind of society based on traditional religious family values. They consisted of existing nuclear families, mostly young parents with two or three children, who wanted to save them from the corrupting influence of liberal society. They were not just escaping a sick planet but, in their eyes, a sick culture that was ridden with too many moral greys. They had identified a planet 11.9 light-years away in the Goldilocks zone around Tau Ceti. A probe had been sent at the maximum possible speed of half the speed of light some thirty-six years previously. Now it had reported back and the prospects looked good – good but not without a challenge.

This was not Danny's group. They were quite the opposite. His 'faction' – if you could call it that, which they wouldn't – was determined to be as diverse as possible. In those early days they were limited to just over a thousand people in each space-village mission, so they had sought to include as many races, backgrounds, cultures, languages and faiths as possible. To ensure a diversity of ages, they even included a few older people who were certain not to see the day of arrival. They ranged from scientists to dancers, philosophers and builders. They wanted to see that the new colony was as full as possible of the riches of human achievement. They were also conscious that diversity meant strength in the genetic reservoir, which was vital with only a thousand in the first fleet.

They had identified a planet in the Epsilon Eridani system that had been a focus of research since the end of the 20th century. Back then, it had featured in a sci-fi TV series – which did not bear any resemblance to reality. This was the most appealing option at 10.47 light-years, nearer than Tau Ceti. The planet spun on its axis at a rate almost the same as Earth's – twenty-three and a half hours – and it orbited its star at just the right distance with a year of 298 days.

Danny had breathed in the fresh morning air. The south of England in summer was still a beautiful place, and he would miss it. He knew the adage, "You can take the boy out of Earth but you can't take Earth out of the boy." But as he left his room, he met the smiling face of Natasha, who greeted him with a slightly accented 'Good morning" and he smiled back. Like him, Natasha was sixteen, bright and happy. He might be saying goodbye to Earth but not to her and not to the cheery group they joined in the breakfast hall.

That day, they were merely going to move into their cabins in the space-village. They would remain parked on the base for a month. The plan was to see how they settled before they made their final commitment to going. There would be online contact with their families at the end of each day, which was otherwise to be filled with the work or education they had signed up for. Danny was continuing with his chosen A-levels of maths, physics and chemistry. Lessons were taught by resident teachers located on one of the modules or online with Earth-bound tutors. Even at half the speed of light, this arrangement would still be possible for as long as Danny needed to sit his A-levels. Beyond that, they would be increasingly on their own. 'Live' lessons from Earth would cease. On arrival on the planet, two-way communication with Earth would take nearly twenty-one years. So not impossible, but news of 'home' would always be over ten years out of date.

This was one of the things that was emphasised by the village elders. Don't come if you aren't prepared to look forward. Once we're off the ground, there's no going back – ever.

The space-village had been called 'Space-Village Ad Terra Spei' – 'to the land of hope' – the name they would eventually call their new planet. Each village consisted of ten 'ships' – a central hub and nine habitation modules, named after the first ten letters of the Greek alphabet – Alpha being the hub. They were each connected by retractable corridors called gangs to enable all one thousand inhabitants to mingle. Danny had found himself in a cabin on Gamma, which was bigger than he imagined it would be. His sixth form centre was located on Kappa. Along one side of one of the classrooms was a big window with a shutter that could be opened to view the panoply of stars displayed in all their glory. For now, it was firmly shut – shut against a view of the space base that would seriously detract from the life they were going to have to learn. Instead, it was decorated with a spacescape with a view of the solar system from the outside with Earth as a pale blue dot. The school was to feel like it was already in space.

In their second week, one girl in Danny's maths class had had a serious wobble. She was missing her family after a Zoom chat in which her sister had had to leave the room. She knew she still had a choice; she could go to the elders and tell them her doubts, but once she had done that, there was no going back; they were not going to try to persuade her to stay. They had made that clear. They didn't want anyone aboard with doubts. Danny, Natasha and a couple of others had surrounded her and listened. It was then that Danny knew he was not ever going to change his mind. There was no going back for him. This is where he wanted to be. And that was where they all wanted to be – the girl did not go to the elders. Getting this far – actually on board the space-village – had been a long process, and many had fallen by the wayside. Those who had made it were under no illusions about what they were letting themselves in for, and they all had wanted it. Now Danny wanted it really badly. He couldn't wait to feel the shudder of the engines lifting them into orbit to begin their journey. Earth was history.

One month from the day of boarding the village, the gangs were retracted and the ports made safe behind airlocks. Gamma's engines began to hum, and the floor shuddered. Then nothing – no more sound. The speakers in the village had announced that all ten modules had taken off safely. The gangs would be reconnected at 2 AU when they had reached the travelling velocity of half light speed.

Two days later, Danny had been back in the chemistry lab making bad smells and learning what to do about them in outer space. They were on their way to their new planet, Epsilon Eridani h – Terraspei, 'land of hope'. A planet of promising new beginnings.

That had been sixty-two Earth years ago. Danny stretched himself in the warm, bright Eplight of the Terraspei morning and smiled. He had never regretted being adventurous. The primitive space-village had been comfortable – even fun – and, after twenty-one Earth years, the delight of stepping out onto the pristine planet had been amazing. Truth to tell, he had felt unclean. The human invaders were a blot on the landscape of this wonderful place. But the planet had welcomed them. They quickly set to learning its ways and treating it with care, encouraging, tending and even pampering its native life. Earth at its best could be stunningly beautiful, but Terraspei doubly so.

3

Earth 2330

Sam Brooks was five metres from the D; the midfield was pressing – they needed to level the score. A breakaway was on! He raced down the pitch into space behind the forwards as the wing-back slid the ball two paces in front of him; the pass was perfect. Sam ran onto it and connected with it. Sweet. He saw the alarm on the face of the goalie as he made a despairing leap towards the top corner where both he and Sam were certain the swinging ball was headed. But a couple of metres out, the ball swerved upwards and smacked against the angle. The post and bar both quivered as the ball ricocheted beyond the reach of the forwards, and Sam, instead of receiving the acclaim he was expecting, was running at full speed back towards his own goal in an attempt to intercept the counterattack. The fact that he got a good slice of the ball as he took his opponent out was probably what saved him from collecting a yellow card.

The match was lost. Sam was dejected, but he had played well, and he knew it... just five centimetres lower and he would have scored a stunning goal and been the hero of the hour.

"Well done, lad," said his coach. "Next Saturday it will be different."

"Thanks, boss."

Sam showered and changed and said goodbye to his teammates. They were all going in different directions, and he found himself on his own as he made his way to the bus stop. He cheered up a bit as he went; he had been appreciated by his coach and his friends. Football had been his joy, like, forever – a consuming hobby. And now in year 11, it was a welcome distraction from coursework and the impending exams that seemed to be the way society worked for people when they were sixteen – at least in Britain.

Sam's football match had been in Wells in a small stadium up the road from its ancient cathedral. Since the former Somerset levels had been abandoned to the rising sea levels, Wells had become a seaside town overlooking the Glastonbury Tor island. Sam, however, lived in Harptree, a small town tucked under the edge of the Mendips and extending into the Chew Valley as far as the lake – a reservoir created in the twentieth century. Back then, Harptree had been just three villages: East and West Harptree and Compton Martin. Those people, Sam learnt, were remarkably welcoming of change compared with some places. Like most country towns in the twenty-fourth century, Harptree did its best to be self-sustaining – people growing and planting in areas that had once been devoted only to cattle and horses – luxuries no one could afford in Sam's time.

The young people of Harptree mostly went to one of the secondary schools in the area. Sam attended the long-established school called Stanton Wick, northeast of the town. This school had a long history – it hadn't always been among houses. When it was first built in the middle of the twenty-second century, it had been surrounded by fields.

Getting on the bus, he spied his friend, Amy Huck, who also attended Stanton Wick. She smiled at him from under a mop of long fluffy dark hair topped by a bright blue beanie. They had both gone to the same primary school. As young kids, when whether you were a boy or girl didn't matter so much, they had been good friends. Now, of course, both boys and girls avoided one another unless they were intent on becoming an item. But on this occasion, he couldn't ignore her. She was on her own, and it was either sit with her or ask a man lost in a book to move his backpack off a seat. He returned her smile and sat beside her.

"Hi, Sam. How's it going?" She asked.

"We lost."

"So not a good day."

They chatted on about life – football, school teachers and exams. They both liked science, unlike the girl he had been paired with in chemistry, Tanya Payne. She had been a real pain because all she wanted to do was muck about. Amy was different. Together they would have made a good lab team. In their conversation, they even got round to what was happening in the news – which most kids seemed to ignore. Sam felt safe with Amy.

The bus took the coast road to Cheddar, where a lot of people got off. They were replaced by others headed by none other than Tanya and her entourage.

"Oh, hi," she went, as they passed them to sit on the newly vacated the back seat where they could pull faces at the driver behind.

"Oh, hell," said Sam.

"You don't like her?"

"I do not. And now she has seen me sitting with you, it will be all round school that we're, like... like... dating."

"I can cope with that. There are worse things."

"Well, I guess... It's just, like, sooo annoying."

"Why do you dislike Tanya so much?"

"She's a liability. I almost got banned from chemistry practicals altogether because of her."

"How? I mean, why?"

"I was, like, paired with her for chemistry. You don't get to choose."

"I know. So..."

"In one of the lessons, Miss Brankhurst gave us Bunsen burners, which, of course, came with strict rules. Tanya doesn't care for rules. She decided to conduct her own experiments with it. She began with burning scraps of paper and then a false fingernail, which she pulled off and nearly freaked me out."

"You're not allowed them."

"I know, but if you tell Tanya not to do anything, that's a reason to do it. Then she went to stick a bit of foil from a sweet wrapper in the flame and a rubber—"

"A rubber?!"

"Yeah. You know for rubbing out pencil..." He went bright red. "I don't mean in the American sense."

"Oh." Now they were both embarrassed. He hastily continued with his story.

"And finally, she got some strands of hair from her hairbrush. The smell was vile. I should have tried to stop her, but trying to stop Tanya from doing what she wanted to do would have been like trying to stop the tide coming in... and, stupidly, I was actually interested in the different colours the flame turned when different things were burnt... Miss saw it all, of course.

"'Miss Payne!' she went. 'And you, too, Mr Brooks. In case you hadn't heard, there are strict rules for using a Bunsen burner. When I said if anyone disobeyed them, there would not be a second chance, I meant it. The two of you can take yourselves off to the office and report to the headteacher at his convenience. Now go.'

"When I tried to tell her it was really all Tanya's doing, she didn't want to listen. She went, 'I mean it, Samuel Brooks. No appeal. You are dismissed from this lesson, and I shall recommend that neither of you be permitted practicals in chemistry for the remainder of this term.' And she chucked us out."

"So what happened?... Oh. Are we here already? This is my stop coming up."

"I got given a let-off. Tanya didn't."

"Tell me about it sometime."

"OK. Bye."

4

Space-Village Talbot-Theta. Earth date: 2330

Hurtling through space at half the speed of light, Joseph McPherson and Fran Davies huddled over their computer on board Space-Village Talbot-Theta *en route* to Pure Haven.

Sixteen-year-olds, they had both been born aboard the space-village. This was their home. They had never breathed the free air on the surface of a planet, smelt the scent of a forest or looked up into a night sky and witnessed the expanse of stars without a metal and multi-paned acrylic dome around them. The sights and sounds of the surface of a planet had all been captured by the lens of a camera and a microphone, but it was a poor substitute for actually standing in a real place. They had VR decks they could enjoy, but it was never going to be like truly being there with all six-plus senses coming into play. The virtual world was just that – virtual not real. But now this was all going to change; within a few months, they would arrive at their destination. Pure Haven would become their new home with all its delights. The prospect was exciting.

"What do you think it'll be like on Pure Haven?" wondered Joseph.

"It's very green. You can see that from here," said Fran.

"No. I mean. What will the people be like? Do you think the young people will like us?"

"It's meant to be much better than on Earth. They're supposed to be kind, generous, peaceful, good..."

"The fruits of the Spirit, I know. But will they want us there? Maybe we will be, like, too different from them. To be honest, I'm not great at being good. I mean, I try to be all those things but I know I'm not most of the time."

"Nobody is. And they won't be, either. But they should welcome us. After all, they do want new people to arrive. They say so in their videos."

"It's great being close enough for comms to talk to them now. The lag is less than a day, Dad says."

"So what are they saying?"

"I don't know. Dad says they haven't been exactly chatty. He asked but, apparently, they have never mentioned anything about children or young people. He says that it's all quite formal. But I guess it's their comms operators. I'm sure it won't be like that with the teenagers when we get there."

5

On Planet Earth in 2330, a new sense of optimism was seeping into the collective consciousness. The climate catastrophe appeared to have peaked around the turn of the century. 2330 was definitely better than 2300. In the twenty-third century, a significant amount of investment had gone into rescuing the planet as well as ensuring the future of the human race by sending people into outer space.

The latter enterprise had so far been a success. Terraspei was thriving. At least it had been ten years ago in the latest news they had received. Pure Haven was eleven and a half light-years away, so not much further, relatively, and that colony reported stability, too.

Sam was fascinated by the idea of living on another planet. At first, as a kid, the thought of applying to become one of the lucky few and going himself was his dream. One day, perhaps he could fly out there too. There would be nothing to prevent him from heading for the stars. He would be free of all that constrains a person on Earth.

But the older he got, the less inviting the idea had become. First, there were the twenty-plus years shut in a space-village, which sounded more cooped up than free. He might be flying in space but he would be trapped in a spaceship they called a village – a village without a bus service to take him to a football pitch somewhere else.

And then there was the out-of-date news. That from Terraspei might have been encouraging but Pure Haven was a different

18

story. Sam did not care for the rhetoric and the paternalistic way they seemed to view Earth. Earth was not the kind of hell they claimed it was. It was a great, resilient and beautiful planet whose people had eventually put some of their differences behind them to tackle the climate catastrophe. Somehow, the threat of being obliterated had overcome some of the old tribalisms. The surge of refugees from coastal areas in every part of the world was not possible to resist, no matter how many walls some people wanted to build. Back then, Sam's people had had to abandon the Somerset levels for the Mendip villages, which had quickly become towns as houses big and small replaced the tents. Planning permission and building regulations had been relaxed, and tower blocks twenty storeys high had sprung up in Whitchurch and Keynsham. The nimbys could not hold on to their perfect views – it was no longer just about solar panels in the fields. Refugees from Bridgewater and Weston had jostled for space alongside the displaced from the Thames Valley, Holland, India, and the Pacific islands, not to mention countries like Bangladesh, and housing was essential. For almost two centuries, it had not been about aiming to be prosperous but to survive.

But now in 2330, the sea levels were at last beginning to recede as the polar ice caps began to re-establish themselves. Rainfall was becoming more predictable, and the plains of Africa were attracting new populations which were not those who had fled the droughts of their ancestors. Earth's population had become mixed up, everywhere hosting a mix of races and cultures – the Earth's land masses had shrunk. Solar, wind and tidal energy extended worldwide, and the old dependence on fossil fuels extracted from one place and transported elsewhere no longer existed.

A new world economy was taking shape. A locally-based tourist industry had sprung up, and, in Britain, people were going to the seaside as in past centuries – albeit in different locations, of course.

Sam had ambitions for a career in the ever-expanding digital communication industry. They had been working on new methods of faster-than-light communication for decades, but the speed of light had always had the last word. Sam saw himself as being part of that research.

For the present, communications remained digital, relying on electromagnetic waves. On Earth the time delays were negligible, and the VRDs – virtual reality devices – most students carried meant they could be virtually present in a classroom setting and able to interact with anyone else also virtually there.

Nevertheless, the tutors – whether actually present or otherwise – as in every age, demanded attention. In year 8, Sam had frequently been in trouble, sometimes even getting detentions for interacting with a fellow pupil instead of concentrating on the lesson. However, that became a thing of the past in year 9. It had occurred to him that his teachers were trying to help him make the most of his capabilities and, unlike the likes of Tanya Payne, he had set his cap at pleasing them and doing his best. Nevertheless, no matter how far technology advanced, it could not replace exams, it seemed. Nor could it replace physical exercise. That was one reason why Sam enjoyed the football – as well as it getting him out of the valley.

He was the younger son of two, living in a third-floor apartment overlooking the lake. His brother was not a bad kid, but Sam didn't see himself as a kid anymore. He had a good collection of digital chums. They were located all over the world. The delay caused by the speed of light as he connected with his favourite mate, Tom, in Warwick, Queensland, was hardly noticeable. It hadn't prevented him from being taken on a tour of the city in Tom's car. Cars were still the thing in inland Australia. In Harptree, everyone – well, nearly everyone – owned a personal electric scooter – either two or four-wheeled – for short journeys. So virtual Tom had to be lent a four-wheeled one for his return tour of Harptree. Amazingly, he just couldn't seem to handle the two-wheeled variety. What they discovered was that learning to ride a bike had to be done in reality. If the brain is not accustomed to balancing in the real world, it can't seem to manage it in the virtual.

Although Tom was Sam's best digital friend, it would be unlikely they would ever meet in person. The idea of jetting around the world – common a couple of centuries before – had long been a thing of the past. The truth was that he was unlikely to meet many new people in person while meeting thousands online.

Sam liked where he lived; it was a cool place with its trees and lake, but he could be stuck with the likes of Tanya Payne around the corner for life. He recalled the rest of that awful day when he had been thrown out of the lab, and it still made him shudder.

They, he and Tanya, had sat on the chairs outside the head's office for what seemed like hours. Sam had perched carefully on his, but Tanya had spent most of the time slouched with her already hitched-up skirt sliding up her legs; she was barely decent. And she was actually chewing gum. If Mr Gilbert had opened his door at that moment, he might have exploded and excluded them altogether. Sam had had to say something, do something about it.

"Tanya, I... I... I think you need to sit up a bit and get rid of the gum."

"What?"

"Tanya. I mean... Why don't you...? If I were you, I would just, like, scooch back a bit in your chair... and ditch the gum. If Mr Gilb–"

"What!" Tanya shot him her best sour look. A look designed to wither. Sam withered.

Eventually, the head's PA came out and invited Tanya – only her – to follow her into the head's presence. She got up slowly, taking out her gum and sticking it beneath the chair.

Ten minutes later she emerged, giving Sam another withering stare as she was escorted to the door into the yard by the PA, who then returned and invited Sam into the august presence. Sam had been scared to death.

"I take it", Mr Gilbert began, "that you, Mr Brooks, did not disobey Miss Brankhurst."

"No, sir. It was Tanya who burnt things."

"Why didn't you stop her?"

"I... I... She doesn't listen to anything I say."

"So you sat there just letting it happen. It may have started a fire."

"Yes, sir."

"Miss Brankhurst recommends that you do not take part in chemistry practicals. Do you want to take part in them?"

"Yes, sir."

"Why?"

"Because I need them to learn the stuff properly. And I like actual lessons. Especially in chemistry."

"Indeed. In virtual lessons, you miss the smells. You want to learn the curriculum, giving you the best chance of a good exam result?"

"Yes, sir."

"Samuel, I am going to ask Miss Brankhurst if she would consider allowing you back into her lab lessons on the condition that you sit at the front and that you distance yourself from Tanya Payne in future. What do you say to that?"

"Thank you, sir... I never asked to be paired with Tanya, sir."

"You won't have to be. Miss Payne will no longer be doing chemistry practicals."

After that, Sam had done everything possible to avoid her and her gang. He wished there were more people he could team up with – like his footy mates – and Amy. There were a few ways people could travel non-virtually beyond his Mendip home but probably not for him. Becoming a professional football player was one way, but he was probably – definitely – not that good. Another way super-clever people left home was to go to live in an actual uni hub. He was not super-clever, so that, too, was out of the question. A third way was to apply to join one of the space-villages preparing to depart for Terraspei or Pure Haven. *But twenty years plus in a spaceship would send me bonkers*, he told himself. So that was not an option, either, even if Terraspei sounded inviting. He guessed he would just have to give thanks that he lived in a good place, one that was not bad to spend a lifetime in.

6

anny's birthday came round more often than if he had been on Earth. There, where he had been born, he would be only ninety-two; here on Terraspei, orbiting Epsilon Eridani, he was one hundred and thirteen. Every year, there seemed to be more people gathered around him to sing *Happy Birthday* – the family was growing just as he and his fellow space-villagers had hoped. Grandpops was the last remaining of anyone in his space-village. He continued to think in Earth years despite the general acceptance of the shorter Terraspei year.

He might be one of the oldest on the planet, but Danny was as alive as the day he arrived. He took a keen interest in everything about the new colony. Terraspei had proved as good and fertile as anyone had dared to hope. The vegetation was quite different from that of Earth. It was alien. Nevertheless, it was, for the most part, carbon-based and used photosynthesis and was deliciously green. And some of it was luscious; it tasted like nothing on Earth – literally. The planet had a stunning beauty quite unlike that of Earth – an experience that required the new arrivals to invent new names for things. One common translucent-green plant was dubbed 'tishbop' because of the sound it made – it gently crackled as it grew, releasing an intoxicating perfume. Another acquired the name 'quilt plant', as it had large, thick, soft pale-green leaves.

Grandpops took a keen interest in the way the young people were developing things – especially when it came to his nineteen-year-old – sixteen in Earth years – great-granddaughter,

23

Elle. In his eyes, she was a shining star. He recognised the sparkle that betrayed her deep-down happiness with life and why she had been nicknamed 'Bubbles'. Surrounded by a loving family, she had no problem giving the respect due to her great-grandfather. Grandpops was a hero – someone to look up to. He was also adorable.

"So, Grandpops," she asked, "tell us again why you joined the first batch of space-villages in those far-off ancient days."

"Not so far off!" laughed Grandpops, "but it was a bit primitive then. I just wanted a change from Earth. Eleven billion people always at odds with each other. The climate was barely improving after the twenty-first-century catastrophe... ah, but you've heard it all before. You're just teasing me, you wicked girl. You just want the old fool to get into his groove."

"No, seriously, Grandpops. Tell us more about Earth. Why was it so bad that a few thousand people got into a set of primitive space-villages and travelled for twenty-one years, raising children and hoping that their new planet would turn out to be OK? Earth must have been a scary place."

"It wasn't so much scary as depressing, lacking hope – especially for the poorest. The space-villages provided a kind of good news story in a dark world. Millions of people invested in them. They represented hope – a lifeline. When my number came out of the hat to receive an invitation to be among the company, I was delighted. Our family were all – apart from my sister – insistent that I should go, despite the separation. There was a period of mourning but communications in the early months were not so difficult. However, the further we travelled, a year turned into two, then three and four, and sensible two-way conversations were no longer possible. The isolation was virtually complete long before we reached our new planet, so aboard the space-village we forgot about Earth most of the time. You can't live in the past, and there was much to do. Your great-grandmother Natasha, and I were the same age – sixteen like you when we boarded – and we were soon wrapped up in each other. We never looked back... And I still don't."

"Do I look like Great-Grandma Natasha?"

"A bit. You've got the same eyes. And the laugh."

"Is that why I'm your favourite?"

"Now, Elle, don't be so wicked. Vanity doesn't become you. Your great-grandmother was not vain. You and your brother are both my favourites, and you know it."

Younger brother, Squirt, piped up. "Thanks, Grandpops. Bubbles *can* be a pain at times. But she is only wicked *some* of the time – only about 90% of it."

Squirt was two and a half Terraspei years younger than his big sister, but these days, he was taller than her, and the name Squirt no longer reflected his size. But Squirt he had been, and Squirt he remained. Like Grandpops, no one used his given birth name, which was also Daniel.

At Terraspei sixteen, Squirt was top of his class in maths. His great-grandfather was proud of him. "How's the maths going, lad?"

"It's great. I'm well into calculus. Some kids say it's hard but it isn't once you've seen the pattern and know where to start."

"You're still making trips to the observatory, Elle?" asked Grandpops.

"Yeah. They've set me on to calculating the distances between stars based on the right ascensions and declinations."

"I'm glad to hear that. I always liked astronomy." Grandpops gave a wistful sigh. "Sadly, my eyes are no longer up to it even if they would let me into the observatory."

"It was your job."

"No. It was my hobby. My job was in the fields."

"Everyone back then was in the fields."

"We were. But it was not all outdoors. I can't say I was up to much labouring. Anyway, they didn't let me. I was set to researching the native flora while others were trying out the seeds we brought from home – behind closed doors that was, so we didn't pollute the place. It was always best to see how much we could live on the stuff which grew naturally because we knew it would always be there unless we upset it with our earthly pollutants. We had to be very careful."

"And that's why 75% of what we eat today is not originally from Earth. And you were the one who went around tasting it all. It's amazing that you didn't poison yourself."

"Now, Elle, you know it wasn't like that. You know it was all done in the lab. We used state-of-the-art methods."

"Like chromatography paper?"

"A bit more advanced than... Elle, you're teasing me again. Squirt, I don't know how you put up with her. We used Fourier transform infrared spectroscopy, thermogravimetric analysis, electron microscopes and many other ways."

"Including feeding them to pets," added Elle.

"We had to use animals to be completely sure before we tried eating it ourselves. But we knew if we had done our homework well, they would not suffer. And you know jolly well that they didn't."

"And now we have robots that can mimic human digestion, so we will never have to do even that again."

But Grandpops was tired. He was not about to rehearse the arguments for and against vivisection in his past. Elle was right, though. With recent developments, it was probably more accurate to test food substances and medicines using the human gut simulator. This was just one of the new technologies that were being worked on. The lab was in constant touch with similar labs on Earth. The only drawback was the time lag – twenty-one years two ways. You could be working on something quite unaware that the problem had already been solved out there on Earth. But it was also true that they on Terraspei had contributed insights that had forwarded their earthly partners' research. In cosmic terms, 10.4 light-years is tiny – well within the local interstellar cloud. But 10.4 years still demanded a lot of patience. And to all intents and purposes for everyday living, Terraspei was isolated.

Ten years after the arrival of the first fleet, a further three space-villages had arrived. There were still villages and ships traversing the space between Earth and Terraspei, but the fashion and urgency that had driven the first fleet's development had soon tailed off. The goal had been achieved; humanity had been seeded out in space. The species would survive, even if Earth failed. But on Earth, there were definite signs of recovery. A new hope was spreading, and the need to flee was over. Now it was not so much about survival as about new opportunities.

The people of Terraspei no longer depended on new immigrants or the equipment they brought with them. In 55 years, they had tripled the population and were founding new settlements, building new roads and advancing agriculture. They had managed to circumnavigate their planet, and they no longer thought of themselves as immigrants from another home world – they were Terraspeians.

Charity's grounding wasn't lifted until after breakfast, and she was sent to school hungry. Her friends wanted to know why she had not been replying to their calls.

"Lost me phone," she said. They didn't believe her, but it was quite obvious she didn't want to talk about it.

In her free periods, Charity sloped off to the library. This was allowed, although she couldn't take a book out that was not in her permitted section. Most of the good stuff was digital, however. So long as they welcomed regular space-village arrivals, Haven did not lack supplies of electronic components. The villages came fully equipped with a huge stock of hardware – more than enough to keep the few thousand interested adults and teenagers going until the next ones arrived. And the next one, Talbot, was not far off now. It had been more than seven and a half years – fifteen Earth years – since the last one.

Software and data came with the space-villages too. The contents of the files had been mostly downloaded from the educational textbooks published on Earth. The Ruling Council saw that it was heavily vetted so as not to allow anything that could corrupt young minds with flawed Earth-based cultures but this did not apply to science subjects other than theories of evolution. Yet a lot of it seemed to get through, nevertheless.

Girls were not officially permitted to study science, but Charity found she could download what most girls never went near and no one in the library suspected her of it. If they did, they didn't say anything, and the algorithms appeared not to object or flag up anything that would draw unwanted attention to her.

She looked up nutrition, and keyed in the three staple crops grown on Pure Haven: wheat, sorghum and sweet potatoes. They were all good foods but green things seemed to be essential, too. Did they eat enough of them? Then there was mention of a crop called 'tomatoes'. What were tomatoes like? She had never seen one, let alone tasted one. *'And why don't we try to eat some of the local plants? 'Has anyone ever tested them?'* she asked herself. It just seemed common sense that you would eat what grew naturally unless it was poisonous or useless. She was bursting to ask whether her forebears had tried that with the lush green that grew abundantly around their house. She daren't ask, of course. That would only lead to a grounding without dinner for another day, and she wouldn't get an answer in any case. And, of course, the science on the computer couldn't tell her either because it all came from studies on Earth. Or did it? No. There was a sizeable section contributed by Terraspei because they had done precisely that – testing for native foodstuffs. If only the people with the power to do anything about it would cast a glance at what was happening on Terraspei. But Terraspei was officially despised.

She didn't blame the few guys in Haven's 'Department of Agriculture'. One of them had been there for decades. As she had dared to point out, testing what grew in the local environment wasn't their job. Their task was to make sure the crops that had been introduced from Earth thrived. They had done a reasonable job for the colony for it to have lasted four generations. After all, despite the lack of diversity in the food, Charity had, herself, survived until her seventeenth Earth year.

Sixteen. She emitted a long Charry sigh. The next big step for a girl was betrothal. She had done her best to ignore that fact as the years advanced. Marriage would mean the end of all education; she would be parted from her brother's science books and would have no access to the school library. She would also be subjected to motherhood. Perhaps it would be better for her to be sent on the threatened correctional programme for dissidents, whatever that entailed – no one had ever dared test it. She shuddered. On the plus side, betrothals lasted five Earth years. She would be safe until she was twenty-one. *So, counting my blessings, I still have five*

Earth years, she told herself. Just hang on in there, girl... Maybe I will be allocated a kind husband if such a thing exists... Boys, ewgh!

8

Charity let her eyes settle on the horizon. Through the rudimentary glass panes of the school window, she could make out a line of ancient Pure Haven oaks along the ridge beyond which she had never ventured. That wasn't unusual for a girl in her teens – third-generation teens – on Pure Haven, but Charity had now become increasingly aware of a disturbing longing somewhere deep down inside. Her mind drifted from the embroidered cushion cover she was obliged to finish. The previous evening, in the same direction, Raph had pointed out the faint light reflected off the soon-to-arrive space-village. That would be exciting. There were bound to be teenagers on it.

"Miss Charity Susanna Williams!" It was Mrs Parsons, the sewing mistress. "Your work will not get done gazing outside. You are by the window so you can see your stitching more clearly. Your future husband will value a mind that can concentrate on the task at hand."

Get lost, Miss Bossy Boots! Who says I want to have a husband, anyway? I don't want to be a girl. What I want to do is go downstairs alongside the boys and do science and technology like them. Why should guys have all the fun? "Yes, Miss. Sorry, Miss."

"I hope that's not meant sarcastically, Miss Williams."

"Of course not, Miss." *One of these days I'm going to travel outside of this valley, beyond that line of oaks – as far away from this prissy planet as I can get. Somewhere where girls can do more than make cushion covers to please their husbands. Perhaps I could sneak aboard that space-village command module on its way back to Earth.*

Charity thought of her grandparents. Both her parents' parents had been settlers. They had been part of the waves of young people set on founding a new home based on clear-cut values – a place where 'right' would be sharply divided from 'wrong'. And right, it had turned out, was where the female of the species knew her place and men decided on the laws and customs. Women were to be their helpmates – devoted, polite and dutiful. At fourteen, Charity had decided she didn't agree with that. No way was she second in anything except power and opportunity. She was cleverer than her brother – and most of the boys. Now she was sixteen and believed evermore keenly that women had not been created inferior to men.

The bell rang but the girls carried on sewing until Miss bid them put away their work and stand demurely behind their desks. In the silence, while waiting for Miss to allow them out of the door in an orderly line, Charity could hear the raucous shouting of the boys already kicking a ball around on the field below the window – the boys' field. The girls' place was on the other side of the building, where there was little room for running around and where ball sports were definitely not permitted. *One day,* thought Charity. *One day...*

In the girls' yard, Charity sought out Leah Donaldson. Leah was a tonic. She was a real rebel, frequently in detention. She didn't care that she had been paraded before the school to suffer the required derision of the boys; she had a brother who said that his friends admired her for daring to challenge the system. Her defiance was alluring and sexy. She assured him that that was not her intention. He also said that, secretly, many guys wanted to escape the strict expectations of the society they lived in too.

"Wanna come round my place tonight?" Leah invited.

"Love to. But you forget I'm banned from your house. My dad says you're a bad influence. If he had his way, he'd get you and your brother on the next space-village flight back to Earth."

"Can't think of anything better."

"It's a pity it takes twenty-three years to get there – forty-six there and back – or I'd be all set for a trip, too."

"If I went, I would not come back. I wonder what it's like on Earth?"

"The planet's in a state. Mass extinctions caused by climate change. Pretty uncomfortable."

"I know that. What I mean is, what is the culture like? I mean, do men rule the roost as they do here? Are people free to say what they think?"

"I guess the answer is probably yes in some places and no in others," suggested Charity. "There are billions of people on Earth."

"What we have here comes from Earth. Our culture comes from the people who came from Earth."

"Fled from Earth and its evil ways, Granddad says."

As they chatted, Betty Jenkins, a short, round-faced girl with frizzy hair, waddled up to their bench. "May I join you?"

"Course, Betty," Leah smiled. "The teachers already think we three are in league to upset the applecart."

"Apples. There's a thing. Would love to have tasted one before the trees all died." Betty sighed.

"My father has," said Charity. "But he said it wasn't really that great anyway."

As Charity and Leah chatted on, Betty became quiet. She looked straight ahead, unfocussed on the world around her.

"You OK, Betty?" asked Leah.

But Betty just sat, her hands under her thighs, lost in thought, so Charity and Leah gave her space. Somehow she seemed to kinda relax in their company; it was important for her just to be.

As they had grown up, Betty had never been popular among other kids. She was too different – her dumpy appearance set her apart. But Charity and Leah liked her. You could say what you wanted to her, and she understood more than most gave her credit for. Charity and Leah were among the few people who accepted her. Some kids were desperate to be cool or popular; Betty just wanted to be treated as if she hadn't got two heads. And it wasn't just at school; home for Betty was an especially difficult place. Her father and mother didn't rate her. To start with, she was a girl and, of course, as their first child, they had wanted a boy. Nor had she been the sort of cute kid that drew compliments from other mothers. She had grown up on the clumsy side and, worst of all, she was hopeless at needlework and drawing. She was, however, an above-average reader and devoured everything she could lay her hands on. But this didn't endear her to her parents.

After her came two brothers. The older one, Abe, wasn't just intolerant of his sister but went about telling untruths about her. Even in primary school, he had spread lies. At first, she asked him why he did it, but he simply denied he was lying dnd that she was off her trolley.

On one occasion, it had involved the family dog. Dogs were rare and valuable, but Betty loved theirs because he was so uncomplicated. One day, Abe had told her teacher that she had kicked him. She would never do that and she had challenged him.

"Abe, why did you tell Miss that I had kicked our dog? You know that's not true."

"You did, though."

"I did not."

"I see you. You're always kicking him."

"That's a lie!" Betty had shouted.

At that point, their father had come in. "What are you two arguing about?"

"Betty's lying about kicking the dog."

"I did NOT kick him. It's you who's lying!"

Her father drew himself up. His face went puce. He raised his hand as if to hit her. She cowered. He didn't strike her - not on that occasion - but ordered, angrily, "Go to your room, girl. Doing something bad is awful, but lying about it is far worse. No supper for you." And when Betty hesitated, thinking about how to right the injustice, he reared up again, and she knew she would never win. The truth was what they believed about you - nothing else mattered; facts were irrelevant. As she left to retreat to her room feeling a mixture of anger and fear, her father called after her, "And leave that library book outside the door. I'll not have you reading it. I don't know why they allow you to read those things. You have a Bible. If you must read, read that." And then she heard him say to her brother, "Don't argue with her. Just tell me when she misbehaves, and I'll deal with it..."

That occasion hadn't been a one-off. For Betty, this was most days. If it wasn't one brother, it was the other. Her teachers believed everything that her brothers said about her, and so did most of the other girls.

"No one will want her when it comes to auction day," one was saying, as Betty passed the door.

"I know. Who would want *that*?"

"She'll get a fiancé, though. Everyone has to have one."

"It'll be an old creep, for sure." And they laughed, knowing that Betty had almost certainly overheard them.

Charity and Leah, though, had always been different. They knew that she couldn't have done most of the bad or stupid things she was supposed to have done. She wasn't capable of most of it. They had no idea which stories were true and which weren't – they couldn't tell. No one could. Even Betty, herself, got to wondering, even doubting herself; sometimes she couldn't remember what was real and what wasn't. Charity and Leah were the ones who kept her sane. She could depend on them being straight and honest at all times. They were always getting into trouble, too, but, somehow, it didn't seem to faze them.

"You with us, Betty?" This was Leah.

"Oh, sorry. Just daydreaming... What were you saying?"

"We were just wondering what the culture's like on Earth."

"I'd have all sorts of questions to ask if I ever got to talk to a real living person on Earth," smiled Betty. "But hey, even if we were allowed to send messages, which we're not, it would take twenty-four years to get an answer."

"And then it would be out of date," laughed Leah. "And, anyway, who would we ask on Earth? We don't know anyone to ask."

Charity just sighed. *What I would give for a real live correspondent on Earth... or, maybe, even Terraspei. There's a thought – only twelve years for an answer from there. That's something to aim at."* Now it was she who was daydreaming.

"Now you, Charry," laughed Leah. "You two. Sometimes you're here but your mind sometimes seems to be elsewhere."

"Sorry. If you must know, I'm working on how I can get a pen friend on Terraspei."

"Terraspei! Impossible. Anyway, same as Earth. Light-years away," said Leah.

"Only six. Raph and I did the maths. Six light-years – mathematically proven."

"You're lucky. I mean learning maths with him."

"There are advantages in having a kind brother."

"Charry, forget any idea of pen friends." Betty was on the verge of panic. This was just the kind of thing Charry might actually try on and get them all into more trouble. Charry didn't know when to give up. She seemed so keen on getting into bother. "Forget it. I mean, corresponding with Terraspei."

"Don't worry, Betty. I know it's impossible. Besides, as you say, I don't know anybody there, even if it were. I've got more immediate things to get into trouble for."

"Like getting out of being betrothed," sighed Leah.

"If only. Short of doing myself some mischief, I haven't come up with a way."

"You wouldn't?" exclaimed Betty. "Do something to yourself?"

"That would be, like, cutting off your nose to spite your face," said Leah.

"Could do that. Literally cut off my nose." Her two friends looked horrified. "But I wouldn't. It's a close call, though. I mean, being paired with a 'boy' – yuck."

All three made retching noises.

"You girls, ill?" It was Mrs Parsons. She had sneaked up on them – deliberately.

"No, Miss. Just rehearsing for the play," replied Charity, quickly.

"And what play might that be?"

Charity hesitated. "Err..."

"'Macbeth'," said Leah, rescuing her friend.

"Good. But remember that no matter what the play, you are to behave like young ladies."

"Yes, Miss," said Charity, but thought, *Not if we're the three witches! Just imagine...*

9

Elle sauntered along to the compulsory citizenship period with an obvious lack of enthusiasm.

"I thought we would be done with these lessons once we'd started A-levels," she muttered to her friend, Anna. "I mean, what more do we need to learn?"

"I guess it's the only input the elders have in our curriculum – all the rest being the A-level syllabus from Cambridge, Planet Earth."

"So? We're nineteen Terraspeian years. We're adults."

"Not until we're twenty-one. That's the same on Earth – eighteen Earth years."

"Maybe. But we're not kids."

They entered the classroom and took their seats. The chairs had been set out in rows. Elle was not looking forward to this period one little bit. Resentment was brewing. What she really wanted was a free period to get on with her astrophysics, which at A-level was deep and interesting. This lesson was, in her opinion, going to be boring and probably puerile.

Poor Mrs Bannister was judged even before she arrived, despite being bouncy and cheerful.

"Today," she began, "you've got me on child-rearing." Mrs Bannister loved children – she had six of her own, so was at least experienced even if she wasn't that organised.

Elle groaned – audibly.

"A new baby is the most exciting thing that can happen in this world. The first fleet had just a thousand people when it set out; now we have nearly three times that just in this secondary school. And by the time *your* children are at secondary level, there'll be a choice of schools on Terraspei. I don't have to tell you how important it is to get it right for children right from the start—"

Elle raised her hand.

Mrs Bannister stopped. Flustered at an interruption so soon in the lesson, she looked at Elle with a terrified expression, which only served to embolden her student.

"Yes, Miss..."

"Elle Fisher. I don't plan on having any children. Do I have to stay? I have some important stuff to do on physics..."

Elle tailed off as Anna pressed her foot – the flesh and blood one – hard against her leg. She became aware of the collective gasp of those around her. *Not have children!* Having children – at least two and preferably more – was the foundation of everything on Terraspei. At the founding of the colony, to choose not to have children would have been to commit the worst betrayal imaginable. The truth was that Elle had not really given any thought to having children. She was so into learning that such a thing hadn't entered her head. She had not actually decided *against* children; it had just slipped out as a reason to escape this unwanted class.

Elle thought Mrs Bannister was going to faint. She hadn't breathed since Elle's first syllable. She staggered to the whiteboard and sat down on a chair.

"S... sorry, Miss. I... I didn't mean to—"

"Get out! Get out of my classroom," spluttered Mrs Bannister, recovering. At least, the teacher had not totally collapsed.

Elle stood and walked to the front and hovered at the door.

"Thank you, Miss." She hadn't meant it to, but it sounded wrong. It wasn't meant to be rude. "S... sorry," she blurted again.

"Get out! Be gone!"

Elle stepped out into the corridor. She had never felt so bad. She was wicked. Not knowing what to do, she went to the library and tried to read a book on the formation of stars. Even here, it was about new birth. The majesty of the birth of a star made her feel so small – and the enormity of her trespass.

It didn't take long for her to receive the summons to meet the head of year. Anna brought the message. No one else had volunteered.

"I've done it now, haven't I?"

Anna nodded.

"But... but I just can't think about having babies. It's not my thing."

"Maybe. But what did you think would happen if you said it like that?"

"I know. I didn't intend to be rude, but, Anna, I feel so trapped. Now. I want to study the stars – not change nappies... It's not fair."

"It isn't. But if you fight them, they'll make sure they tie you down even more. If I were you, I would just comply for now. Anyway, to have babies you need a boy—"

"Yuk!"

"You need a boy, so just don't find one. Easier than campaigning for your rights."

"I guess... But it isn't right. You should be allowed to—"

"No, it isn't just. But the apt time to make a scene is not now."

"Someone has to."

Anna sighed. Maybe Elle was right to protest. Up to now, Anna had always managed to get her way using what her mother called 'feminine wiles'. Could that be described as wise... or was it underhand?

The head of year asked Elle why she thought she was in her office.

"Because Mrs Bannister asked me to leave her class."

"And why was that?"

"Because I wanted to study physics instead."

"You were rude to her. I am surprised that it is you, Elle Fisher, sitting where you are. You have an impeccable record at this school. What have you to say for yourself?"

"Sorry, Miss."

"Are you?"

"Yes, Miss. I didn't mean to upset Mrs Bannister."

"You told her you didn't plan on having children."

"I didn't want to be in her lesson. I had interesting – urgent – physics to do. A-level–"

"I have no doubt you are taking your A-level studies seriously. But that doesn't mean you are excused from citizenship classes. Every child has to do them on Terraspei. Why not you?"

"I am not... I don't feel like a child."

"But you are until you are twenty-one. I take it you didn't truly mean to imply you do not wish to have children when you *are* an adult?"

Elle's mind moved swiftly. She recalled her conversation with Anna. "No, Miss."

"Good. So I want you to reassure Mrs Bannister of that when you write your formal apology."

"Formal apology?"

"You know how to write a letter of apology?"

"Yes, Miss."

"Now go. And let this be an end to it."

"My parents–"

"Will be kept informed."   So it wasn't over. They would be livid. She would be properly in the doghouse. If only she had kept her mouth closed. *I bet it's not like this on Earth*, she thought.

"Yes, Miss."

That evening was the hardest time Elle had ever had to go through with her family. Perhaps the worst part was seeing Grandpops so upset he couldn't speak. He didn't care tuppence about cheeking a teacher – he had given his share back in the day – but the idea that the dream of establishing a healthy population had been questioned, that his line would falter – as it had almost done before – was unthinkable. How could Elle say such a thing?

Elle didn't sleep that night. As Ep rose above the horizon, signalling a new day, she came to a conclusion. *My mistake was to say what I did in that classroom. I should have been a lot more patient. But I am not wicked for thinking I might choose not to have children. I have the right to choose whether I get married and have* a family. Just like Grandpops and Great-Grandma Natasha chose to leave Earth. It was their dream, and there would have been plenty of people on planet Earth who didn't like their choice. They opted for an adventure. What if I want an adventure? Maybe I could apply to travel on a space-village one day. But now I just want to study for my A-levels.

Unlike some girls her age, she didn't have a boyfriend. There had been no pressure to do so from her family for which she was grateful. But what would they say if there *never* was a boyfriend...? But she knew they would love her, whatever she chose to do.

10

Space-Village Talbot was on its preliminary approach. In just two months they would decouple and begin to orbit, preparing each module to make a gentle vertical descent to land at the hastily refurbished spacedrome on the outskirts of Pure Haven Town. Then over the course of the next six months, the 3521 new immigrants would gradually leave the hubs and integrate into the community. At the end of that period, the Alpha module would take off, leaving the nine others containing the hospital suite, the laboratories, the hydroponics decks, the technical equipment and spares, and a multiplicity of other supplies, animal, vegetable and mineral.

All was anticipation, both on Pure Haven and in the space-village.

What happened next, however, was not anticipated at all.

The village commander on Talbot-Alpha, Commander Pritchard, was in the process of taking stock of the things they would hope to take aboard from the surface of the planet after landing, when he received a knock on his door. It was the chief of communications.

"Come in... Hi, Matt. I'm amazed – the chief of comms in person. I'd expect you to be messaging me on my phone, even from just outside my door."

"I did not want to convey this electronically, sir... Security."

"Go on then. Take a seat. I'm all ears."

"Two days ago, we became aware of some disturbance among some of the paired electrons – you know, the entangled ones."

"The paired particles? I've never heard of any of them being

43

'disturbed'. We only have them aboard because it's procedure. They've done nothing but sit there for nearly a century."

"They began triggering alarms on the system."

"Hmm. Maybe something has happened on Earth. I hope it's not catastrophic. We're ten years now behind the news."

"Over thirteen, actually, sir; taking into consideration time dilation."

"Ah. Of course. Special relativity – you can't travel half the speed of light for nearly twelve light-years without incurring a very noticeable time difference. What would that be, Matt? Three years?"

"More like three and a half, sir. Our clocks tell us it is December 2326 – but on Earth it's May 2330."

"Quite. So what's with a couple of years? It makes no difference to us here. All the emigrants to Pure Haven run on the same time as us. That's what's important. The time on Earth has no meaning for us here."

"Not any more, sir."

"Matt, what are you talking about?"

"The people on Earth have contacted us... Through the paired particles. There appears to be no time delay as with electromagnetic waves."

"But the speed of light?"

"No longer applies."

"How do you know this, Matt?"

"Earth has made instantaneous contact. We have deciphered what is happening with the particles. Earth is saying that the technology has been developed to send instant messages across the universe. The speed of light, it seems, is no longer a barrier to interspace communications.

"It didn't take Izzy, the watch officer, long to recognise a simple repeated Morse code message containing instructions. In her enthusiasm, she followed them. After just four strokes of her keyboard, we had obtained voice comms. Now, we seem to have established a permanent microportal."

"A microportal? A tiny doorway? Into what?"

"A spacetime tunnel, sir."

"A wormhole?"

"A very small one, sir. But it connects us directly to Earth – Cambridge, England, to be precise. And a professor is saying it's 25th May, 2330."

The commander sat upright but in total silence. Communication of this nature would be a complete game-changer.

"I know she should have consulted with me, and then we should have come to you. But you can't blame the girl; she's a bright cookie, and monitoring ten-year-old news can be dull at the best of times. Anyway, as soon as she heard the operator from Earth, she came straight to me. She was a little alarmed, to say the least."

"So, you're telling me we have some unknown person from Earth talking to us live on the phone?"

"Yes, sir. So far we have not ventured to respond, of course."

"Are you sure it's Earth?"

"Yes. Unless the speaker has done some serious homework on both Earth and our mission – including the names of our crew who departed ten years ago – twenty plus years ago for them. And by our calculations, the time dilation is accurate to the day. I think they have anticipated we might be sceptical."

"Who knows about this?"

"Myself and Izzy, and James who was also on shift in comms. No one else on this vessel or any other module, other than yourself now, knows anything. As far as I am aware, none of the other modules carry entangled particles."

"Good. I'll take a comfort break and will join you down in comms in ten minutes. Order me a strong coffee."

Commander Pritchard arrived at comms in silence. He took the offered gas lift chair, took a deep breath, relaxed and made himself comfortable. He didn't want any distractions from his not-so-young body. He listened to the man at the other end of the line. He was saying...

"This is a message for Commander Pritchard if he is still the commander of the Space-Village Talbot *en route* for Pure Haven. You may be confident that this technology is end-to-end encrypted and, by definition, only accessible at your portal and ours. If you enter "VIDEO" on your keyboard, you will see a picture of me. I am Professor Richards, the head of communication at Cambridge University, England." There was a pause, and after a couple of minutes, the message was repeated, only it was obviously newly spoken – it was not a recording.

The commander entered 'VIDEO', and there he was – a well-dressed man in his fifties against the backdrop of the River Cam and Trinity College Chapel. It appeared to be late spring. It was easy to forget seasons aboard the space-village but they kept to the Earth calendar, so that would be right. Of course, AI could do anything, but one thing was certain: AI or not, this message would have to be coming through a wormhole – albeit a very narrow one – with its other end in Cambridge, England. Izzy was quite sure it was not from the planet beneath them.

Pritchard took a sip of his coffee and spoke. "Commander Pritchard here from Space-Village Talbot-Alpha *en route* for Pure Haven. To whom am I speaking?"

The response was instantaneous – it was as if he and this professor guy were in the same room.

"Ah, Commander. I'm delighted to hear from you. You are the first quantum communications we have achieved beyond Terraspei. If you have a camera, F10 should allow me to see you."

Pritchard adjusted the camera and pressed F10.

"Your years since you departed have not aged you, Commander." Professor Richards was comparing the face he saw on his screen with the mug shot in his records. "I am now confident with whom I am speaking. I am Professor Richards from the computing department at Cambridge University. As you see, my office has a magnificent view of the Cambridge backs. Now it is time for me to explain."

Professor Richards summarised the transformative developments from Terraspei. Pritchard listened intently. This was indeed a game-changer.

"Can we only connect with you?"

"You can connect with anywhere you share paired particles with. I will talk you through how you can activate them. When they wake up, they will instantly establish a microportal. Our records show that in your case this includes both Pure Haven and Terraspei, but if you get stuck, we can patch you through to them and help you set up the link. You also have pairs with partners in two other places on Earth: Yale in New Haven, Connecticut, and Shanghai University, China."

"So we have twenty-four-hour access?"

"Indeed. Wherever the university hubs are in relation to you, however, makes no difference. You do not need a clear line of sight with this technology. But it does mean some of us can go home to bed at night if others are listening in."

"Got you. We are in radio contact with Pure Haven. We are on schedule. We have increased in numbers since we launched. We have had six hundred or so new babies born during our twenty years on route, including some third generation."

"That is excellent news, Commander. We have been concerned about the colony. So far they have not picked up on our messaging. It is a relief to hear they are responding to your radio calls. Perhaps you might ask them to check their paired particles."

"I will. Thank you, Professor. I will leave it to our comms crew to note all the current news on Earth. There remains one final question for now. When our people learn about this development, they will immediately want to contact their families. Would that be possible?"

"That can be arranged, Commander. We can establish a standard electromagnetic link to a private phone through our university hub. At your end, you can patch them through to your comms deck. You can also call up Terraspei, of course. It was their scientists who made the final breakthrough in this technology. They have nicknamed it Wormcomm – a name that is beginning to stick. Your families will need to book a call so that when it arrives here, we can direct it through to the desired phone number on Earth. We have already begun doing this with calls from Terraspei with great success.

"One thing, however, I must warn you about is the psychological shock this may cause. When someone finds themselves opening their phones and hearing a voice they have long since accepted that they will never hear again – at least in this life – it can be a highly charged emotional moment. And sometimes the news they receive is not always good."

"I hear you, professor. The first thing I am going to do is inform my officers, then the wellbeing team and the chaplaincy."

"Unlike on the planets, this is going to affect almost all of your people personally, commander."

"We will prepare for this. Forewarned is forearmed. Keep us in your prayers."

"Certainly. We will await your reports, Commander. Have fun!"

"Thank you, Professor. I will meditate on this and take it all in."

"May God be with you. *Au revoir*."

Commander Pritchard leaned back in his chair and took a final gulp of his coffee. He was a believer in God, but he found the religious views of some of the villagers hard to cope with. He had given up arguing with them a long time ago. He had no say in the moral or life choices of the inhabitants, but he still retained the responsibility for the health and welfare of all aboard. He was the commander, and only he and his trained officers had the know-how to navigate space and the demands that made on the wellbeing of human beings. He needed time to allow the impact of this development to subside before he did anything else. It felt like someone had flipped him upside down and righted him again.

"I shall be in my cabin. Allow no one to disturb me except for emergencies. Meanwhile, keep this carefully under your hats until I decide when and how to break the news."

"Understood, Commander," said the chief of comms. He hoped the commander wouldn't leave it too long.

Three hours later, the captains of each module were summoned to the operations room beneath the bridge of Alpha. When they had been made fully aware of the situation, the chief consultant of the medical team, the wellbeing consultant, and the leading chaplain were requested to be present in the administration suite of the hospital bay.

A debate about how to spread the news was entered into. There was no easy way of doing it. Bearing in mind the common denominators of those headed for Pure Haven, it was eventually agreed to do it in the notices before morning worship the coming Sunday when most people would be together in their various worshipping groups. Those who weren't present could then be told by someone close to them.

A month before Talbot was due to arrive, the time had come for Charity and her whole cohort to be allocated their marital partners. They would not marry until they were twenty-one, but the designated five Earth years of engagement had to begin in year eleven. The so-called 'boys' – actually young men – were twenty before they went through the process, four years later than the girls.

Most fathers allowed their sons some choice in whom they were partnered with so long as they didn't choose beneath them. Status was everything. Consultation was not a privilege extended to the girls, of course; females had no say in the matter. The official line was that women existed to keep house, breed and feed children, and otherwise remain silent. Men knew best – in the case of a marriage partner, the decision was the father's.

Nevertheless, before the betrothal day, Charity had studied the field. All the girls had. Even in the third generation, the colony was not that big, so everyone knew who was up for allocation. At one end of the scale, there were the 'gross toads', and at the other were the guys most girls thought of as 'cool'. In between were the 'drips', 'creeps', 'weeds', 'tolerable' and 'OK'. She dearly hoped her parents – rather, her father – would avoid the boys she rated to be in the bottom half of that spectrum – even the bottom two-thirds. And the 'cool' guys were probably nightmares to live with, anyway; she couldn't stand those who fancied themselves. This rating of the field by the girls was a pointless game, though. The criterion that her father would apply would be, first and foremost, status. The nearer a boy was to the ruling class, the better. Positive connections would benefit him. And that would also be true for his daughter. Wealth and influence always went together, and her father would want his daughter to be comfortable and her children to have the best as they grew up. Next, he would look at their breeding potential; he would try and avoid any siblings of children who had died or got sick or who had had bouts of illness themselves. Finally, he would look at intelligence and possibly appearance if there was a tie.

However, the system did not allow the father of a girl to approach the father of a boy. All the offers were made at an annual betrothal festival. Bids were made by the fathers of the boys in a silent auction. If a girl was popular, then her father could choose from the offers received. If he received no bids, his daughter would go into a second round and then as many rounds as it took. There were often a few more girls than boys in each cohort. These would be offered to widowers of any age as a second wife, so there would be no female with breeding potential left without a partner. Of all the outcomes, that was the fate the girls of lower status most dreaded.

This whole process made Charity feel that growing up sucked. The only consolation was that there would be no immediate change to anything; the engagement would last a minimum of five years.

12

All too soon the 'auction day' was upon them. Charity called it that, although its official title was the Annual Betrothal Festival. The main floor of the Town Hall, the colony's largest building, was packed with fathers and their twenty-year-old sons in the front with the fathers of the girls at the back. The girls were corralled across the street in a building used most of the time as a barn. The sheep that generally lived in it had been turfed out for the occasion. It was the middle of the long winter lasting twelve Earth months, but the sheep had woolly coats; they would survive a couple of days. Despite an open fire in one corner, the girls, dressed in their finest, huddled together for warmth.

Whether it was down to the cold or apprehension, a tense silence pervaded the assembled sixteen-year-olds. Only a few girls ventured to say anything. At the end of the day, they would all know their fate. They had no family with them; their fathers were across the street and their mothers were at home supervising their siblings or keeping house. The girls were overseen by half a dozen men, all of whom made Charity's flesh creep. At least two of them were people she knew girls should not be left alone with.

Through the cracks in the barn wall, they had witnessed the 'boys' being shepherded into the Town Hall by their fathers. They mostly looked as reluctant as the girls. The fathers, on the other hand, were all full of a 'bonhomie', which Charity thought was probably false. They were in competition with each other after all.

Inside the Town Hall, a hush fell over the chatter of the men as the leader of the Ruling Council for that year called for order. 184 girls were up for bids. The previous week, their names and numbers in alphabetical order had been posted with a ten-word bio for each one. On arrival, fathers and sons were asked to select their top five and put their bids into boxes positioned around the hall.

When all the bids were in, the boxes were wheeled onto the stage. A man stood beside a large blackboard with the numbers 1-184 entered into columns. The boys had similarly been numbered 1-176. As the primary bids were read out, the man wrote down the numbers of the boys against those of the girls on the board. It soon became clear that half a dozen girls were going to get more bids than there was room for, while a third got none at all. It was like this every year. These girls would have to wait until the second round when the second bids were counted.

At the end of the first round, Charity's dad inwardly rejoiced to see that his daughter had received two bids, while Leah's father was proud that his daughter had three numbers beside hers on the board. Of course, in the barn, neither had any idea of what was happening in the hall. Leah couldn't see that at least one of those who put her first she had rated as 'cool'. But Mr Donaldson quickly moved from pride to disappointment when he checked out their social standing. He was not going to allow his daughter to be betrothed to someone below his station as he saw it. He decided to gamble and rejected all three bids and put Leah into the next round. It was a risk, but one he felt he should take.

Two young men's fathers had put Charity first. That was unexpected. As a family, they were not so high in the pecking order, and Charity was not one of those girls who stood out in any way. Well, her father didn't think so. He loved her, but that was because she was his. He looked up the numbers. The two guys were both acceptable to him, although one was decidedly lower status in his opinion, so he opted for the one whom he thought was the better. It wasn't an obvious advancement, but the family was at least on a level with his. Nothing would be lost; beggars could not be choosers. At least his daughter had not had to continue into the second round. With a bit of luck, he could improve his status when his sons came up for their turns. He hoped Charity wouldn't be disappointed, but then he hadn't really any idea what would satisfy her – he hadn't asked. After all, it was his decision. He was amazed to have had a say even if the choice had been between only two; not all fathers could claim their girl had had more than one bid in the first round. For the Williams, he decided, the event was turning out to be a success.

A break was called, during which the first-round girls' and boys' fathers met and the preferred bids were accepted. Round two then began. Charity's number was crossed through along with those who had already been claimed. Leah's remained.

In the second round, Leah received two bids. Her father could not afford to go further, and he accepted the boy who sounded the most promising. She was, of course, his second choice, and Leah would be aware of that.

This process was repeated until all five choices had been exhausted. The fathers of the boys who got none of their choices came forward and submitted bids for the remaining girls. This continued until all 176 boys had been allocated a partner. It took a long time, but no one was allowed to leave the hall until the process had been completed.

At last, the shivering girls were sent for to be introduced to their allocated boys. In the midst of a giant mêlée, the three friends were torn apart in different directions. Leah was the first to find her husband-to-be. He was in an emotional mess. He had been set on his first choice, but his father had been outbid by one from the Ruling Council. His dream girl was gone from him forever, and he was left with Leah, who was by no means a disaster for him. Just not his choice. Leah had thought of him as 'OK', but nothing compensated for being paired with a disappointed boy. They were introduced, shook hands, made a date for him to visit her home and then parted.

It became obvious to Charity that for the most privileged, some of this must have already been fixed beforehand because the highest-status girls didn't seem surprised. Some couples appeared to have formed a previous liking for each other and were clearly relieved and delighted, while others were upset, having been claimed by someone other than the ones they had hoped for, including the girl Leah's new partner had set his heart on. Charity had entered into no previous arrangements; it hadn't occurred to her that it was possible – it wasn't, officially. The higher-status families seemed to operate with different rules. However, it seemed more than one had bid for her in the first round. Amazing.

Jonah Williams introduced Charity to a young man called Nathan Rogerson, with whom she was told she was to spend the rest of her life. She had seen him around but didn't really know him. He was not one of the 'cool' guys, nor among the 'creeps', 'drips' or 'gross toads' at the other end of the scale; he could have been a lot worse. It was clear, however, that he was pleased with getting his first choice, so, at least, that was a good start. Charity couldn't see what he saw in her – why he had chosen her in the first round.

"So, why choose me?" she asked, bluntly, when they had been allowed to speak privately to one another.

"I've watched you in the library. You're not like other girls. I've seen you sneaking science books. I liked that."

Charity rolled her eyes but inside, she was alarmed. *He has been spying on me in the library studying science!*

"I like the fact that you are interested in science... and I also like it that you are prepared to defy the rule that the subject is off-limits to girls."

"What?!"

"You're a rebel. I like that."

"I don't get it. You're supposed to like the way I make cushions."

Nathan smiled. "Am I? How do you make cushions?"

"Badly. I hate needlework."

"But you do like science. And you're clever. Your brother Raph says so."

"You've been quizzing my brother?"

"Not exactly. Raph talks about you to my friend, Zac. If you were having to select a fiancée, you would use every research tool at hand."

"Raph never said anything to me."

"Zac didn't let on I might be interested in you. I was very 'casual' in my enquiries."

"Creep."

"If you say so. But I'm glad your father accepted my offer. It wasn't the only one you got."

"Sought after, then." Charity said with a smirk.

"He was looking for status."

"And you're not."

"No."

"So tell me about you."

After ten minutes of dull resume, Charity decided Nathan was boring and a bit geeky. Physically, he wasn't attractive, but neither was he repulsive. He was OK. His social standing didn't matter a jot to her, except that she was glad he was not among the elite. Like her, he didn't stand out, and that was good. The best part of the proceedings for her was that she hadn't had to go through more than one round.

As the bargaining drew to a conclusion, the festivities got underway. Musicians began to play ballroom dance music. The six unallocated girls had been whisked off discreetly back to the barn, where they would be put up for grabs by one of eight widowers. *That*, reflected Charity, *must be awful.* She thought she had spotted Betty among them but couldn't be sure. She begged to be allowed to see what was happening with her friend in the barn. Nathan said that he was cool with that, and, to her astonishment, her father reluctantly concurred. *Interesting,* she thought. *Maybe this betrothal thing has not turned out totally evil. Dad would normally have said no.*

She got back to the huge cold barn just as the last of the girls were being bid for. It was Betty. Charity sidled up to her.

"Oh, yuck, Betty. I'm so sorry. You must feel, like, awful."

"Nah. I expected it."

"But Betty, don't take it personally. It's not about you but the status thing and all that."

"You sure? But, frankly, Charry, I don't care."

"You're going to get given a widower."

"I know. I hope he's, like, so old he won't last long. He could be of status even, then my dad will be happy."

"That doesn't sound like a place you'd belong—"

"Betty Jenkins!" A guy with a megaphone bawled. She had been claimed.

"Wish me luck." Charity gave her a quick hug.

"At least we've got five years..."

Put like that, it sounded like a death sentence.

13

According to custom, Charity's family invited Nathan round for dinner. Lamb was on the menu – the most expensive food on the market and rarely on their normal list of foodstuffs. But this had to be a very special occasion when the prospective son-in-law was to introduce himself properly.

As they took their chairs, Charity's father, as was his due, spoke first.

"So, Nathan, tell us why you put our Charity's name as your first choice?"

He doesn't mess around, my father, thought Charity.

"Because I find her an attractive, well-brought-up young lady." *Creep.*

"But why, when you had 184 to choose from, did you go for her?"

"Whenever I saw her, she seemed to be very polite and softly spoken and—"

He was interrupted by a guffaw from Luke.

"Luke," admonished his father. "She *is* softly-spoken. Although she may not be to you when you are rude to her."

Or to you, thought Luke, but he didn't say anything.

"Do continue, Nathan. As you were saying..."

"I know she is quite gifted."

Shut up, Nathan! Charity began to panic. *He's going to spill the beans about me in the library.* Her normally pale face noticeably reddened; she was gripped by fear.

"In what way?"

Now it comes.

"The embroidered cushion she made last term was by far the best. As soon as I saw it, I thought, 'That's the girl for me'."

Charity's mouth dropped open. That was absolute rubbish. She had to admire his guile. Her mother, however, glowed with pride, and her dad was pleased. But Charity's mouth still gaped in amazement. This was so a lie. Compared to Leah's, if not Betty's, her cushion didn't compare; after all, she hadn't even tried. And he couldn't have seen it or known it was hers if he had. So now she knew that he wasn't going to let on the real reason. *Have I been chosen by an astute, intelligent guy? One who can work the system? One who has sussed me out even when the librarians haven't? Maybe he can keep me in science books forever. He's a great liar at any rate. Maybe God's listening.*

This betrothal caper hadn't proved so bad after all. At least, not for her. It was clear her family were delighted with the outcome of the auction, and, amazingly, so was she – something she would never have believed a week ago.

During the meal, Nathan was quizzed about his prospects working on one of the colony's farms – something which he seemed passionate about. When they had finished eating, Mr Williams suggested the newly betrothed might like to walk out in the garden together so they could continue to get to know each other better. Luke was put on washing up – mainly to keep him from lurking behind the fence – and Raph retreated to his room to do his homework.

Charity began. She should have let the boy speak first, but to hell with that. "So. All that rubbish! What you said about my cushion. You've not even seen it."

Nathan grinned. "The bit about being passionate about working on the farm is true, though."

"You like farming?"

"I like trying out new things."

"New things? Farming hasn't changed in decades. I mean, the sheep aren't any better than they were a generation ago. Probably worse."

"I know. They are considerably worse. But hopefully, that will be improved when the next space-village arrives. They're supposed to have some fresh frozen embryos and some straws of semen – well, as fresh as they can be after travelling for twenty-odd years in a deep freeze. But that's not what I mean by new things. I'm trying out what's already growing here."

"You're what?!"

"Trying out new things that might be good to eat."

"Wow! That's just what I think we should be doing."

"I know."

"How...?"

"Zac. Raph told Zac, and Zac told me you came up with the suggestion, and your father squashed you."

"But..."

"You're quite safe. It hasn't gone any further."

"What else has Zac told you?"

"That you help Raph with his homework and you're a whizz at science even though you're self-taught."

"Polite and softy-spoken..."

Nathan laughed. "You do have attractive feminine graces."

"So when we're married—"

"You'll be my Marie Curie."

"Really? The renowned husband-and-wife science team. You mean that?"

"Absolutely."

"But how are you – we – going to pull that off on Haven? I'd never be allowed, even with you on my side. I'm already breaking the rules."

"No idea... yet. But we'll come up with something. At least we can work on the farm things together. And, maybe one day the culture will change on this planet."

"Some hopes."

"There are more men around who want change than you think. The founders of Pure Haven left Earth to found a new colony. Maybe that's what we could do one day."

"For now, though, Nathan, you have to keep that thought to

yourself. Seriously. It's dangerous."

"I know. Working on the farm helps me to cope with it."

"Maybe I could come and help you. You know, before the five years are up."

Nathan laughed. "Not so fast. You're supposed to check I'm honey all the way down."

"What? What are you on about? Honey?"

"It's *Winnie-the-Pooh*. He has to check that his pots have honey right to the bottom – no cheese. Have you read those books?"

"No."

"I'll lend them to you. Storybooks make a good break sometimes – a change from science all the time. And they say things about life."

"If only. I'll look for it."

"Can I call you Charry, like your friends do?"

Charity smiled. "Yeah, so long as you don't do it in front of my parents. Dad doesn't like it."

Nathan smiled. "Don't worry. I think I've got the picture. You can call me Nat if you like... so long as you don't in front of your parents."

Charity giggled. *Maybe I could even fall in love with this guy.*

"How do you like your betrothed?" demanded her father after Nat had gone.

"He's OK. He'll do."

"Is that all?"

What do you want me to say? I didn't choose to be betrothed. "I've only just met him, Dad. I haven't got my mind around being betrothed yet."

"She has five years," pleaded her mother. "Don't rush her."

This was brave.

"It's all right, Mum. As boys go, he's pretty good."

Raph laughed. The tension was relieved.

"He was trying super hard," said Charity. "I like him for that."

"Good." Dad was satisfied. Clearly, this was as much as he

was going to get. He only wished the boy was higher up the social pecking order. Charity was right, though; it could have been much worse. He would do. He would have to. When it came to Raphael, though, he would be doing the choosing, and he would be aiming higher.

14

Anna, adjusting her prosthetic limb, clumped up to her friend, Elle, as she was rummaging in her locker in the school corridor.

"What do you think about the latest?"

"The gossip line? Do I need to hear it?"

"It's not about people – about anyone. It's about phones."

"A new model? That'll affect me, like, in ten years. You know I don't keep up with all that."

"No. It's not about a new model. You can do this on your existing one – even yours."

"Do what? Come on, Anna, we have to get to registration."

"This new thing: 'super-connectivity'. It means we can talk to anyone. Like across the whole universe, instantly."

Elle stopped. Had she heard this right?

"That's not possible. Nothing can travel faster than the speed of light. It takes ten years to even talk to Earth – more than twenty to get an answer back."

"Not anymore. That's what's new."

"You mean you can phone someone on Earth and talk to them? Like, live?"

"Yes. Live streaming, live everything. With this, you could communicate with someone a zillion light-years away. It doesn't matter where."

"Rubbish."

"No. For *real*. Honest. I'm not fibbing."

"I'm not saying you are, Anna. But... who told you this?"

"This guy from the uni–"

"The cool one you fancy? Oh, Anna."

"No, not him. An old guy. Well, he's a lecturer. He's like fifty years old. He told my dad about it."

Elle was all ears now. Could this be true? She fizzed with curiosity. Anna giggled. Her teenage friend was so predictable.

"Ah. Stop, Anna. I nearly fell for it. You're a rotten tease. I'm such a sucker."

"No. No tease. Honest. This. Is. For. Real... really real... or so he said."

"I'll believe it when I see it. What are they calling this, then? Has it got a name?"

"Yep. 'Wormcomm'. Apparently, the signal is relayed through some wormhole thing, so it doesn't have to travel through spacetime and be restricted to the speed of light. Don't ask me the technical details. I never could get my head around science. I mean quantum mechanics like Mrs Patel teaches is, like, insane."

Quantum mechanics. Is she talking about quantum entanglement? The paired particles. That could be it. Have the scientists devised a method of using it? Elle adored innovation and was ready to push the boundaries of discovery. There was no doubt in her mind she was going to be a scientist one day and be at the forefront of everything. But this could not possibly be true.

"Quantum entanglement. Was it that?"

"Yes, that's it. How did you know?"

"I didn't. But for centuries physicists have suggested paired quantum particles could work to forge a sort of wormhole. But no one has come up with how to do it... until now, it seems. Where did this tech come from, then? Has this come from Earth?"

"No. He told us it's ours. Here. It was our scientists here, on Terraspei. I'm amazed you haven't already heard about it."

"I haven't. Amazing. That's so... like... They've kept that quiet."

"But how can these quantum things actually do it? I don't get it."

"Entanglement? No one knows. Honestly. Nobody truly gets their head around quantum mechanics. It just works; that's the thing to remember."

Elle began to imagine how she was going to get to quiz the

scientists. She was daydreaming; she was already knocking on the lab door. She stared ahead of her, focused on nothing. Anna waved a hand.

"Elle. Elle, come in, Elle. Tune back into everyday life. We're late. Come on. We'd better get to class."

Elle couldn't concentrate. How could anyone think about anything other than this news? At morning break, Elle spotted Mrs Patel heading for the staff room.

"Miss."

Oops. She'd better calm herself. Mrs Patel wouldn't have long before she would have to make her way back to the lab for her next period.

Mrs Patel stopped.

"Well, Elle?"

"I... er... heard that... er... about something called 'Wormcomm'. I wondered if you were going to mention it in your next lesson with us."

"Elle Fisher. I should have guessed that you would be among the first to want to delve deeper."

"But is it true, Miss? I mean being able to phone anyone in the whole universe, like as if they were on our own planet?"

"It is true that we can create a microportal between our university hub and a paired hub elsewhere. It depends on the whereabouts of the paired particles... We'll talk about it all in physics. But I suspect that the implications for other subjects are going to be just as interesting."

"How do you mean, Miss?"

"Use your imagination, Elle. If you were in your parents' shoes, what would you think?"

Elle stopped and pondered the question.

"It won't go down well with those parents who don't like us using social media. Plus those who like Terraspei to be isolated, I guess. They would be scared of who their kids were talking to. Earth could be dodgy."

"To put it mildly. Your great-grandparents who set off from

Earth have protected four generations of children from the corrupt ways of that planet since they left."

"And now all that might be damaged."

"Fear not, Elle. I will talk about it in the science class. Now I think I need to pay a comfort visit before my next period. How about you?"

"I guess." *How can anyone think about going to the loo when something as exciting as this has just happened?*

Back at home later that day, Elle was on the phone with Anna.

"You know, lots of people won't like this."

"Why? It's great news. We won't feel so off-grid anymore. I mean, things are not bad on Terraspei, but we are so limited. All the things they've done on Earth – all the history of humanity – are only the things they've chosen to send us. And now we can ask questions. Just imagine—"

"But that's the problem, Anna. What's to stop us from getting the rotten as well as the wholesome?"

"How do you mean?"

"Isn't it obvious? Our forebears set off on space-villages which took 20.8 Earth years to find a new place to live. Why? Because it was all going wrong on Earth. The last thing they want is those things infecting Terraspei."

"But *you* don't think it's better being isolated. Elle, you of all people don't believe in that. I mean, shutting the universe out. Just because horrible history is associated with Earth, it doesn't mean the people who live there now in the twenty-third century are all corrupt and horrid. No. You are definitely not an isolationist."

"You're right. I'm not. I'd love to know more about what's happening on Earth. And even Pure Haven, but right now I'm trying to see it through Grandpop's eyes."

"Now, *they* are isolationist."

"*They?* Who are we talking about? I wouldn't call Grandpops an isolationist; he's just—"

"No. Not your great-grandfather. Pure Haven. New ideas won't go down well there. From the little we hear, I'd hate to live there. Girls and women are second-class citizens."

"So they say. Who knows what the ordinary young people there want? If I were one of them, and if that were the case, I'd revolt."

"Not if you were brought up to do as you're told and never get to read anything other than the approved books. Or perhaps no books at all if you were a girl."

"Maybe. I'd still hate it. I'd never believe men are better than women. They may be good at some things, but mostly they're stupid."

"That's absolutely not true. Men can be every bit as good as women if they want to."

"You're right. *If they want to be.* Thanks for pointing out my prejudices."

"You're not prejudiced. It's just that not everything you say gets properly thought through."

"Oh dear. I'm just so awful—"

"There you go again. You're not awful, just Bubbles."

"Thanks. I'll try and lessen the fizz. But you know, Anna, I am sooo grateful to have been born on Terraspei and encouraged to explore things."

"Me, too. That's why our scientists have been working hard on this, I guess. This has been developed *here* – we don't want to shut ourselves in and keep the rest of the universe out. Now we can get to explore what it means – what it feels like – to be people on Earth and even, maybe, Pure Haven. Listen to them... and perhaps even help them."

"And any other race of intelligent beings who might have paired particles. Imagine every alien species with this technology could just phone us up and—"

"Bubbles. You're fizzing. Let's do one thing at a time."

Elle and her family were glued to the screen that evening, along with the entire population of Terraspei as scientists talked about the breakthrough that had taken place. They had secretly subjected it to a year of testing – they hadn't wanted to say anything until they were sure they had done it, a spokesman explained.

"We sent messages across the lab, then across the city and finally to the other side of the planet. Each time with complete accuracy."

"The other side of Terraspei? Through the planet?" asked the interviewer.

"Quantum entanglement doesn't worry about what is or isn't between quantum pairs – not even a hypergiant star. That was established in the twentieth century. What's new here is that we've been able to use it to induce a stable microportal."

"So you're saying that it doesn't matter where the microportals are; the communication is instant, no matter how far apart."

"Succinctly put."

"When will this tech be rolled out beyond your lab?"

"A signal to Earth has been up and running for our leading academics for a couple of months. All space-villages have carried paired quantum particles just in case from the beginning of interplanetary travel."

"This was planned from the start?"

"The possibilities of this occurred to people centuries ago. And we've been working on it all the time – on and off. This is a massive achievement. We're now ready to do some trials outside of the university."

"So," said the interviewer, supplying a note of doubt in her voice, "how do we get it working on our phones?"

"Through the hub, subscribers will access the uni hub via the usual microwaves."

"Just call the uni?"

"The uni hub. But at present, we're going to restrict this to just a few well-monitored pilot schemes. So, everyone, please be patient."

The interviewer then adopted a graver tone. "What worries some people is what's to stop the floodgates opening and us – our kids – getting all the latest horrors from Earth just as they're happening?"

"There will be safeguards. It won't connect with everyone on

Earth. They will all have to subscribe to a hub, same as here. As I said, initially it'll be restricted to just a few people. We intend to connect them with similar people – parents with parents, teenagers with teenagers. All will be closely monitored. AI will step in to prevent anything unsavoury."

"But kids could soon be gaming with someone on Planet Earth?"

"Gaming's OK. So long as it satisfies the algorithms and the hubs regulate the traffic. This won't be a free-for-all. Even on Earth, safeguarding online was quickly applied after the initial devastating impact of uncontrolled access was experienced. Everyone will have to apply to participate. Initially, in the pilot phase, we want people who are good communicators and listeners."

"What about Pure Haven?"

"That'll be up to them, I guess. They have paired particles from Earth, too. All they need to do is build their own hub, and it can be three-way traffic all the way... If they want it. We're activating their pairs, but so far they haven't responded."

"They may not be aware."

"Oh, we're pretty sure they've noticed the signs. And, in any case, they have a space-village approaching them which has responded. We have a connection with them up and running. They have passed the news to them using conventional radio waves, so they have been made aware that way."

"This sounds very exciting. What is the next stage for us?"

"In the next few days, we'll be calling for interested volunteers to become part of the project."

In the Fishers' living room, Elle did a fist pump. "Yesss. Can't wait."

Unnoticed by the young people, however, a tiny tear trickled from Grandpop's left eye. His great-granddaughter worried him. And the rate everything seemed to be changing also worried him.

<h1 style="text-align:center">15</h1>

Sam stared at his computer screen. He had developed his own revision timetable for his exams. Today was history – just so much to learn. There was an endless bank of facts, sources, speculations, and goodness knows what else on every period. Layer upon layer of material. How deep should he go? Not so deep because he had only 40 minutes for each question in the exam. Nevertheless, the more he knew, the more he could pack into his answers, and the higher his grade would be.

Sam sighed as his screen flashed a communication from his school. *Ugh. What now? Do they want me to revise or not?* He had deliberately avoided his usual social media, even texts from his friends, in order to concentrate on his work. And now the school was saying something about coming in urgently. So what about exam prep? Couldn't they leave him alone to get on with it? But when he read the text fully, it was about a significant scientific breakthrough – something that would seriously affect young people. And their school had something really special to share with their years 11, 12 and 13 students.

He turned on his news feed. "Scientists receive groundbreaking information technology from Terraspei University." *Groundbreaking? It must be over ten years since they sent it. Can't it wait till I've done my exams?* But the implications seemed to be that from now on, interplanetary communication would no longer be restricted to electromagnetic waves with their limitation to the speed of light. "Imagine having a live conversation with people on an exoplanet!" smiled the newsreader.

Sam strolled up the path to his school. He thought he had been done with it until the exams started. He spotted his friend James, backpack on his shoulder, making his way to the same door.

"Hi, James. So, what's all this about 'Groundbreaking IT'? How's it going to affect our exams, do you reckon?"

"Hi, Sam. Dunno. They can't ask anything that's not in the curriculum. It must be something important, though, for them to call in the whole year 11 in our revision break."

They wended their way to the hall where the year 11 students were assembling.

"Hiya, Sam." *Oh, botheration! Not Tanya. Sam sighed – inwardly. Tanya, again! When would she give up on him?* She had accused him of getting her into trouble, tormented him at every opportunity and even dated his footy mates, so he had to listen to her screaming on the touchline. But she, thank goodness, was not going to continue into the sixth form. When both lessons and the football season ended, he had breathed a sigh of relief. He had not expected to see her around the school again until the exams.

"Oh, Tanya."

"Good to see ya."

"Yeah."

Like a leech, she walked with him to the entrance. At the door, Sam held back and let her go in first, and once through the doors, he dived off to the side and headed for the boys' loos. When he emerged, he looked for a seat in the back row, only to find himself next to Amy Huck. She smiled at him and went, "OK?"

"Oh. Sorry. Saving this seat for a friend? I'll—"

"Yeah. And you're it. Sit down."

"But..." She didn't seem to care what people might say. Before he could say more, a hush spread across the hall as Mr Gilbert, the head teacher, entered and climbed the staging.

"Students," he began, "thank you for coming back into school in the middle of May when, no doubt, you are applying yourselves diligently to your revision." A titter emanated from around the hall, which Mr Gilbert ignored. They knew the implications of failure, and he was not going to waste time spelling it out again. But they needed to hear this news. Schools across the world were teaching their pupils about the new super-communications that would be taking their planet – their planets – by storm in the next few months, and he had some very interesting news. News he was bursting to share with his students.

"Ladies and gentlemen..." Up until last year, it had been 'boys and girls', but at the beginning of year 11, they were being addressed as adults. "You will have seen in the news feeds that our friends on Terraspei have developed a new form of communication that will revolutionise the history of humanity.

"As you know, around a hundred years ago, the technology to build engines to travel at half light speed made it possible to reach the nearest habitable exoplanets in our region of space. It took our predecessors from the twenty-third century no more than forty years to successfully colonise these planets – well within the lifetimes of the enterprising young people of the time. They are now into the fourth generation.

"These planets have worked well – Terraspei in particular. But the distance – more than ten light-years – means it takes over twenty years to hold a reciprocal conversation. This is especially difficult for interplanetary cooperation towards advancing science and technology. By the time the communications have been received, things are long out of date in our fast-moving research. Even the arts suffer from being cut off. Isolation serves no one.

"But now, today, all this is about to change. Our friends on Terraspei have been especially busy. As a small population, they have more to gain than we do, and that has lent impetus to their research. They have developed a form of super-connectivity. In a moment I'm going to hand over to Miss Brankhurst, our head of science, to explain the details, which I urge you to make careful note of. But I cannot emphasise how important this is for all subjects – indeed, our whole lives.

"In your history studies, you have learnt of the impact of the innovations in communications technology in the late twentieth and twenty-first centuries. Young people were faced with a connectivity that vastly superseded that of their parents, let alone their grandparents. This came with a cost; mental ill-health and online social abuse rocketed. Learning the psychological skills and safeguarding to cope with it lagged behind the technology. Today, we have learnt that lesson.

"We know this works precisely because we are in communication with Terraspei using it. At the moment, it is only usable by those in the university laboratories who have the materials required. As I said, scientific details to follow from Miss Brankhurst." He shot her a smile.

"But allow me to get onto the social implications for us here in this school. The British government has commissioned a hub in Cambridge. I understand that now we have all the specs from the team on Terraspei; building the system will not take more than two months. There will also be hubs in America and China, but we will have to take great care how much we bombard our interplanetary friends with.

"Those who wish to exploit us via the airwaves will no doubt try to take advantage of the opportunity to profit from this too, just as they have been doing ever since the Internet was invented.

"So now I come to the most exciting part."

The head smiled from ear to ear.

"We, at Stanton Wick, have been selected to be a school link. Our school and *our school alone* in the whole of Europe. Exactly why we have been selected I do not know. But we have. This is very exciting but also quite daunting. We are determined not to mess up this opportunity.

"So, if any of you would like to be part of a pilot connection – I want just two people – I invite you to contact my office through the usual channels. Thank you, ladies and gentlemen." A wave of amazement rolled across the hall as the implications of being one of the first to talk to other young people across the galaxy sank in. "I will now hand over to Miss Brankhurst, who will give you the science."

Sam did his best to get it. He struggled, though. Miss Brankhurst went too fast.

As they walked out of the hall, he mumbled to Amy, "I don't get that bit about microportals. I mean, how does speech get through?"

Amy explained, putting it over better than Miss Brankhurst for Sam.

"Thanks. How did you get that from what she said?"

"I went into it before I came. It's on the news."

"Oh. So this isn't a surprise?"

"No. Not Wormcomm. But that we have been selected to be a school to pilot this is *amazing* news."

"Yeah. I mean, just imagine having a connection with someone on another planet."

"Absolutely. You're good at virtual connections – you've got a VR friend across the world."

"Yeah, but...on another planet! Live. Amazing."

"Would you like to have a go at this?"

"You mean being part of the pilot thing?"

"Yeah. They want two people."

"Yeah but *me*. There are all those who are predicted to get A stars. No point in applying."

"Being good at stuff doesn't make you suitable for everything. They've already got their scientists and top-flight people in the universities. No, this is about having ordinary kids involved. That's why they have come to our school and not one of the posh ones."

"Makes sense."

"And you are already communicating across the world, so you know how to do it."

"Suppose..."

"And if we apply together, that may give us an advantage."

"You really want to do this?"

"Of course. It's really, like, exciting. I mean... another planet..."

"OK."

"Let's both message the office and say we want to do this together."

"Now?"

"Of course."

As Sam took out his phone, he felt that, actually, this was, like, cool. Really cool. He was going to be jealous of the kids who were chosen because it wouldn't be them, would it? There had been hundreds in the hall that day. How many of them would be applying?

16

etty bounced up to her friends at break. There was a sense of real excitement in her that Charity and Leah hadn't seen before.

"Haven't you heard?" She asked.

"Heard what?" replied Charity.

"There's been a breakthrough in interplanetary communications. Someone on Terraspei has produced some kind of quantum thing that can connect planets almost instantaneously across the galaxy – the universe even – if we know there is anyone there. You could get your pen friend on Terraspei after all."

"Wow! How? I mean, how... do you know that? It's made up. It can't be true. Nothing can travel faster than the speed of light."

"Abe, my brother. He said it was supposed to be a secret but—"

"Like the best secrets, known about but not talked about in public."

"Exactly."

"It's a hoax."

Leah struck a serious note. "I think my brother said something about it, but I didn't take it in. I thought he was talking about one of his sci-fi books."

Charity was still sceptical. "So this means we can add Earth and Terraspei to our social networks – on our phones."

"That's what the boys are saying," confirmed Betty. "But, of course, it wouldn't be permitted on our networks. I mean, we're already restricted to approved female friends and family – even if you have a phone. My brothers told my dad I was doing things I wasn't – as per usual – and he's confiscated mine. Says I can have it back when he thinks I deserve it."

"Aw, Betty. That's awful."

"No worries. You guys keep me sane."

Leah laughed. "Charry keep you sane? You're joking."

"You two are about the only people I can trust. Sometimes I don't know what's true myself. I'm not joking. You keep me sane. They do it deliberately – tell me one thing one day and another the day after and say I'm imagining it all. They, like, make stuff up all the time on purpose. They want me to lose it. I know they do."

Charry gave her friend the biggest of cuddles. "You're OK. Stick with us. This planet is mad. But we're solid. Keep believing in yourself, girl."

"It would definitely help to be able to talk to people in a place where lies aren't passed off as the truth," said Leah. "But they'll never let us use our phones, that's for sure."

Charity put on her determined look. The one that came before she got herself into trouble. "Not if we used a guy's phone... assuming all this is true. I mean, Terraspei!"

"You wouldn't dare," laughed Leah.

"You'd get him, whoever he is, into deep trouble," said Betty, anxiously.

"Where there's a will, there's a way. You just watch me."

"That's scary."

"Yeah," agreed Leah. "Don't get yourself and other people into trouble, Charry." Coming from Leah, this was serious. "Some things are, like, just too dangerous."

"Yeah." Betty nodded. Her face showed alarm.

Charity breathed out a big sigh. "I guess you're right, guys."

"Getting banished won't help anybody," said Betty. "I need you guys."

"You're right. I'll be careful. And, don't worry, I won't say anything to anyone. I won't even give them a clue I've heard the rumour." That was the dangerous thing. True or made up, talk of it was banned, wasn't it? It was time to change the subject.

"So, how's it going with your allocated young man, Betty?" Betty screwed up her nose. Her chosen 'young man' was a widower in his mid-thirties, who smelt.

"He stinks... literally. And I mean 'literally' as in he's probably not washed in years."

So, Charity thought, as they talked about unwanted human pairings, I'm going to have to find out whether all this talk of faster-than-light connections has got any truth in it. If it has, I will need to get hold of a phone that will connect off-planet, which won't get anyone into trouble. Maybe I could modify my own phone. It can't be that difficult. And when I have, I won't breathe a word to anyone – not even Leah and Betty, for their sakes.

17

Raph decided to call his friend Zac. Zac could be trusted. You could say anything to Zac – including sharing your frustrations with the Ruling Council – and it wouldn't go any further.

"So, what's with this new super-connectivity rumour?"

"Super-connectivity? Don't understand it, mate. Probably a hoax. How's Charity?"

"She's OK, so—"

"I'm free right now. Is she in?"

"Yeah. Didn't know you were keen on her. She's just got betrothed."

"I know. It isn't like that. She left her sports bag – at least I think it's hers. That's why I need to see her. I'll be with you in ten."

"What's the rush?"

But Zac had ended the call... and Charry couldn't have left her sports bag; her kit was all hanging on the washing line.

In under ten minutes, Zac was at the door.

"Charry is in her room."

"I haven't come to see her, Raphael. That was for the regime."

"Régime? The Ruling Council? Your phone being monitored or something?"

"Can't be sure... but I've got this sneaking feeling. Anyone with academic parents invites attention."

"Just your parents? What about you? You've got potential."

"No. I haven't."

"You have. Anyone deemed to have potential can be invited to study at the Institute. You'll get an invitation."

"I won't. I won't be going to the Institute."

"Why? To be asked to attend the Institute is an honour. It's an elite college."

"I'll tell you what it is. It's a way of making sure the brains are on their side – controlling the narrative. There is no way I want to go to the Institute."

"If you're invited, you can't say no."

"Exactly. So I'm thick."

"But you're—"

"Not clever enough to go to the Institute. They have to think I'm only interested in sport and pretty girls. I am officially totally disinterested in science... or things that are, like, 'groundbreaking' or sensitive."

"And super-connectivity is groundbreaking and sensitive?"

"Of course. Just imagine the implications if the population could chat in real time with people on Earth or, worse still, Terraspei. Our grandparents left for this planet to escape the challenges to traditional culture. Why do you think they named the planet Pure Haven?"

"Because they left behind any tendency to criminal, selfish behaviour – a place to put the common good above the individual."

"And in practice, it's turned into keeping everyone in their allotted place in society, so there is no threat to the Ruling Council."

"Like girls can't study science."

"Yep, among other things. Talk about super-connectivity on the phone could get us into hot water. I overheard the head talking to Mr Noakes in the lab. 'Wormcomm' is not to be talked about – all rumours quashed under pain of banishment from on high."

"But it could all just be a rumour, just be a hoax."

"It could, but I doubt it. I mean, the head could just have told Mr Noakes to ignore it. Why the draconian response? I reckon they're rattled. I would be amazed if it were not true; it's something that has been on the cards for centuries, so not exactly new."

"Centuries? How do you mean? That's, kinda ridiculous."

"Yeah. It's the ability to manipulate the process that's been the problem. What I'm hearing is that it uses quantum entanglement, which was discovered around 1930. Back then, it defied the laws of physics discovered by Einstein, and he didn't like it. It took decades to be actually accepted because it seemed to defy the rule that nothing can exceed the speed of light."

"But... I thought nothing *could* travel faster than the speed of light."

"Unless a pair of quantum particles are entangled and can be enticed to open up a microportal... Look, don't try and apply logic here. You get two particles – say, electrons."

"The particles that you get in electricity."

"Right. Two subatomic particles that are twins of each other. Whatever one of them does, the other does too."

"They communicate."

"Well, no. They just seem to know *without* communicating."

"How—?"

"I said don't try to apply logic. In the 20th century, they separated pairs by a big distance so that if they were communicating, there would be a delay – the time it takes for the message to travel, which cannot be faster than the speed of light. But there was no delay. Wherever the paired particle is in the universe, the other does what its twin does. They act in unison – instantly."

"So if we had one of the pair here and the other was on Earth..."

"Or Terraspei. Bingo, instant copying of their quantum state."

"And we have sets of twins here on Pure Haven?"

"If I were establishing a colony light-years away, I would equip myself with a bank of them, wouldn't you? Especially as trillions of them would fit into a space no bigger than your little fingernail. I would say our grandfathers packed a few in their luggage – just in case someone down the line invented a use for them."

"And now they have."

"It would seem so. Somehow or other they have got them to

create a tiny wormhole through spacetime to order."

"That's, like, amazing. If you could just chat with people on other planets live, that would change everything."

"Precisely. And if being isolated suited you, you wouldn't want every teenager, whizz-kid or not, to have access to them."

"They could go ahead and contact Earth; bypass them."

"Or Terraspei?"

"Yes. So it would be possible for *anyone* – they wouldn't need to be a scientist. I could connect *my* phone. Wow! How do we get hold of..."

"Raph, forget it. If you want to end up banished where no one even knows whether you're alive or dead, then ask questions. Otherwise, just listen and wait."

"Got you."

"And don't call me a whizz-kid in front of other people, or they might send me to the Institute or sign me up to work in a government lab... or just disappear me."

"But you'll pass your Level-Eighteen grade A, and they'll know."

"No. Lower B."

"You mean you'd deliberately fail?"

"And you should do the same."

"*I* would not have a problem doing that. I don't shine."

They heard footsteps on the stairs. A smiling Charity had bounded out of her room.

"Hi, guys. What's the secret? What are you two whispering about with serious-looking faces?"

"N... No secret, Miss Long-ears," said Raph. If you really want to know, we're discussing the Level Eighteen exams."

"Hi, Charity. You OK?"

"Yeah. I wish I had your lessons. I'd love the chance to study physics and chemistry."

"I know. Not so easy for girls."

"You can say that again."

"It's not so easy—"

"Don't bother. All you need is a kind older brother who lets you read his textbooks and stuff."

"You mean his Eighteen-Level books? You have to hand in the Sixteen-Level ones. That'll make you more advanced than the cleverest sixteen-year-old boys."

"Charry! You promised not to tell anyone."

"Zac's OK. Nat says. And anyway, you were sharing secrets just then."

"I wasn... OK. But this doesn't go any further. My sister here has read all the Eighteen-Level stuff, including the chapters we haven't got to in class yet. She's a bright girl, much cleverer than me."

Charity laughed at her brother's compliments.

"How about you guys coming up to my room and telling me about what you're doing in class... and, by the way, what's with this rumour about super-connectivity that might allow us to get stuff from other planets?"

"Charry! You're not supposed—" began her brother but Zac was already saying,

"Yes, let's."

When they were altogether in Charity's room and Zac had checked she didn't have her computer running, Zac began, "Charry, you do know that this knowledge is, like, toxic?"

"Yeah."

"Really dangerous. If the Ruling Council got wind—"

"They won't."

"OK."

Half an hour later, Charity had been made completely aware of the quantum mechanisms at play. She understood quicker than almost anyone Zac knew, despite being only sixteen and not having had any science lessons.

"Raph and I are not going to discuss it openly. The regime will want to sit on it... hard. And your brother – and me, too – could get into a lot of trouble just talking science to a girl."

"Yeah, I know. I don't ever let on what Raph lets me into. Except to you now... and Nat, since you helped him spy on me.

Not even Mum and Dad know. Apart from Leah and Betty, who was the one who told me, Nat and you, there's no one. I promise."

"My little sister's not only clever but wily and cunning. The best actor I know," confirmed Raph.

"You can share everything with Nathan," said Zac. "He's your betrothed because he's a science nerd – quite the cleverest guy around – and he's watched you in the library sneaking a peak at the science shelves."

"I know."

"The reason he bid for you was because of your brain... mainly."

"So if he's that clever, why isn't he in the Institute?"

"Same reason as I won't be. Because he fluffed his exams."

"On purpose?"

Zac nodded.

"That clever?"

"Just be grateful you're a girl and won't be made to go there."

Zac looked into Charity's eyes and saw depth. She was really bright. A stirring in his stomach surprised him. No girl had done that to him before. *Am I jealous of Nathan? I hope there's someone like you in the space-village that's coming.*

18

Towards the end of harvest, Pure Haven became a hive of anticipation. The new space-village was in orbit preparing to descend. The settlement was seriously going to expand; three and a half thousand new people were going to have to be accommodated over the course of the winter. They would, at first, remain in their cabins aboard the space-village, then after six months, the Alpha hub would leave and begin its return to Earth. When that happened, there would be no going back; both immigrants and existing residents would be fully committed. These were to be the first influx for fifteen years; the tension among the Pure Haven elite was palpable, and the people felt it.

The Williams kept their heads down. Charity's school was obviously making preparations, but no one dared ask what the plans were – especially not the girls. And no one – not even the other kids – talked about the rumours that had been circulating about super-connectivity. They had all got the message. It was as if that news had never existed. It was abundantly clear that Pure Haven was not going to take advantage of this new tech. Charity concluded it would go the same way as the AI that had served them well in getting to their planet. The Ruling Council were determined to turn the clock backwards.

Far from super-connectivity, Charity could see a time – perhaps not so far off – when personal phones would exist no more for ordinary people. They would begin with the females. It was getting harder and harder to replace phones, and battery recycling had been scaled back in recent months, which was affecting privately owned home computers as well as phones. It didn't have to be this way. There were perfectly serviceable recycling facilities, and more would be arriving on Space-Village Talbot. The elite had no problem keeping their electronics powered – nor did the marshals.

Charity was really looking forward to the arrival of the new space-village. Apart from some fresh faces, they would have some cool stuff on board, and their expectations might stimulate the Ruling Council to do some updates. She doubted, however, that there would be any cultural reforms – emigrants to Pure Haven were traditionalists by conviction; they might be in favour of totalitarian rule. Experience showed that the trouble would come when some of the new people were placed lower on the social ladder than they expected to be, while, at the same time, some of the existing residents would have their noses put out by being demoted. Integration of immigrants had always caused a problem.

On the eve of the expected arrival, Charity felt both excited and apprehensive. The usual social interaction had cooled, and she thought it best to stay at home. School was having an untimely holiday, and so, along with her brothers, Charity busied herself with some 'improving' reading – the Bible. She enjoyed some of the scandalous tales in the Old Testament but also some of the sayings of Jesus, which seemed to contradict the official line – Jesus had been a rebel and had been put to death for being one, but, of course, he was officially revered in the settlement. It occurred to Charity that the Ruling Council resembled the people Jesus criticised and who had got him killed. But, for some reason, that didn't seem to bother those who determined the way Pure Haven worked. They saw Jesus on their side, whatever. And, despite the much-quoted verses about women remaining subservient, in practice in those New Testament days, they seemed to have had a bigger look-in than the male-dominated society around them; there was no shortage of girls and women in the Christian stories. Some of them had even been put in charge of things, which was clearly different from the way things generally worked in the Bible lands at that time. *It's a good job my parents can't read my mind,* thought Charity. *They think I'm reading this Bible because I'm a dutiful daughter. But, to be honest, I like it when the high and mighty guys in the stories who fancy themselves get brought down – especially when Jesus punctures their pomposity... Oh, and I look for the juicy bits... and the saucy ones. The Song of Solomon is hilarious: 'Refresh me with apples. I am weak from passion...'. Apples? I wonder if there are any apples on Talbot?*

The day wore on. Even her mum ran out of chores for her to do, and Charity became bored. And there, as if by magic, was her Nat.

"You're going to have to give up coming round like this, Nat. People might think you fancied me."

"I do. And I'm bored."

Charity laughed. It was amazing how he seemed to reflect her mood. "So when you've got more interesting things in your life, you'll forget me?"

"Nope. I'll just do them with you."

"You say all the right things. You'd better mean it... So, are you dreading our new arrivals?"

"I'm reserving judgement. Let's wait and see which way it goes."

"They might have some lovely attractive girls."

"I hope so. But you're not going to get out of it that easily. Living on this planet for a whole lifetime is going to be hard. I need to have someone whom I can love and trust when I'm trying to live a lie."

"You can trust me in that."

"Thanks."

"But we do need to be careful where we talk. Walls have ears."

"George Orwell."

"Who's he?"

"A guy who wrote a book in 1948 called *1984*. You can find it online. It's subversive, but somehow it missed the censor. Probably because it's labelled dystopia and the algorithm decided it is just another bit of young adult sci-fi."

"Like the Bible you're reading."

"Whoa. You, too? You see it, too? The subversion. It's packed with females. Jesus' life is bookended with Marys. It was a Mary who saw the angel and said yes to bearing Jesus, and it was another Mary – Mary Magdalene – who was the first one to see him alive when he rose from the dead. The stories were revolutionary when they were written."

"They still are. If you listen to Jesus, you know there's authority out there beyond our Ruling Council."

"You frighten me sometimes, Nat. You shouldn't talk about the Ruling Council like that."

The kitchen door opened. "Are you coming in, Nathan?" called Charity's mother. How much had she heard?

"I'm not sure I should leave my daughter and her fiancé together for too long on their own. After all, you have only just become betrothed."

19

"**Y**ou young people worry me, Elle," said Grandpops. It seemed to go with being a great-grandparent.

"You're always worried about something these days, Grandpops. Don't you trust us?"

"Of course I trust you. I'm proud of you. We just don't want you to get hurt. Terraspei has always been a safe place. There are fewer people, and it's far away from all the bad influences on Earth. You know, when we volunteered to be part of the third travelling village—"

"Yes. You've told us about fifty million times, Grandpops."

"Yes. But all that's different now. This new... 'thing' they've invented is going to change everything forever. We'll be like just another country on Earth. All their corrupt ideas and ne'er-do-wells will prey on our beautiful young people and lead them into bad ways."

"Or we could lead them into good ways. What sort of bad ways could they come up with that you haven't already told us about?"

Grandma broke into the conversation. "... or discovered for yourselves in all that reading you do? Bad ways are somehow built into what it means to be human. There is a dark side to all of us. We have to work on being good."

"Yeah, I know. And let the Spirit in to help us."

"Precisely."

Elle's dad looked up from his tablet, on which were stored generations of classics going back to the Ancient Greeks. You never knew which century he was in. "Worry about it or not; it's happened. And it's our scientists who have done it. You cannot stand in the way of progress." He brandished his tablet. "History teaches us that. What counts is what we do with it."

"All my friends think it's brilliant."

"So long as you understand the dangers – what you might be getting into. As soon as anything new comes out, there will be criminals on both our planets wondering how they might exploit it."

"Even on Terraspei?"

"Even here. I wish I could say otherwise, but I can't."

"I promise I won't do any communicating without you knowing, Dad."

"Perfect. Two brains are better than one."

"Yeah. And you tell me all you're communicating too."

Her dad sighed. "I guess it's not so much about being answerable as remaining safe."

Grandpops smiled. "That makes a lot of sense. Only don't ask me whether anything's safe or not. It'll blow my brain." He was happy. He was sure he could trust these younger people. In the final analysis, people are protected not by isolation but by their own understanding and values. That way they can identify the lies and separate them from truth and goodness. They'll no longer be vulnerable but wise.

20

On Space-Village Talbot, the decision to break the news about Wormcomm in the worship services simultaneously throughout the connected modules proved to be a good one. Nearly all the residents were present at a service somewhere. They were able to look after each other as the implications dawned on them. If anyone thought that the technology should not be used, no one voiced it. Congregations were left speechless.

The atmosphere on board was electric. The question on everyone's lips after the shock had subsided was, "When do we get it?" and, "Who are we going to phone on Earth?" It was strange seeing older people getting excited about new technology; of course, the kids took it all in their stride.

In the event, the question of who they should contact did not arise for most people. Within twenty-four hours, comms was inundated with calls from Earth requesting to be put through to their relatives. The chief of comms had four more computers patched into the system and draughted half a dozen members of the crew from other duties to act as operators.

"This is what it used to be like in the early days of telecommunication," observed one. "My great-grandmother to the power of ten was a telephonist in the twentieth century."

"I'm amazed she had any time to have any children," came the quip.

After a couple of days, however, the immediate rush was over. Now the emphasis was on caring for those suffering stress. It was a challenge being connected again to parents and siblings after so many years. The tears flowed. Those who received the saddest news found it hardest, of course. When your neighbours were excited about getting a call from Mum, it was tough to learn that yours had died in the last few years.

But there was no going back to Earth. Being reconnected changed very few people's minds. The kids were far more excited about what lay ahead than any contact their families made with the past. This generation belonged to Pure Haven, not Earth. It helped to be in touch, but day after day, as they orbited the planet, families were looking down at their new home. The bright green lands and huge craters filled with water between snowy peaks, all topped with fluffy white clouds, looked pristine and inviting. And the little town that became visible through the telescopes, although small, seemed homely.

All would have to wait but, with Wormcomm the kids had a new way to use a phone. It was a new fad they could buy into. Joseph and Fran met after a science lesson.

"I'm going to ask if I can chat with someone on Earth my age," said Joseph. "There must be teenagers in the family that would like to link up – maybe do an online game or something."

"Yeah, why not?" said Fran. "What do you think the elders will say?"

"'Yes' probably. Can't see what harm that will do?"

"There are corrupt influences on Earth."

"It'll only be with one person. I wouldn't be going on some free-for-all thing, would I?"

That evening, Joseph asked his parents if there was anyone his age in their family on Earth he could connect with.

"I don't rightly know," answered his father, truthfully. "But we can always ask."

"Some wholesome young man," insisted his mother.

"Of course. I'll enquire next week. More people from our family plan to be present when we next call."

"What about Beth?"

"Your sister is too young," said his mum. "The same rules that apply to interacting with friends digitally within the village will apply when it comes to communicating outside."

"She's twelve Earth years."

"Yes. So she's going to have to wait a few years."

"Soon we'll be on Pure Haven."

"And they will have their own ways, but I doubt they will be less diligent. And anyway, during the six-month integration phase, those who remain living in the space-village will be sticking to the onboard rules."

The members of the Ruling Council gazed doubtfully into the night sky. The space-village would be making its final approach within a few hours. How all these people could be integrated worried them. Would they become a bad influence? Had the onboard children been brought up in the right way? They must be prepared to absorb them slowly and ensure they acknowledge and respect the social order, especially the established authority of the Ruling Council.

What didn't occur to them was that of the 3561 people ready to descend on their planet, most were already chatting away to people on Earth. They had successfully – or so they thought – buried the super-connectivity tech. They were not aware that the space-villagers above were settling down very quickly to using Wormcomm in their everyday lives.

On Pure Haven, Christmas alternated between winter and summer. That winter Christmas was to be the last major event before the modules made their final approach.

In the space-village above, the decision was made to maintain the gangs between the modules until after the festival, which saw the same comings and goings as they had done for the past twenty-one Christmas Days. Videos of the worship on board were shared with the assemblies below while they sang the praises of the gift of the newborn Christ, too. The same carols that had endured down the centuries were ever popular, and the space-village musicians looked forward to teaching the colony some of the new ones that had been written since Pure Haven had been founded. And to top it off, for the first time in twenty years on board Space-Village Talbot, there was the screen-sharing with families on Earth. Since Talbot had left, they had celebrated Christmas three times more on Earth than on board; such was the impact of the time dilation. But, despite it being June, the Earth-bound relatives and friends were not averse to entering into the spirit of things with their newly rediscovered connections.

On Talbot, there was a magic about that particular Christmas that was really special. They were heartened when they heard the positive vibes coming from the old planet; things looked as if they were beginning to turn a corner in the battle against climate change. That Christmas would become a time that, in years to come, they were to look back on as a major highlight in their lives.

21

To Sam's complete amazement, he and Amy found themselves summoned to the head's office. Miss Brankhurst delivered the message. She had a broad smile on her face and told them it was good news. They weren't in trouble.

"I told you," said Amy, as they traced their way through corridors and across a yard. "It's us. For Wormcomm."

"Maybe more like, 'Thank you for your interest, but not this time'."

Amy sighed. He was being a misery guts, but he was probably right.

However, a beaming Mr Gilbert sat them down and said they had been the preferred applicants. He was attracted by their enthusiasm and had been impressed by the work they had put into obtaining a good result in all three science subjects. He concluded with, "I'm especially pleased, Samuel, that you have decided to associate with a more diligent student since the last time you were in this office."

"Yes, sir. I didn't choose Tan—"

"History, Samuel. All history. Expunged from the record."

"Thank you, sir."

"Report to Miss Brankhurst, and she will set things up for you."

"Thank you, sir," replied Amy, struggling to keep the excitement from bubbling over.

There was something about talking to someone nearly twelve light-years away that was, like, wow!

A family were looking for someone of the same age to connect with two people on board. It sounded cool. They didn't have to establish a regular link if they didn't get on. Sam thought they probably wouldn't. From what he had heard, they were probably rather religious – especially as they were about to land on Pure Haven.

That evening after tea, Sam and Amy were told to be ready to get a call from a guy called Joseph. At half past seven, Sam's laptop blinked a live connection.

"Hello."

"Hello, is that Sam?" It was as clear as a bell. It was as if the guy was only just down the road.

"Yeah."

"I'm Joseph, and I live on Space-Village Talbot-Theta. Are you really on Earth?"

"Yeah. And are you really over eleven light-years away?"

"We are. I can see your Sun as a tiny star through my porthole. It's quite dim compared to some of the others. I can't believe you're so far away."

Amy broke into the link. "Hi, Joseph, is it? I'm Amy."

"Oh hi."

"Let me look out our window," said Sam. "I think I know which of the stars is Tau Ceti if it's up... No, it isn't at the moment – you're around the other side of the planet."

"That doesn't make any difference, does it?"

"No. This new tech is, like, amazing."

"It is. You're the first person I've spoken to ever who doesn't live in our space-village."

"Meet Amy." He moved the laptop to include Amy beside him."

"Hi, Amy. Fran's coming to join me in a mo."

"How many are there of you all together?"

"Counting everybody, just over three and a half thousand but not very many of us were born on board. There are forty- eight of us in my school year."

"Which year is that?"

"Year twelve. We keep to the same school years as on Earth and we do most of the same curriculum as you."

"Only forty-eight in your year. That sounds kinda small."

"It's like we all belong to one family. It'll be good to be able to meet new people. How many are in your year at your school?"

"Let me work it out. In our year there are five forms and about thirty in each form. That makes 150 in our year group, but they come from a wide area."

"We don't know most of them to talk to," said Amy.

"Wow! That's amazing. You can choose your friends."

"Yeah. It's not just our school, either. My best mate doesn't even go to my school. There are three schools in the area."

"That's, like, incredible... Oh, here's Fran. Fran is one of the girls in our year."

"Hi. I hope you don't mind talking to me."

"You're welcome, Fran," said Amy. "I'm Amy and this is Sam."

"You can't be short of friends with all those people," said Fran. "You must be very busy."

"Yeah, we are," said Sam. "Not just with friends, though. There are exams and all that. And the football. If I were in your place, I'd be longing to talk to someone outside... You haven't got many to get up a football team."

"And nowhere to play if you had!" exclaimed Amy. "I can't imagine not having a field to play on."

"True. We do play indoor football, though," said Joseph. "We use the largest gym. When we were younger, we liked to play boys versus girls. But now we're bigger, some people say we should be allowing the girls to become ladies, which means they have to stop doing most sports, so the girls miss out more than the boys, I guess. My younger sister, Beth – she's twelve – says there's no way she's going to become a lady and stop running about."

Sam felt cooped up just thinking about sport in a space-village. "That's, like, crazy. It would drive me mad. How do you put up with it?"

"Oh, it's OK. We've never known anything else. To be honest, the idea of leaving this village and stepping onto the surface of a planet is scary. We're all looking forward to it in one way, but we've no idea how we'll do it. The good thing is that no one has to leave the village straightaway. We can stay here, living in our cabins, for up to six months. Then if we really don't like it on the planet, we can choose to return to Earth, I guess. Talbot-Alpha is returning anyway."

"Which will mean another twenty years plus in space without a gym."

"Over twenty-four."

They chatted on for over an hour before Joseph's parents called him for dinner.

The following morning, as they and their tiny year group came together in one of the school rooms, Joseph and Fran shared with them what they had talked about with Sam and Amy. An air of excitement fizzed around. Joseph and Fran became the centre of attention. All of them wanted a Wormcomm connection with someone on Earth. It also made them increasingly impatient to land and get out onto the surface of a real planet. These were indeed exciting times with so many new freedoms beckoning. It was kinda scary but cool nonetheless.

The maths teacher arrived, and they did their best to concentrate on the topic of the day. The teacher couldn't quite make out what all the buzz was about as he tried to explain the complexities of multiplying surds. Even he failed to find surds quite that exciting.

On Earth, Sam and Amy were still trying to get their heads around the fact that Joseph and Fran were so far away when they sounded like they were just across the street. The more the chat had gone on, however, the more they had become aware of just how different living on a space-village was from what they took for granted in the Chew Valley. They had a lot to learn and a lot to share. Mr Gilbert was one of the most keen to hear how the first contact had gone.

22

The intense interest in the rolling out of Wormcomm was not limited to Earth and Talbot. Elle had been increasingly excited at the prospect of chatting to someone her age on Earth. The powers-that-be had gone to some trouble in trying to identify possible links. But it was a school on Earth which had approached them first – Stanton Wick.

Apparently, the school had already begun forging links with a space-village in transit, and they were keen to be the first school in the country – if not the world – to establish links with Terraspei, too.

Elle applied without hesitation. Bubbles knew what she wanted, and if she wanted something, she generally got it.

"Already!" exclaimed Anna. "You never cease to amaze me. Like, you never gave this a second thought. The next thing is that you'll be on a space-village going somewhere no one has ever been to before."

"I might if they ever invent one that applies the quantum tech to transporting human beings and doesn't take a lifetime to get anywhere."

"Bubbles by name and Bubbles by nature."

"I got the name because of how I am."

"Look. Just promise me that you'll be careful. You know what they're like on Earth."

"I know their reputation. I've read the history books. But there are billions of people on Earth, and they can't all be like that."

"But you don't know who they might pair you with. It could be a modern-day Henry VIII or a Joseph Stalin."

"Hardly. Whoever it is, they'll still be at school."

"I hope you don't regret it. I mean, you could have talked about it first."

"I am now."

"I don't mean to me. I mean your family."

"Who would most likely say, 'Don't do it'?"

"Bubbles, you're wicked. Presenting them with a *fait accompli* isn't right."

"Look, don't worry. If they turn out to be a Henry VIII in training, I promise I'll dump them... It would probably be a girl, anyway."

"Boudica."

"What?"

"Boudica. She rode into London in a chariot with iron blades sticking out of the wheels. Supposed to have killed 80,000 people."

"So, OK. If she turns out to be a Boudica in the making, I'll cease communications. Whoever it is, it'll take them twenty years to come after me on the fastest space vehicle known to humanity. Oo, scary... not. I don't know what you're worrying about, Anna."

"That's the worrying thing. You just don't see the dangers."

When she got home, Elle didn't breathe a word to her family about her application. She didn't want to risk anyone calling the school to cancel it. *Am I committing a sin? Is deceit a sin? Maybe. But it's not my fault if people are over-careful stick-in-the-muds.* She hoped the connection would be made soon and that she didn't have to explain that the initiative had been hers. She could just come home and say that she had had an invitation to link up with someone who didn't appear harmful. *I wonder who I'll get?*

The following Monday morning, Elle and the others who had applied for an Earth-based Wormcomm friend were called into one of the classrooms nearest the entrance lobby. There were twenty-four of them. The teacher explained that the school in Britain had only a few students selected to become pioneers of the new technology. Of these, two had been chosen to connect with a space-village.

"The staff have decided the best way to begin is to choose just two of you at this stage," explained the teacher. "Please write your name on one of these pieces of paper I am passing around, fold it in four, come forward and put it into this hat."

Elle sighed. She thought she would be guaranteed a friend. She was on the cusp of saying that she had applied immediately. Her name was down early; it should be done on a first come, first served basis. But she didn't get to say. The teacher offered the hat to someone to draw a single piece of paper. As the first name was called and it wasn't hers, Elle thought she'd faint with frustration. *This is, like, so unfair*, she thought. But she knew that wasn't true. The chosen guy drew the second name; it was not hers, either. The winning girl uttered a cry of delight, "Cool." Elle, it seemed, was not the only keen kid on the block that day. She was gutted.

"Sorry you missed out," commiserated Anna, as Elle approached her with a sombre face.

"Thanks. It was cruel, but there were only two spaces, and the guys who won are as enthusiastic as me, so I'm glad for them. Sir says they have to report back their experiences. Even write about it."

"Essays. Yuk. Every exciting thing is an excuse for the English teacher to set an essay. It's guaranteed to suck all the fun out of anything cool."

"My teacher gives us the option of writing a story of imagination, which is not so dull."

"I guess. If you've got the gift of imagination. Unlike me."

"But, surely, you can imagine stories."

"I can't. Last week, teacher said, 'Imagine you were walking into an unknown wood. What do you hear?' All I could hear was my mum calling after me, telling me not to wander off on my own. When I told the teacher that, she said I had no imagination."

"That's a put-down. They're not supposed to do that. I guarantee you do have imagination. All you need to do is discover what sets it off. The trouble is too many adults squash us. They mean well, but they rein their kids in too much. They forget this place was built on the imagination of the pioneers of interplanetary travel. They should allow their kids the freedom to be, to explore... to grow..."

"... and want to connect with kids on Earth. Are you going to tell your parents your name went into the hat?"

"I... don't know."

"Bubbles, you should. Keeping things from people is dangerous. It'll come back and bite you one day. If you want them to trust you, you got to be honest."

"I guess."

"I know."

That evening, Elle decided to fess up. She had not been selected, and there was no indication of when or if there would be a second wave. But with a bit of luck, they might not think of asking the school to remove her name from the teacher's hat.

She waited until halfway through the evening meal and just threw it out there as if it were of no real import.

"Oh, by the way. It didn't happen for me, but the school asked for volunteers to have a Wormcomm friend from Earth. I said I would be interested but they only wanted two students."

As Elle predicted, her mother didn't see it as a small thing. She rounded on her daughter and was about to launch into the reasons why Elle should not have allowed her name to be considered. "And you didn't think you should, at least, have asked us first? Elle, I—"

To Elle's surprise, Grandpops intervened. He had rarely done this. He was usually quiet and soft-spoken but not today, it seemed. Elle winced internally. She had predicted her mother's reaction and was prepared for it but she hated upsetting Grandpops.

"Ever since I learnt about this new Wormcomm thing," he said, "I have been considering this possibility of it being accessed by our young people. Well, 'possibility' is the wrong word. The right word is 'inevitability'. This will happen whether we like it or not. This tech exists, and denying it won't get anyone anywhere. Every new invention has its drawbacks, and I can see many in this, but it also has its benefits and avenues for growth. The question now is not *whether* we use it but *how*. Given that fact, I think it is highly desirable that our family is involved from its inception. That way we can influence its roll-out. And there is no one I think I would want more to be involved than Bubbles. She might be quick to jump in but it's not the speed of the takeoff that matters but the accuracy of it. I'm sure we can trust Elle not to be influenced by the wrong kind of person on Earth."

Elle sat open-mouthed. No one said anything.

"But you haven't been paired up with anyone yet?" confirmed Grandpops.

"N... No. Not yet. Only two people got chosen."

"Then let's hope it doesn't take too long. We need the right kids in this."

"Thanks, Grandpops. I think the ones they've chosen are sensible students." As she said this, she reflected on the twenty-four in the room. There were certainly no doubtful ones there. "Thank you for saying I'm trustworthy. I hope I can live up to that."

Grandpops smiled, "I'm sure you can. Just remember, leaving out your parents rarely works well. It's generally wise to get them onside."

"Like, when you decided you wanted to fly off-planet."

Grandpops smiled. "They hated it, but I told them *before* I applied, even though I was technically an adult."

"But you still did it."

"Yep. I still did it. They were brave people, my mum and dad."

That night, as Elle lay in her bed, she thanked God for Anna and her grandpops, and for their wisdom. She had to admit to herself – and God – that she had been going down the road of deceit. She prayed for her mother. She told herself that if she changed her mind and became a mother herself one day, she would try not to be so protective of *her* daughter. Because that was it: her mother just loved her too much to let her take risks.

23

The landing sites were given a final mow of Pure Haven's native 'grass'. The fence around the spacedrome had been made extra secure. Whether it was to keep the newly arrived in or the existing residents out, Charity couldn't decide; there was no livestock in the area.

Some of the men decided to go to the perimeter to witness the sights and sounds, but most stayed away and watched on their televisions. When a space-village takes off, there is an enormous throbbing vibration that can be felt for many miles, but when it lands, it does so with barely a whisper, and, of course, no one is going to emerge for days. So when the ten very large modules had gently descended one by one from the sky, the show would be over.

The commander stood on the bridge of Alpha with his eyes glued to the screen in front of him. Officers shouted out altitude, lateral distance, engine speed, rate of descent and finally, "Touchdown," and, "Landing engines off." The craft settled and relaxed as the short legs beneath the hull took the weight and the cushioned hover skirts deflated.

The commander relaxed too. "Thank you, ladies and gentlemen. I think we can say that was an excellent landing for Talbot-Alpha. How are things with the others?"

"All in order, sir. Talbot-Beta is on course for landing in fifteen minutes and Talbot-Gamma fifteen after that, as planned."

"I'm going to my cabin. Keep me patched in."

105

"Yes, sir."

The Williams watched their screen as the cameras followed them landing a hundred metres apart. They hovered like Earth birds eyeing their prey and then slowly – really slowly – dropped to the grass. As they settled, they gave out a soft whoosh, as if relieved that they could rest after so many years on the move at half the speed of light. When all ten were down, everything was silent. The craft would spend several days slowly absorbing the Pure Haven atmosphere and adjusting their internal settings to those of the planet to allow the villagers to acclimatise and become accustomed to the gravity, feel and smells of their new home.

Three hours later, all ten modules were side by side on the large, close-cropped field. It would be six days before anyone could step outside. That would be a new experience for those born on board, and most of the others had forgotten what it was like to be outside under the stars with no windows or metal surroundings to protect them. No matter how spacious a space-village was, it could not prepare its inhabitants for the sensations of the open air.

24

Over the following six days, the villagers were gradually treated to the wonders of the fresh Pure Haven atmosphere. It was sweet and pleasantly rich with the aroma of the 'grass'. For the first time in two decades, some began to feel cooped up in their cabins and were impatient to get outside.

However, the protocol for the first contact had been established. The chief representatives of each village would step out first to meet the Ruling Council of their new planet. They were mostly men accompanied by their wives, but two were women with their husbands in tow. Everyone was extremely nervous but trusted that God would protect them. After all, God was God wherever you might be in the universe, and they were all under him. These people of Pure Haven were his special people, weren't they? They were free of the corruption and violence that epitomised Earth – that was why they had chosen to embark on their ambitious venture.

At last, the time came for the hatches to be opened and the leading representatives in their finest clothes emerged into the winter Taushine. When the wife of the first representative from Talbot-Beta stepped off the ramp, she found herself confronted by a large group of men all wearing dark-brown linen suits. They were lined up inside the high fence that surrounded the field. The gates appeared shut, and more men, not so finely dressed, stood beyond them. There were no females to be seen anywhere, and the ladies became increasingly uncomfortable as they were totally ignored by the greeters.

One of the women stepped forward, purposefully introduced herself to one of the men on the periphery of the group and demanded, "Have you no women on this planet?" The thought of being outnumbered by a planet of men was extremely perturbing, if not frightening. The man replied.

"Oh, yes. Of course. They are at home watching this on their television sets." And he pointed to a man with a primitive-looking camera standing on a wooden platform just beyond the fence. "We have television here most evenings," he said, with a proud air. "And today, it is operating during the day to witness this significant event."

'Significant' seemed rather too small a word. And then he left her and joined the queue to talk to her husband.

"I can't wait to see them come out," stated Charity. "I wonder what..." She tailed off. *Oh dear. I must learn not to be so... speaking my thoughts.* Her parents ignored her; she was relieved. They were staring at the TV as if something dramatic was going to happen. It didn't. The drama was yet to unfold. Not even Charity could imagine the way the arrival might impact their world.

The first was an older gentleman who seemed to be someone of rank among the new arrivals. He was greeted by a gathering of the Ruling Council with profuse handshakes. He was followed, surprisingly, by a woman. Charity wanted to cheer. She appeared alongside the elderly gentleman and walked with a confident air as if she were a person of some importance. In that moment, she was the only woman in the field. No women accompanied the members of the Ruling Council, nor was any to be seen in the ranks of the security staff or onlookers. This was entirely to be expected. Was this woman being deliberately provocative?

However, as more people emerged from the modules, almost half were women. Clearly, the customs aboard concerning women did not reflect those of the colony. The company milled about around the ramps, meeting and greeting, and then the newcomers, led by the women, filed back into one of the modules, and the TV closed down until its scheduled hour.

Charity was bursting to talk about it but dared not even suggest that anything had happened that was out of the ordinary.

Later that evening, Raph softly tapped on her bedroom door.

"Hi?"

"It's me. Can I come in?"

"Sure."

Raph tiptoed over to the bed and slumped back on his elbows. He spoke quietly – he did not want his parents to know he was talking to his sister. "I told you things would change."

"How? What do you mean?"

"Don't tell me you didn't notice. All those women coming out alongside the men. They're going to change things around here."

"Yeah. I wanted to cheer. But let's not count our sheep before they breed. The men of this place will prevail. You watch."

"Why so negative?"

"It's too soon."

"There are three and a half thousand and half of them are female. That's going to be like around... like..."

"One in eight females on this planet. That's not enough."

"Assuming all the women in Haven are happy with the status quo. Which they're not."

"You mean we'll, like, storm the Bastille?"

"The what?"

"Revolt. Riot."

"Well, I guess..."

"Most women are too busy trying to feed their families to riot."

"But they won't be on their own. There are men–"

"Men? The best of them are just pretending to be thick so they can keep out of it."

"Zac, Nathan."

"And you. You might be on our side, but you're not strong enough. And I don't blame you. I don't want you to get banished. And that's what's going to happen."

"So what about three and a half thousand people in the space-village?"

"If they don't convert – play ball – they'll just get sent back to where they came from."

"But what about the supplies, the new tech?"

"The Ruling Council doesn't care. They have enough for themselves already. Keeping the rest of us poor helps them."

"You mean making people deliberately poor?" Raph was shocked.

"It's happening already. Phones, batteries, electricity... food even."

"What about Wormcomm?" Raph persisted.

"What about it? Banned. Pretend it doesn't exist."

"But if someone were to get hold of it... Give it to the kids... I mean, all the Earth stuff could change things forever on Haven."

"It could, but... it's not going to happen, Raph."

"But don't give up, Charry. I like the way you are. You're an inspiration for the future. You've changed me. At least, you convinced me that you're right."

"But I can't say anything outside of this room. If I said anything out there, I would get grounded. Or out in the town, I could even be banished." *And perhaps I might have risked that, but not since Nat came on the scene. I have to stick around for him.*

"Banished. You never know," said Raph, "that might not be as bad as all that. Could be the best option. If you get banished, I'd make sure I got banished, too. And out there, wherever it is, we'd be free."

"Or dead. And that's not going to help anybody."

25

After only half an hour, the women began to make their way back into Talbot-Alpha, and the men soon joined them. They headed for one of the community spaces. A few of the women came together.

"I don't think I have ever been so uncomfortable," said one.

"Me neither. At least they could have had the thought that we women would like to have met their wives."

"Perhaps they didn't expect us to come out on the first stepping," suggested a third.

"They didn't. Perhaps women just don't do that here," said her friend.

"Well, I'm not going out there again until I see someone other than a group of rude, dark-suited men."

"Agreed. That was so embarrassing."

"To say the least."

"I had fondly imagined being greeted by some excited women offering to take us to a church hall or somewhere for a cup of tea and a piece of cake."

"While what we got was a load of rude formal men inside a locked gate. Do we need to be guarded?"

"Kept in, more like."

Their husbands joined the group.

"May I hazard a guess as to the topic of this animated conversation?" asked one.

"You may."

"Where were their women?" He gave a rueful smile.

"Apparently, they were at home watching it all on old-fashioned TV," said the woman who had been bold enough to ask the question.

"I have decided I am not going outside these walls again until there are women to greet us."

"Is that what you all think?" asked an elder. The gathering had now turned into a general meeting.

"Well, *I'm* not, whatever anyone else wants to do."

"Nor me," said another.

"I think I can speak for us all here," said his wife, loudly. "In future, we will wait until we have women to greet us." This was followed by the women's applause.

Back on the bridge, the commander was welcomed by the watch officer with the news.

"We have a situation, sir. The women are refusing to keep to the schedule."

"That doesn't surprise me. They must work out for themselves how they go about their integration here. They have until the end of June, when we will be in the Pure Haven spring – six months from now – and then we leave for Earth. If people wish to return, we can attach the required number of modules, plus the supplies we will need. So long as there are not too many of them, we can manage that."

"If they all came, we would need to restock the abiogenesis plant with fresh chemical products... there are losses in the recycling over time."

"Of course. But that's assuming they will all refuse to stay, which I doubt. Anyway, worst-case scenario, we can head for Terraspei – we'll have plenty for twelve years, if not twenty-three."

"Do you think that will be the case, sir? I rather fancy Terraspei for a vacation."

"I have no idea. All I know is that this vessel is my home, and my home leaves this forbidden planet on 30th June. Not a day later."

The next day a further group of people stepped out of the space-village. This time, however, they were all men.

Watching on her TV screen, Charity wasn't surprised, but she was delighted to see that her brother seemed disappointed. If things were going to change, it wouldn't be soon... maybe in a generation or two when their generation was in charge. *I wonder what the young people in that space-village are like. What could change things is what the boys on board think. That's what I'm waiting for.*

26

At their second meeting, the people of the space-village proposed that some of the children and young people on board should be allowed to meet with a couple of dozen youngsters from the Pure Haven community for a party. You can't beat a party. It needn't be long but would be informal and relaxed.

The Ruling Council agreed. There could be little harm done, and it would lift some of the mutual anxieties. After all, where do you begin if not with a children's party at which none of the complicated issues such as integration would be discussed? The kids would not want to do anything but have some fun. It was therefore arranged for the following day between two and four in the afternoon. The parents of the Talbot kids hastily threw together a few party treats, but it never crossed the minds of the Ruling Council that the space-village kids would always assume a party involved food. They rarely did on Pure Haven.

The villagers chatted among themselves about which two dozen children should take part and who would accompany them. The right people would be their teachers, being the adults they would all be familiar with. The fact that all four of the teachers most suited were women didn't cross most people's minds until after the choice had been made. Maybe that was how it should be. Why change what seems right just to please someone else's prejudices?

Joseph was to be among the three chosen from the upper end of secondary school. He and two of the girls from his year group were told to help with the little ones if they became shy but to try

114

and chat with young people their age if they could.

Among the children chosen to attend the party from among the townspeople was Charity's twelve-year-old brother, Luke.

"Hey, they look like dolls," volunteered one of Joseph's classmates when they spotted the kids from the town crossing the grass. Indeed the girls of all ages were dressed in long, plain dresses. The boys wore suits – miniature versions of what their fathers might wear on a Sunday.

"I guess they've put on party clothes. We didn't think of that. For us, it's the first time outside ever, but for them, it's, like, just a party occasion."

"Anyway, it's too late now," said Joseph, as he herded two shy little boys onto the grass. "Where do we put the food?"

"On the grass, I suppose. There's nowhere else."

Grass. It was amazing. They'd seen pictures of it but never touched it, felt it, or smelt it; it was the scent of newly mown Pure Haven grass that captivated them. One of the little ones got no further than a few paces from the ramp before she began to kneel and then roll on the ground. Soon they were all playing with the grass, scraping the mowings together and tossing them into the air. The half dozen littlies from the town needed no second invitation, and, long skirts or suits notwithstanding, they joined in. The teenagers soon got to playing alongside them. This was fun. Amid the squeals, the older ones introduced themselves. The adults, too.

The Talbot teachers had some ideas for games, and they organised the kids into circles of juniors and seniors, each playing ice-breakers that used names. The older ones went around the circle, saying, "Hi. My name's Joseph, and I like carrots." The next person had to say, "Hi. My name's Zeb and I like dancing. His name's Joseph and he likes carrots," and so on until all twenty-odd had had a turn. Of course, it was really hard remembering all the names and likes, but they gave each other clues.

When the game was over, Joseph said to one of the teenagers from the town, "Until today, it's only been us. Now there are so many new people to meet."

"We feel the same. We are more in number than you, but we've mostly all known each other from being little. It's nice to meet new people."

"It is," agreed Joseph. "A week or two ago we got Wormcomm for the first time, and now we're here on this planet. It's hard to take it all in in just a few days."

"Wormcomm? What's that?"

But at that moment a large raindrop from above landed on Joseph's face. He stopped and stared upwards. He felt the wet drip run down his cheek. Then another struck his forehead. "What's...?"

"Don't worry. It's only rain. It won't hurt you."

"Rain? I've seen it on the reels. It's wet."

The local kids thought it strange how the space-villagers darted about in wonder.

As the raindrops increased in number, the local parents in charge were calling.

"Come on, children. We must get you undercover before you're properly soaked." The nearest cover was Talbot-Theta. It was some way to the nearest farm buildings, which were outside the perimeter fence anyway.

"Come aboard," shouted one of the teachers above the excitement. "Joseph, Fran, grab the food, will you?" She led them up the ramp into the module. Now it was the turn of the town children to be awed with amazement. They had never seen anything like the interior of a space-village. It was a completely new world.

The locals hadn't thought about party food, but the teachers and children of the space-village were now the hosts, so they quickly arranged for some snacks and pop for everyone.

As the children shook off the raindrops and dried their hair, they all fizzed with laughter. It was such fun meeting new children. A game of port and starboard was suggested, and soon they were all surging this way and that from one end of the gym deck to the other. Up until now, this had been the furthest the onboard children had to run but they, like everyone else on the long voyage, were used to regular gym sessions including the bleep tests. It soon became clear that the Talbot kids were fitter than the planet-based ones. But the teachers were wise. They called turnarounds, which allowed the last to be first sometimes, and so the fitter children were eliminated as often as the others.

At last, the food arrived. It consisted of bean-flour flapjacks and sweet stuffs produced in the food labs along with fresh salad from the hydroponics decks. All was received with enthusiasm. A hydroponics facility was something the colony had long since abandoned.

"What are these round red things?" asked Luke. "They're, like, amazing... like nothing I've ever tasted before."

"Oh, these?" answered Joseph. "These are tomatoes."

"Tomatoes. I've heard of them. My sister goes on about them. She's read that they are highly nutritious, but we don't have them on Pure Haven."

"No tomatoes! That's sad. I like tomatoes. Maybe we can get some growing here."

One of the parents tasted the fizzy pop. "You have lemons on board, too? Amazing. We tried growing them here after the last settlers arrived but without much success. I tasted this when I was a kid. The trees didn't thrive, and there aren't any now."

"No. We don't have lemon trees," responded a teacher. "There are no trees on board. This is flavoured with lemon balm from the cultivation decks below. All our fresh food is grown in sealed rooms imitating different climates. We vary the LEDs for each stage of growth... Would you like to see it? I'm sure we can show some of you around."

"Yes, please. That would be lovely. But shouldn't we get permission first?"

"No problem, I've already asked. So long as we all wash our hands thoroughly after touching the grass... Ah, here is Commander Pritchard. He has come to greet you."

The commander of the whole village was relaxed and informal – even joked with the children. No one seemed to treat him with any particular deference. And the way women were part of everything stood out. How these female teachers were put in charge of such an important activity was almost breathtaking for the town parents.

The children and young people were now properly dry and, having washed their hands, were taken on a tour of the module. The sixteen-year-old boys, accompanied by Joseph and his female friends, talked together and tried to answer all the questions that arose from both sides.

"You girls are both sixteen?"

"We are," said Fran. I had my birthday just last week.

"Are you betrothed yet?"

"Betrothed? No way!" They looked shocked at the idea. "We're far too young for that."

Her friend began to giggle. Were these guys already trying for a relationship? "Haven't found, like, anyone my age who I fancy." She jabbed Joseph with a mock sour expression. He teased her with some kind of remark that indicated that if she were the last girl aboard, he wouldn't fancy her either.

"But here – I mean on Haven, the boys have to be over twenty, not sixteen. And no one chooses. The boys can give their fathers a clue who they fancy, but girls just, like, get bid for."

"Yuk." The village girl grimaced. "That sounds rather... Is it always like that on this planet? Will I be put up for some kind of auction?"

"If you're in year 11, I guess so. It's always been like that. All the girls in our year are now betrothed. They won't have to marry until they're twenty-one, though. We held our Annual Betrothal Day last month. They will probably put you in next year."

The girl gave a little shudder. This planet sounded scary. They sat silent for a moment, then a Haven boy asked, "So what's this 'Wormcomm' thing you're talking about? We haven't heard about this. Where does it happen? And how does it work?"

"Wormcomm? Don't you have it yet? It's very new to us, but we thought you would already have it on an established and populated planet. I guess you have another name for it. It's what we call communicating with other places faster than the speed of light. Instantaneously, in fact. So you can talk to people on Earth and places. You must know..."

"No. Never heard of that. It sounds—" His mate gave him a tap on his shin.

"Some of us *may* have heard about it, but it isn't a thing that we can talk about. You'll get into deep trouble if you even admit that you know about it. So I reckon this conversation stops here, and no one ever says anything about it, like, out there..."

Joseph stood with his mouth open.

"But we're *not* 'out there'; we're in here," declared Fran, hotly. "And no way am I going 'out there' if it means I have to get betrothed to some old guy who just bids for me in some kind of slave market, and I can't keep my Wormcomm buddy on Earth."

Her friend began to weep quiet tears and cuddled her. "Me, too."

Joseph recovered himself. He felt he had to say something.

"Why are you all boys? It would have been nice for some of the girls in your year to be included. Someone who could tell our girls that they needn't be so scared."

"At sixteen, they are not minors like us. They're all betrothed. They are not free to go to parties... Look. If the three of us agree to say nothing 'out there', I want to know more about this Wormcomm."

What none of them knew was the younger children had already shared their excitement about chatting with boys and girls on Earth. Why wouldn't they? Until then, it had been the largest innovation in their young lives. There was no way the parents of the Haven kids were not going to hear about everything their children had learnt that day. The unspoken secret was out. The Ruling Council had been unaware of the extent of the Talbot Wormcomm connections. They were soon to be disabused.

27

"They did what?" Luke's dad was furious. He yelled at his poor wife, who had had no more control over what Luke and his friends had done than he had. "That is not going to do us any good whatsoever. I'm struggling to maintain our status as it is."

"I'm sorry, dear. But really it is not our fault. Luke's twelve and just did what the others did. The people to blame are the supervisors. I've already expressed my disappointment, but they are men, and so my voice doesn't hold much impact. Maybe you should file a personal complaint. That way, they'll know you are not pleased, and it will be to your credit."

"I shall do it immediately." He tore back down the garden path and headed for the Town Hall.

When he arrived, he found he was not the first. Other fathers were there, all expressing their anger. If they didn't complain, it might appear they didn't mind or were even complicit.

Meanwhile, Luke was sharing his exciting adventure with his siblings. Charity and Raph were transfixed as he described the mind-boggling bridge, the engine room with its 'HASOL' unit – the half-the-speed-of-light power generation matrix. That was followed by a theatre equipped with eight-track surround sound – although, by no means state-of-the-art, it was something the kids on Pure Haven had never before encountered. Next, there was the hydroponics deck with foods they could not but be impressed by, the recyc-plant where they turned poo into dough ready for the ovens in the bakery, the galley in which the chefs produced the most exquisite aromas, and, last but not least, the personal cabins where the Talbot Space-Village kids lived.

"It was all, like, you... amazing... sooo cool. What I don't get is why they plan to get off and live *here*."

"You haven't shown them around the sights, sounds and scents of the planet yet. I think I would miss that stuck on a spaceship, no matter how cool," said Charity.

"Yeah. I guess. They really couldn't get over the grass, which was about as much of the planet as they got to see – apart from the rain... Oh, and guess what else?"

"Yeah. Tell us," said Raph.

"They can talk to people on *Earth*. Like, *live*. Like *now*. They've got this thing called *Worm* something... something which means they can call up kids on Earth and actually talk to them – pictures, I mean video, as well as sounds."

"Wormcomm," supplied Charity.

"Yeah... Er... You already know about it?"

"Everyone does in my year. But – listen carefully, watch my lips – we DON'T TALK ABOUT IT."

"So you shouldn't either," said Raph, sternly.

"But... are you saying it isn't just something that works in the space-village?"

"It doesn't work here because it's forbidden," insisted Raph. "So cool it. Right now. OR..." And he drew a finger across his neck. "Get it? Shut it. Say no more to us or anyone else... ever."

"OK. I get it. I don't like it b—"

"Not ONE MORE WORD." This was Charity.

Luke nodded.

"And it would be better if you didn't go on about how cool the space-village is, either," said Raph. "Certainly not in front of Dad... or Mum... or any grown-up."

Luke was learning fast. It was not what he or his friends – or any of the kids liked – but what their parents liked, or rather, the Ruling Council. *They* decided what was good and what was bad. They even seemed to decide what God should think was right and wrong. In the Bible, even Jesus got into trouble with the Ruling

Council in his day, didn't he?

"I don't care for Ruling Councils..."

"SHUT IT!"

"OK. Keep your hair on. I get it. I promise, not a word." But it was hard to bottle up all that excitement. Luke and his friends had had the most amazing day of their lives.

28

Elle couldn't sit still. She had been anticipating her visit to the observatory all that day. She hoped the sky would remain clear. She knew some gardeners were praying for rain, but she asked God to hold off until the next day. *Was that a selfish prayer? I don't care, she told herself. Although she did.*

At last, Epsilon set, and the stars emerged brilliant in a still cloudless sky. It seemed God had taken notice of her prayer above those of the gardeners. Full of excitement, Elle made her way up to where the telescope was trained in the direction of Gliese 677, a triple star group. The smallest star, Gliese C, a red dwarf, was thought to have a habitable planet, but why anyone would want to go there, Elle couldn't imagine. Apart from anything else, the light was bound to be a shade of red. Nevertheless, it could well harbour life, and that was what was intriguing to the scientists on both Terraspei and Earth.

To look up at Gliese from Epsilon Eridani, an observer has to look in the approximate direction of Tau Ceti, and Elle's imagination was triggered. *There, there was definitely life – human life. We should now be contacting them, live, through Wormcomm. Why is it no one has been able to make contact?* They used to fear the colony had failed and everyone had died, but that was not the case because the space-village about to land on Pure Haven had made Wormcomm connections, and they had confirmed they were in radio contact with the planet.

Rosie, the controller, welcomed Elle as she stepped into the telescope's control room.

"Hi, Elle. You're just in time to set the scope. Remember how to do it?"

"Key in the coordinates using this keyboard."

"And how do you find the correct coordinates?"

"Ah, yes. I remember. I have to select the star by name and number from the database with a couple of... I've done it. Gliese 677. Can I just cut and paste?"

"By all means."

Elle complied, and they heard the telescope's motor start up and begin locking onto the star."

"Don't forget to confirm that you want it to track... Yes, that's it... So what's been happening with Gliese 677 C? Nothing seems to have... yes, there it is, a slight change in its radial velocity. That's caused by Gliese 677 Cc – our habitable planet."

"I'd love to be able to see the planet."

"Far, far too small at this distance. It's much bigger than us, though. We know that. And we also have a good idea of it having liquid water."

"An essential for life."

"Yes. But, as they say, not as we know it. There wouldn't be much photosynthesis going on under the dim red glow of their star."

"We're lucky to have found our planet, aren't we? So Earth-like."

"Absolutely. So far we have found only two Earth-like planets in the Earth's backyard. Ours and Pure Haven around Tau Ceti."

"It's a pity we can't travel as fast as we can communicate."

"I doubt if that will ever be possible."

"They can in the sci-fi stories."

"Of course. But sci-fi is what it says on the tin. It's fiction."

"Wormcomm was fiction until this year."

"Indeed. We are extremely fortunate to be around when our scientists have cracked a way of using quantum entanglement to engender stable microportals. Have you thought about a Wormcomm correspondent on Earth?"

"I have. I applied, but they only needed two, and I wasn't one of the lucky ones."

"You applied? You would like an Earth correspondent?"

"Of course. But all the spaces were taken."

"Well, as it happens, the observatory is looking for a couple of young persons to team up with an Earthling. You could be one of our representatives. There's a school on Earth – in the United Kingdom – called Stanton something."

"Stanton Wick?"

"Yes, that's it. In the Chew Valley."

"Funny name."

"Loads of the villages in England have funny names. You up for it?"

"Wow, yeah."

"OK. Ask your mum and dad if I can send them your details."

"They'll say yes."

"Great. Get them to contact me to give their permission... I hope it turns out to be someone nice.

"So do I. Grandpops says he trusts me, but that doesn't stop him from being worried that I'll be in contact with the corrupting influences of Earth."

"He's got a point, Elle."

"I can't wait to see who I get... Why do you think we can't communicate with Haven?"

"Could be they're not using their quantum pairs."

"You sure they have them, though?"

"Absolutely. All the space-villages from the 2260s until now had a flask of them. They have all been properly tested. And they've had three space-village landings since the first one. Now they are just about to get their fourth."

"And *they* definitely have Wormcomm."

"So I hear... Would you like to take a look at Tau Ceti?"

"Yea-ah. Let me do it. First, I find the coordinates... cut and paste and..." They heard the telescope motor whir into life, and a few seconds later they were locked onto a bright star only six light-years away.

"So close but so far. Only twelve Earth years to get there."

"I wouldn't bother, Elle. If you want to travel to the stars, I'd go to explore the unvisited."

"Gliese 677 Cc?"

"Well, maybe not there. You wouldn't get much of a star tan." They laughed.

"When the space-village lands at Pure Haven, they'll definitely have a Wormcomm connection. Maybe I could get a correspondent there."

"I shouldn't laugh, Elle, but you are amazing. I don't know where you get all your energy and enthusiasm from. You'll probably be in deep conversation with half the residents of Pure Haven before the year's out."

29

The two dozen Talbot kids and young people bubbled with excitement. None of them could sleep that night. Joseph lay awake thinking, going over the day. Actually standing on the surface of a planet impacted parts of his brain that he never knew he had. The way the rain seemed to come from high in the sky onto his face and the scents it released from the soil... wow. He recalled the excitement of the local children seeing the module in which he had been born and had taken for granted for sixteen years. Those children in their starchy suits and old-fashioned dresses had stared, wowed at the sight of the vast space-village modules sitting silently in a field of Pure Haven 'grass'. And when they had come on board, they had been transfixed.

That evening, Joseph and Fran had a date with Sam and Amy on Earth, and he would have so much to tell them.

As always, the call went through perfectly.

"Hi, Sam."

"Hello, Joseph. Hello everyone," said Sam.

Amy had to ask her question. "Hi. So what's it like being cooped up in a spaceship all your life? Like, never getting to go outside?"

"Well, funny you should ask that. Today I went outside on this new planet for the first time. It was, like, *really* odd. A bit scary, to be honest. I mean, with no ceiling, it's like... like feeling, well, kinda..." He wanted to say 'naked', but he couldn't say that – not with girls on the call.

"... being kind of uncovered?" suggested Sam.

"Yes. *Really* uncovered."

"Like being outside, naked," supplied Amy. "I get it... I think."

Woah! thought Joseph. *This girl's got... she's different.* "Yes... And it began to *rain!* The sky is just immense, and water came down from it... like from nowhere."

"From clouds?" suggested Sam.

"Yeah. I guess."

Joseph spoke of his day while the Earth-bound young people listened intently. The more they chatted, the bolder Joseph and Fran became. They began to use new words to describe how they felt. Joseph was impressed at just how articulate they were becoming. On board, there was not much discussion about things they all had grown up with, but having to explain things to people who had no experience of all that brought out sides of their personalities and skills they hadn't realised they possessed. Growing out of a shell was what it felt like to Joseph. It was as if his world was cracking open to release the person he truly was.

Fran was particularly articulate. She had read many books and knew a lot of words. She and Amy went deeper and deeper into the inner wonders that surrounded things. It was like they had bottomless wells of emotional knowledge that seemed to resonate. It left Joseph somewhat confused, but he was happy to see Fran so delighted.

Eventually, Sam intervened. "OK, girls. Time to let the guys in."

"We're not excluding you," said Amy.

"I know. But I want to ask a tech question. Do they have Wormcomm on Pure Haven? I mean, if you have, I'm sure they must. But no one here has come across it. When you leave your space-village, will you still be able to contact us?"

Joseph hesitated. But Fran spoke up. "They know about it, but they are not supposed to, and they made us promise we wouldn't talk about it outside... like to anyone on Pure Haven."

"It's kind of forbidden," explained Joseph.

"Why?"

"Wouldn't want to speculate," said Fran.

"Got you," said Amy. "We wouldn't ask you to."

"Actually," said Joseph. "Perhaps we shouldn't have told you that. We were told by the kids here to say absolutely nothing because if we did, we'd get them into trouble. So we'd best forget it."

"Yeah," concurred Fran. "I should probably not have said what I said in case anyone's listening in. And please don't tell any of your family members because if this gets out... the kids here are scared."

"We won't say anything. This is, like, horrible."

"If young people ran things, I guess there would be a lot more freedom and peace," suggested Joseph.

Fran screwed up her nose. "That would depend on the young people. Not all young people are to be trusted."

"To be frank, I think it's fear that drives this colony," said Fran. "I reckon they keep it peaceful by making sure no one ever says anything at all. They're probably scared that if their kids connected with you, you lot on Earth would upset things here."

"We promise no mention of what you've said about Pure Haven will get talked about," said Sam. "We'll keep the chat to other things. I hope you can stay online after you leave your village."

"We have a few months before that happens," said Joseph. "Plenty of time for things to work themselves out."

"In the meantime," said Fran, brightly, "next time it'll be time for you to tell us about what you're up to."

"Yeah. Got to go now, though. Food beckons."

"Enjoy. Bye, guys. It's been good."

"Awesome. Bye for now."

The next day, in lessons, the Chew Valley teenagers shared their experiences of Wormcomm. The class was fascinated. They even got into the headlines of the BBC news feeds on Earth and 'News Terraspei', too.

This didn't go unnoticed by the Ruling Council on Pure Haven, who might not have been transmitting on Wormcomm but were certainly listening in to the news broadcasts.

30

Elle's dad smiled at his daughter. "Never give up, do you? If you want something, you always somehow manage to get it. So you want me to send an email to your professor?"

"Yes, please. It's just like this Wormcomm thing is sooo cool. And if I'm actually being a young rep for the observatory, that's way better than just doing it from the school. That's being, like, important."

"So the fates have determined that the school connections weren't good enough for someone as special as you."

"Dad! I didn't mean it like that. That's rotten. It's not like it has to do with me showing off, just... I don't know, being from the observatory—"

"Makes you sound more important."

"Oh, Dad. That's not..." Her dad flashed a wicked smile. "Aw, Dad. You're teasing me! Give over."

"I'm proud of you, Elle. Not because you're more special than anyone else but because of your tenacity... There, I've responded. They have my permission."

A week later, Elle received an email thanking her for her application and saying that she was on the reserve list. *Reserve list?! Not again! I don't believe it. The whole planet is against me... if not the entire universe.*

Elle turned up at the observatory feeling like it had rejected her. Its dome seemed to look down on her with a malevolent air. Behind it, clouds loomed. There would be no observing tonight, and instead of feeling frustrated as she should have, it was like the elements were on her side. No one was going to be happy inside the building that night. Good, she thought. Angry and flushed, full of jealousy for the person who had been selected rather than her, she stomped up the steps... and bumped into her friend Anna.

Elle couldn't help admiring Anna. She was cool and fresh-faced, always positive and bright but quiet and gentle with it. Anna had plenty to complain about - she had no right foot - but she rarely did. Elle immediately felt dirty and mean. How could she be so selfish? Anna always seemed so perfectly balanced.

"Hi, Elle. You look down. Why so sad?"

"Nothing. Sorry, just lost in thought... You're happy. Good news?"

"Yeah. Have you heard of this new connectivity thing - connecting with other planets, like, instantly through a microportal?"

"Yes. Wormcomm."

"Well, I've just been invited to engage with the link with Earth. I applied, and, guess what, they want me."

"You?!" What! Anna? She struggled to gather her composure. "I mean... er... that's cool... Like, I'm real happy for you, Anna." Elle genuinely was.

"There's this other guy, Lee, too, but I don't know; he doesn't seem that interested."

"Oh. Why did he apply then?"

"I don't think it was his idea. His mum was keen and applied for him."

"I know Lee. He doesn't seem keen on much except football. I kinda gathered that he comes here just to get away from home."

"Yeah. It could seem like that. Anyway, this Wormcomm can be done at home."

"Why select him if he doesn't seem up for it?"

"I think it is because he was the only boy who made an application. At least, that's the impression I got."

"Actually, Anna. I... I need to tell you... to be honest... actually, I applied, too. I'm on the reserve list. I'm happy for you, Anna,. I truly am."

"Oh, Elle. You should have been the one—"

"Why? You're a much better kid than I am – always have been. You don't go around saying things you shouldn't. My mouth is always in front of my brain."

"That's not fair, Elle."

"What's not fair? Only one of us could be chosen, and you got it. That's the way things go."

"I know. But what's really not fair is that Lee got it not on merit but just because he's a boy. They shouldn't do that."

"But the people at the Earth end might be both sexes."

"So? A person's gender is irrelevant. Or ought to be. Whatever they do on Earth, that's not what we do on Terraspei. We have our values, and here decisions are not made on gender. Wait there. I'm going back in and tell them."

"Anna, you can't do that!"

"Of course I can."

"They might take you off the project."

"So? I'm not being involved with anything that's harbouring discrimination. I will ask them straight out if Lee was selected on merit or because he was male. If they say it's because he's a boy, then I will resign."

"Anna, who's the hot-headed one now?"

"Oh. This isn't to do with emotion. This is about a principle," said Anna, calmly. "See you later in the refectory."

Twenty-two hours later, Elle received an email. A decision had been made to include a third person on the Wormcomm project. Was she still interested? For a second or so, she thought about it. After being rejected twice and now being brought in as an afterthought, she wondered whether to change her mind. This development was probably down to Anna – a reluctant acceptance on the board's part to include her after Anna's measured and well-reasoned criticism. Her pride was telling her to decline politely.

But then if Anna had put herself about and made a fuss, she owed it to her to accept the invitation. The email went on to say that on consideration the board would like her to be part of the observatory's project to connect with Earth. Their purpose was to team up with two young people from Earth called Sam and Amy, who were noted for their interest in science. They were to befriend but especially to listen to what was happening on Earth from the point of view of sixteen-year-olds.

Elle swallowed her pride and emailed back accepting the offer. *To be fair, I've got rather too used to always being the girl who gets to things first,* she told herself. She had always been at the top of her class and made a fuss of by her family, and being in the top three on this project was still a massive privilege.

Elle was becoming conscious of the universe around her expanding, while she was feeling ever smaller. *I guess the world 'out there' is just so big, while I'm not going to get any bigger than I am now.*

After school, the observatory called Elle in for a briefing. She met Anna on the way. In the room were several members of the observatory staff, including her professor. He gave her a broad grin, which made her feel a little braver. This project seemed to be a pretty important business for the observatory. There was no sign of Lee.

The project director stood and described where they had got to.

"The university is already listening to the official spokespersons from Earth – the professionals whose job is to articulate their current affairs. What we are about at the observatory, however, is to find out what Earth feels like for two budding scientists in the context of a British school on Earth. Stanton Wick has been selected not because it is special but because it isn't. It has a long history of helping local children of all abilities to fulfil their potential, but it doesn't have a record of sending swathes of people to elite universities. It is neither a top school nor a bottom one – it is properly comprehensive."

As ours is here, thought Elle.

"Our secondary school here on Terraspei is obliged to be comprehensive," continued the director, echoing Elle's mental observations. "The intake is too small. On Earth, in places like Europe, there is often a choice – pupils choose a school, and schools select their pupils. However, we wanted to connect with a school that is primarily chosen because it is the nearest, as well as one whose policy is to accept every local child, irrespective of their background or abilities. Stanton Wick has being inclusive as part of its ethos.

"However, within that school, we do require students who are specialising in science and desire to learn something about astrophysics and astronomy – even if they are not very far along in their course.

"For our part, we have selected two students with a proven interest in things scientific; they are both keen junior assistants in our observatory. They are well-placed to take up astrophysics and astronomy once they have finished their school studies.

Wow, thought Elle, *doing astronomy through the observatory straight after leaving school! I thought I might have to do a general science degree first. Seems not.*

"When I say 'listen,' we want you two to try and establish what these young people on Earth care about, what they fear most, and where they think things are going in their world and beyond from their point of view – in their everyday community, in their studies, and in their relationships outside of their own world. Got it?"

"Yes, sir. I think so," said Elle.

"Got it. Listen to where they're coming from on everything," smiled Anna.

"Exactly. Oh, and have *fun*. That part I think I can leave to you, Elle. Life is too short to be spent doing things that are dull, isn't it?" He laughed.

"Yes, sir."

After the briefing, Elle's professor approached her with a jolly face.

"Well done, Elle. You're on the project."

"I was only a reserve until yesterday."

"I know. We only had two places," said the prof, "but I persuaded them to make it three. As a matter of fact, *before* your friend Anna waded in with her equal opportunities protest. She's right, by the way. The board had the best of motives – it's so easy when you try to give people equal opportunities to positively discriminate for the best of reasons. But, as it turned out, neither Anna's nor my interventions were needed. Lee has decided against being part of the project. He said he had too much on.

Apparently, his parents made him choose between the project and football. The project lost."

Elle giggled. "Easy choice."

"And I'd be right in thinking you would choose this above sport?"

"Every time. Sport's OK but I love science. I love the idea of this talking to science students on Earth."

"Exactly so... Now that Epsilon has set, I have something to show you."

Elle followed him to the screen in the control room. On it was a magnificent view of a spiral galaxy, which Elle instantly identified.

"That's the Andromeda Galaxy."

"You know your astronomy. What can you tell me about it?"

"It's the nearest major galaxy to our own. It's the same size or a bit bigger than the Milky Way – Something like a trillion stars and 150,000 light-years across."

"How long would it take to travel there?"

"It's two and a half million light-years away, so with the fastest ship, about five million years."

"So too far for us humans."

"Far too far. You're... you're not telling me, professor, that we have a Wormcomm contact there?!" Elle almost exploded.

"No, Elle. With the current science, we need paired subatomic particles deliberately transported. But, in the future, who knows? New scientific breakthroughs are happening all the time. Maybe someone on a planet somewhere in the Andromeda Galaxy is already on the cusp of finding a method of talking to us right now."

"I hope they are. It's beautiful."

"It is. And the people who live there – for undoubtedly there are many civilisations – are quite unable to see it," said the prof. "Just as we cannot see the full beauty of our own galaxy. Sometimes, we are too close to things to see them in all their glory."

"Like if we're *inside* something, we never get a complete picture," said Anna.

"Indeed. The important thing to realise is that if we are

involved within anything, we can only see part of the whole."

"That sounds like philosophy," said Anna.

"Indeed. Being an astrophysicist – or any kind of scientist for that matter – leads one into philosophical reflection. No discipline can claim to know the whole truth about 'life, the universe and everything,' as Douglas Adams once famously said. Humility is a prerequisite for being a scientist, or indeed any area of life."

"Douglas Adams?" said Anna. "He wrote science fiction, didn't he?"

"He did. And through it, he helped us to see how puny we are. We learn through his humour that we may never really know the answer to everything, but what we can do is ask the question."

Elle looked carefully through the eyepiece and then again at the screen. "It certainly makes me feel very small. I mean, it's all so far away. What we are looking at is light that began 2.5 million years ago. Long, long before human beings evolved."

"Millions of years before. But remember, Andromeda is still in what we call the 'Local Group'."

"'Local' as in next door? The universe is that huge?" said Anna.

"Vast beyond our imagination. To study astronomy, Elle, Anna, we need to be prepared to see how infinitesimally small and short-lived we are. If you cannot cope with that, then astrophysics is not for you."

"It rather puts football into context," said Anna.

"It puts everything into context."

"So small, so puny, so transient," reflected Elle.

"Can you face that truth every day throughout your working life?"

"Yes," said Anna, "because there's something that is also true: I might be tiny, but I'm not insignificant. I have the power to look at the universe and perceive its beauty."

"If I were in the Andromeda Galaxy," said Elle, "I would love to know that some conscious being is looking at me and saying, 'Wow' - no matter how puny she may be."

"So you matter in the universe?" The prof smiled. There was so much hope in the upcoming generation. He was proud of them.

They would make good ambassadors on Wormcomm.

"Yes. The universe doesn't care how big you are or aren't," said Elle. "Something – some sentient being – that can just go, 'Wow!' makes the whole universe kinda have a purpose... And it's not just brain stuff; it's heart, too, isn't it? I mean, I *love* it. Am I allowed to say that if I am a scientist?"

"Of course, Elle. Without love, we are nothing... You believe in God?"

"Someone who created – creates – all this? I guess so."

"You won't see Him looking through a telescope."

"Because, if He exists, He's not going to be part of his creation, is He?" stated Anna.

"No. Love is the nearest thing we've got to seeing God."

At that moment, Elle felt small, important and loved beyond words, all at the same time. "It's love that makes you special, not how good you are at science."

"Absolutely. And you are loved. Learn astronomy, learn your science, but remember you are loved – loved beyond measure."

"I reckon that's, like, the best thing I heard anyone say this year," said Anna.

The prof beamed. "Remember that in your conversations with your Earth friends... and listen to their wisdom."

✧✧✧

Logging onto Wormcomm was easy. Far easier than Elle had expected. Even in the small community in Terraspei, a line could be delayed or fuzzy. Elle assumed that since Earth was so far away, it could be a patchy line at best. But no, everything was as clear as a bell. All she needed was a good connection to the uni hub. As soon as Elle pressed return, there were Amy and Sam, sitting together at some sort of table.

"Hi."

"Hi."

"Are you on Earth?"

"Yes. And you're on—"

"Terraspei. Wow! It works."

"Yeah. We've already been chatting to a space-village. The signal is crystal clear. It's you guys on Terraspei who have made the breakthrough in the science. Congratulations. And thank you."

Elle caught her breath. *Breakthrough. Yes. And not just in science, today – kinda spiritually, too.*

"Hi, I'm Elle."

"And I'm Anna. We're told you two are, like, good at science."

Sam blustered. "Hardly good at it."

"Don't be so modest," said Amy. "We're studying science in sixth form. I'm especially interested in how things work beyond our planet as well as on it."

It took only a few minutes before Sam and Amy learnt why Elle – Bubbles – had been selected. Their observatory wanted them to find out what it was like for teenagers on Earth. They also wanted these calls to be fun.

32

Stanton Wick had never had so much attention. Schools in Britain, indeed the whole Earth, were watching how the teenagers were working out how to use Wormcomm in an educational setting. There were billions of people on Earth but only a few on the exoplanets. So to avoid flooding the Earth hubs, only the designated contacts and people who had direct personal contact with emigrants were permitted to use it. The three Earth hubs were watching and listening carefully to the Stanton Wick pilot scheme.

Sam, Amy, and a team from the school council met together to discuss what they had learnt from their initial encounters. Both Amy and Sam shared what they felt. Sam was amazed by the people on Terraspei.

"They're so, like, upbeat about things."

"Yeah, that's true," agreed Amy. "But I think we only see the excitement of making contact beyond their own small community. Their everyday life might be a bit boring. I mean, we're used to news about billions of communities – thousands of languages. They all live in one small town and a few scattered farms."

"I guess so. And, also, we only get to talk to the ones who are enthusiastic about wanting to chat."

"They started off, like, keen on knowing what it's like to be living on a dying planet," said Amy.

"I get that," said one of the other students.

"But I tell them that there are signs that it's getting better... finally."

"Don't count your chickens, mate."

"I know. I just want to feel, like, hopeful."

"To be fair," said Sam, "there are signs that we're turning some sort of corner on Earth, aren't we?" He wanted to defend Amy's optimism.

Katie, Amy's friend and a member of the school council, chuckled. "Always the optimist, Amy."

"You gotta have hope."

"So long as it's realistic."

"It is. How gloomy do you think young people felt in the twenty-first century? Yet we're still here, complaining. The worst-case scenario is that we can apply to hop on a space-village and head off to Terraspei or Pure Haven if we want."

Sam sighed. "I wouldn't think about going to Pure Haven."

"Why not?" said Katie. "The indications are that it has a good climate. Good oxygen levels – twenty-two percent. An average temperature of twenty-five degrees—"

"And a narrow, mean culture," said Sam.

"You don't know that. They may have wanted to be morally good, but that doesn't make them mean."

"Believe me, they are, Katie."

"But we haven't made any contact with them through Wormcomm yet. I think we should wait until we do to judge. Sam, what's got into you today? You're kinda hooked on the dark side of things. Sleep badly?"

Sam was stuck. They had promised they would not report on how things were with his friends on Space-Village Talbot. They had inside knowledge of the way society worked on Pure Haven, and the dread their space-village friends had of having to leave the freedom of their modules had to go unmentioned. "I guess so, Katie. Take no notice of me."

But as the conversation continued, Katie was not the only one to notice that Amy, too, was reticent to say much about what their friends on Talbot had to say about leaving their village.

Katie came up with a proposal – the idea of three-way traffic. Of course, many before her had thought about the possibility, but it was left to the teenagers in the project to say what they liked or didn't like and make suggestions for the future.

"OK, guys. What say you to a three-way link? Bring some of our Terraspei correspondents into your group."

Sam looked at Amy.

"Can we talk about this – privately?"

"Ooo," went Katie. "Secrets."

"Just indulge us, Katie. Give us ten minutes," said Amy.

"To devise a strategy of deception."

"If you say so."

"Come on, guys," said Katie to the others. "Let's go and get a coke while they cook up their cunning plan."

After they had left, Sam said, "Amy, we can't just go on not sharing our exchanges with Joseph and Fran with the others. They know we're being deliberately..."

"Obtuse."

"Not saying anything. It's obvious."

"What are we going to do?"

"Well, if we agree with making a three-way, we'll have to let people into things."

"And we can't say no. There is no reason to. And the guys on Talbot might want in, anyway."

"That's it," said Sam. "We ask them, and if they want it, then that's fine."

"So we tell the others we're going to ask the Talbot guys what they want to do. If they're in, then we're all for it."

"OK. Let's get them back."

When they were all together again, Amy explained. "The thing is, the space-village people might not want a three-way. We didn't want to agree with it without asking them. But we've decided we'll ask them and see what they say. If they'd like to do it, then we're up for it."

"If they are, they're going to have to ask their parents or leaders the same as we are," said Sam.

"That sounds fair," said Katie. "We know that you know what

we don't know about what they know."

"Who?" said Sam, lost.

"We don't know," laughed Katie. "Not until you ask the guys on Talbot. Then we'll know."

"Know what?" asked Amy. "I don't know what you mean. Who knows what?"

"Who knows?" blurted one of the others, laughing. Everyone began to giggle. The serious stuff had come to an end; the fun had kicked in. "History tells us that everything is built on deception, one way or another."

"And it's about time that changed," said Katie, firmly. "I don't believe in secrets."

"OK," said Sam. "Be patient. But just pray, Katie, that no one ever tells you a secret and asks you to keep it."

Katie thought about some of the things her best friend had told her that very morning. He had a point.

33

*I*t didn't surprise anyone when it came. The Ruling Council had to act; they couldn't appear to show any signs of weakness because the truth was that they had never been so vulnerable. The twin happenings of the arrival of the space-village and Wormcomm in the same month represented the hugest challenge that they or any ruling council before them had had to face.

The first thing they did was arrest the four parent supervisors of the children who had led their children aboard the space-village. The cameras rolled as their homes were stormed and they were literally dragged away by marshals to the lock-up. Their 'trial' - also transmitted onto people's screens - lasted just one day. They were found guilty of deliberately leading vulnerable children into danger. Innocent lives had been put at grave risk. Such mistreatment of children came with the death penalty. In the short history of the colony, only two people had ever been executed, and those were for murder. In a so-called generous act of leniency, the Ruling Council commuted their sentence to banishment. Most people thought that that was merely execution by another means. Banishment meant being abandoned in the wilderness with one bottle of water and one loaf of bread. How were they ever going to survive? No one who had been banished had ever been seen or heard from since.

Despite their impeccable records - these parents had been chosen for the assignment because they had been beyond suspicion - the sentence was to be carried out immediately. No appeal would be considered, and that same afternoon they simply disappeared. No one even dared to mention their names in public. Their families lost all status; adults were removed from their jobs, and children were excluded from school – even the Institute. They became pariahs of the community – no one dared speak to any of them. Charity saw one family the following week scraping away at their backyard to try to plant seed that someone had risked leaving outside their door in the dead of night.

Top-level negotiators from the Ruling Council were appointed to meet the leaders of the space-village in the privacy of makeshift tents within the spacedrome. Although what transpired were called negotiations, they boiled down to a list of demands placed on the villagers for integration into the colony.

It was decreed that three families would be taken in the first instance to be allocated to homes in the town. The adults would be given jobs, and the young people placed in the schools. The original idea of people getting established and returning to live in Talbot was abandoned. Once in the community, there they would remain. They would not be permitted by the Ruling Council to come and go to the space-village. The rest of the travellers were to remain within the confines of the spacedrome. They could move between modules or take advantage of the Taushine – or rain – but no further. The marshals guarding the gates were ordered not to talk to them.

When the Talbot negotiating party reported back through the onboard messaging system, there was uproar among the villagers. Many were for returning to Earth immediately. After all, life in space had not been that bad, and they were thoroughly institutionalised. However, the commander told them that the village was not equipped for an immediate return journey. Some stocks had to be replenished from the planet.

Later that day, the commander and his senior crew met on the bridge.

"I cannot say I'm surprised at this," sighed the commander.

"What are we to do?" asked the captain of Beta.

"We go nowhere – yet. We can't. And anyway, my crew are contracted to spend six Earth months here."

"What about supplies?"

"The only two things we absolutely require are fresh air and fresh water. The first, the planet is already supplying. One month is going to be sufficient for a decent airing of all the vents and piping."

"And we're already compressing fresh oxygen into the tanks," added the first mate. "Not that we depend on it, but I like the idea of getting in fresh. And we could do with some supplies of calcium if we can get it; I would love some lime. And while we're at it, lithium too. Both of those things will be required to take all three and a half thousand back to Earth. Some fine silicon suitable for making new chips would be good, too."

"I do hear you," replied the commander. "As far as water is concerned, we have already set up rain traps. But we'll need more."

"I'll attend to that," said the second mate. "I'll see that the sheeting for more traps is made ready for deployment."

"In the meantime, it looks as if we are to lose three families," reminded the captain of Gamma.

"That is something we must leave to the village elders," said the commander.

"But what if no one comes forward? I mean, it sounds like a pretty daunting prospect."

"I've thought of that," answered the commander. "If we can't make Earth, we can strike for Terraspei. That is only twelve years of travelling rather than more than twenty-two – well within our capabilities even with a full complement. But do not mention that to anyone at this stage; we don't want a general decision to abandon Pure Haven just yet."

"I concur. A good plan," said the captain of Gamma.

"Excellent," echoed his counterpart from Theta.

"So now we must wait and see what the villagers decide to do," said the commander.

At that same moment, the villagers were all on their screens in their cabins in a joint consultation. The requirements of the authorities on

Pure Haven were set out.

"That is preposterous," said the first to speak.

"I guess they have been scared by us. This place is far more primitive than what we were led to believe," said a second.

"They've gone back in time to the nineteenth century."

"Back in time, certainly. But they do have electricity, transport, and telecommunications."

"OK. Twentieth century. But not much later."

"They have a very rigid society," observed one of the women who had met with the children. "It appears to be quite misogynistic."

"Maybe we should not rush to conclusions. We don't really know them yet," said a softly-spoken person.

After an hour of debate, it was put to a vote. They agreed that three families would go as invited. They would take their phones with them and report back daily on what they experienced and what life was like for them.

The elders asked for volunteers. They weren't surprised when there were none. Some older people might have come forward, but they were concerned for the children.

At the end of another half hour back and forth, they decided that three volunteer families should be sought. An exception was made for those families who had teenage girls sixteen or over; since all the girls of their age on the planet had just been betrothed, it might prove awkward for them if they hadn't got partners.

In their cabin, Joseph's dad muted their microphone.

"That's not easy," protested Joseph's mum. "What about our children? I don't believe this is something for us."

"Mum," broke in Joseph. "Actually, it might be better for us than lots of other people because we've had some of their kids in this cabin. We know them already. They're not so bad. If we went to their school, it wouldn't be like we knew no one at all."

"And that wouldn't apply to other young people?" asked his father.

"Very few."

"That's brave of you, Joseph," said his mother. "But you have no idea what you're taking on."

"No one does. But I'm up for it unless anyone else volunteers."

"It'll be four more years before Beth turns sixteen, and that's not true for quite a few of those with daughters who are already fifteen," said Dad.

"OK. I might regret this. Let's volunteer to be the guinea pigs. If it doesn't work out, we can always come back aboard."

His dad unmuted his mic. "OK, we're up for it, but we wouldn't want to take precedence over other volunteer families. If there is anyone who would really like to do this..."

No one spoke.

"All right, we'll do it. We'll give it a go, but if it doesn't work out, we're straight back on board. Agreed?"

The same was promised to two other families, one from Talbot-Beta and one from Talbot-Kappa.

That evening the three families ate together and made friends. What they didn't know then was that the Ruling Council had decided to separate them as far apart as possible. They were to be sent to different corners of the town and countryside. Isolation was the name of the game.

34

Three days later, Joseph's family found themselves allocated to an outlying farm. On arrival at the Town Hall, his father had been asked about the job he had done aboard the space-village. When they learnt that he worked on the hydroponics decks, food production was the natural choice. A farm was nothing like a hydroponics deck but he didn't argue.

Walking to the farm took three hours. There was no other means of transport other than a few old-fashioned tractor-bikes with trailers, which appeared to be few and far between and ridden only by the marshals. One of the families was put into a trailer but the other two, including the McPhersons, were set to walk.

They were conducted by three marshals who gave them the odd cup of water but no food.

But for the occasional puddle, the road, or track – it became increasingly narrow – was dusty. There were intriguing green plants to right and left, and some of them were tall enough to resemble trees with smooth-barked stems, which opened out to multi-shaped leaves of green and yellow.

After an hour they came across a grove of larger plants, this time of a more recognisable form, which the marshals explained were called Pure Haven Oaks.

"Oaks. You could have fooled me," said Mrs McPherson.

The marshal simply glared at her. After that, she said nothing.

Finally, they seemed to arrive at a plantation of what looked like very poor examples of temperate fruit trees from planet Earth. No fruit or leaves were to be seen on them. And then beyond the 'orchard' was a small farm.

The farmer and his wife looked horrified. They had no idea about any of what had been happening. They hadn't bothered to watch their TV and had no interest in the politics of the Ruling Council. They were given no notice and had no accommodation prepared for their guests. The poor man and wife were, however, obliged to house them immediately – somewhere.

The marshals couldn't get away fast enough. They must have been hungry, too.

It took less than five minutes for Joseph, Beth and their mum and dad to see that the farm was in a sorry state. Everything was run-down; it had clearly been in a better state in the past.

They were greeted with a mixture of welcome and discomfort. The farm consisted of a small three-roomed farmhouse, an outhouse for washing, a barn and an earth closet at the end of the yard. No one had thought about where a new family could stay.

When Joseph mentioned Luke Williams, the farmer immediately thought of finding a bed for him and Beth at the Williams'. The farmer and his wife had failed to have children themselves; like their sheep, they had sadly suffered a series of miscarriages. For labour, they relied on outside help, which currently included Nathan Rogerson and his betrothed, Charity Williams, at weekends. The Williams could take the children. They could house the mother and father in the barn until they could construct something suitable.

Mrs McPherson was devastated. This was not part of the deal. The idea of being in a different place from their children tore at their hearts. She wished Joseph's adventurous spirit hadn't come to the fore and they had remained on board. Being in this dirty place was one thing but they hadn't bargained on being parted from their children. But then again, who knew what lurked in the corners of the barn?

"I hate sending them away from us. But they would have a proper bed in a proper house with other children," he said.

"Why do we have to be separated?" asked their mum.

"No room for all of you here. No room at all," said the farmer, not unkindly.

"Didn't anywhere offer to take us all in together? We are a family."

"Offer? Who said anyone offered? It doesn't work like that. You go where the Ruling Council says. They, in their wisdom, have decided your experience is what we need here on the farm."

"Can we all go to the Williams?"

"No! You have to do what the Ruling Council decides. What happens to the children don't count. The marshals told me you are a farmer. You are here to help us."

"I have not set foot on soil since I was a boy," protested Mr McPherson. "We've been on board a spacecraft for over two decades."

"But you've been farming on board?"

"I suppose you could call it that. The hydroponics decks produce the food for the villages but they are fully automated and computer-controlled with just the right amount of nutrition, light and heat for each crop. The AI sees to most of it."

"But you have to sow the seeds and harvest the crops?"

"Yes. That has to be done manually."

"Then there is no difference. We put the seed in the fields and harvest the crop when it's ripe. Same thing."

"Same idea but completely different knowledge required."

"You'll learn soon enough. Now, let us get your kids sorted."

Mrs Williams took the farmer's call. Her husband was not at home. She was horrified; she knew what her husband would say but she also knew that if they refused to take the children in, they would suffer further social setbacks. Luck had somehow dealt them a second wild card within a week. The family had already arrived. He was making quite a reasonable request. The farmer wanted Charity to come and pick up the children immediately.

The McPherson's could see their host had little choice. They were learning quickly that things were even more primitive than they had already suspected. The intake of the new migrants was going to make their hosts' hand-to-mouth existence even more acute. They and their fellow migrants would be vital for the future of the colony.

As soon as a suitable place had been prepared, they could be together again, suggested Mr McPherson. Joseph was more than happy with the idea, however. The Williams had a daughter his age and Beth was in the same year as Luke. He liked Luke. It could be cool.

The family hadn't eaten since breakfast but although it was now late in the afternoon, there was no sign of any food coming. The parents were concerned about sending their children off without anything inside them but there was nothing they could do about it.

35

Needless to say, Luke Williams was over the moon at the idea. He made sure, though, that he put on a neutral face when his father got in. As predicted, Mr Williams was livid and cross with his wife but there was nothing that could be done about it.

Charity was dispatched to walk to the farm.

Raphael and Luke retreated to Raph's bedroom.

"That isn't fair. Mum's done nothing wrong. She had no choice," said Luke quietly to his brother when they were safely upstairs.

"No," said Raph, "but she's the one who agreed to it. And she's a woman."

"I can't see why that matters. She's a person. If Dad had been here instead of her, she wouldn't have told *him* off. That's not fair."

"Where do you get the idea that women are to be treated the same as men?"

Luke smiled. "You, I guess. And Charity."

"And you agree with us?"

"U-huh. Charity might be an annoying sister but she's definitely the cleverest of all us kids. Being a girl has not stopped her being clever."

"You're a wonderful brother, Luke. It's pretty hard for us who think like this. Some boys are beginning to notice I'm not, like, rude about my sister like they are about theirs."

"I know."

"But what is this Joseph like, Luke?"

"Oh, he's real cool. He was real nice to the girls on board, too. I reckon he thinks like us. And, I guess, most of them in the space-village do... And I know I'm not allowed to mention it but he is one of the ones that's always on..." and he mouthed: "Wormcomm."

"He won't be on it here," said Raph, bluntly.

Luke shook his head. "His phone will be connected to the space-village site. He could still use it via them... Couldn't he?"

"Well, maybe. Let's wait and see."

Making a shortcut through the native flora, Charity soon arrived at the farmhouse to pick up Joseph and Beth. The McPhersons were delighted to meet Charity, who seemed to be a very pleasant sort of girl. She was smiling and welcoming, not at all like the impression they got from their interactions with the Ruling Council, the marshals or the farmer and his wife. Her appearance didn't surprise Joseph because he had already met her brother Luke and he liked him a lot. He wondered how many of the young people on the planet were like them.

"Can we come with you and see where our children will be staying?" asked Mrs McPherson.

"I don't recommend it," said the farmer's wife. It was the first time she had spoken. "It will be very dark and it looks like it's going to be pretty wild tonight."

"What's the weather forecast? And how far is it?"

"An hour's walk. There's no path through the scrub."

"And we told you, a storm's coming," said the farmer, wanting to hurry things on.

Their parents would have liked to have gone with them to see them settled into their new home with the Williams but they couldn't have stayed overnight and it would be too late to walk back to the farm, even if they could find their way in the dark, especially that night – there would be no starlight under the threatening sky. It was pretty scary for space-villagers being out in the elements in the daytime, let alone at night in the wilderness.

Beth was reluctant to leave her mother and father but Charity was really gentle and kind. She came across as a nice friendly sort of girl who seemed to better understand the challenges parting a family posed than the farmer and his mute wife. She assured them their children would be well looked after and that she and her brothers were looking forward to sharing their house with them. And it was clear that Joseph and Beth had taken to her, which was reassuring. At least they were not going off with some monster.

Joseph was a good brother, too, and Beth trusted him, so, tearfully, they cuddled and parted on the front steps of the farmhouse.

"Bye, you two."

"Bye, Mum. Bye, Dad."

Final hugs were shared and then the kids were on their way. They waved as they disappeared behind a fleshy-looking bush. Charity didn't want to get home late – she didn't really like crossing the countryside in the dark either, especially with a storm brewing.

It was after they had gone that it dawned on the McPhersons that there was no sign of a computer at the farm and the TV seemed unused. There was no evidence of anything electronic – in fact, any electricity being used at all. On board Talbot, they had devised a computer programme to analyse the weather conditions on a planet even though they were in a craft designed for living in space but here, on this farm, they were completely cut off. It appeared to have more in common with the 1300s than the 2300s on Earth. What had they let themselves in for?

The farmer described the work before them.

"When this storm's over we'll check the flock. Let's hope it's not too harsh. The animals are not as resilient as they once were."

"They're too inbred," explained the wife. The second thing she had said, other than to invite them to sit on the wooden benches at a rustic table.

Her husband looked at her as if to tell her she had said too much. But he didn't argue the point. "They were too similar to start with. We would have done better with a wider variety of breeds."

McPherson smiled. "I think the solution to that may be in the cryogenic chambers on Talbot-Beta. We have a good collection of straws of semen from across the British Isles. When we set off, we were aware that something like that might be welcomed."

"That would definitely help, I guess, but it's not down to us, is it? The Ruling Council will say what we can and can't accept from your village."

"I'm sure there can be no argument about the value of improving your flock with some fresh strains. Let me pho—"

His wife interrupted him. "We can go back tomorrow and fetch them if you like." She had become increasingly uneasy. She didn't trust these people – or, at least, the man. They must not know they had working phones. They wouldn't be working for long, anyway. There was obviously no electricity to be had in the farmhouse.

As Tau disappeared behind the thickening clouds, the wife showed them to the barn, which was across the yard from the outside earth closet. She helped them to make up a straw-filled mattress bed. "Sorry, it's probably not what you're used to but it's the best we've got. This morning we had no idea we were to have lodgers."

"Didn't your Ruling Council do any planning for our arrival?"

"Oh. They have their plans but there's no telling what they are. And the less you say about the Ruling Council, the better it will be for you... and us."

"The Ruling Council is not popular, then?"

"I didn't say that! If you're going to be useful to us, you will have to keep out of politics, like we do."

"We understand," said Mrs McPherson. "Or, at least, I think so."

"You say too much for a woman. Mark my words, which I can say here and not in front of my husband, you will keep your mouth shut in the presence of men and not even look a man with status in the eye. And never disagree with them – not even your son now that he's a grown boy."

"Grown? He's sixteen."

"That doesn't make him any the less your superior."

"What about me?" asked Mr McPherson.

"That's not for me to say."

"Because I'm a man?"

"Because you're a man and if you want to get yourself banished, that's your business."

"Banished?" asked Mrs McPherson.

"Where dissenters and dangerous people get disappeared to. And don't tell anyone I told you that."

"Don't worry. You can trust us. We've got the picture."

A candle appeared in the doorway. "Why are you taking so long, woman?" bellowed the farmer.

"They're not used to things like we have here. I need to show them everything before I leave them in the dark."

"In the dark? May we have a candle?" asked McPherson.

"Not enough. Like I said, we didn't expect you," barked the farmer.

David McPherson decided to be as polite as possible. He felt sorry for these people. "We are sorry to have imposed and we will do our best to make it as easy for you as possible. I'm sure we have all that we need. Thank you."

Then they found themselves in the dark.

"We have a bed. A loo and water across the yard. And each other," said Mr McPherson. "What more do we need?"

"Our kids."

36

As they walked, Charity noted the way Joseph looked after his sister. He put his arm around her when she cried a bit and told her that he would stay with her. Beth had a good brother. Luke had liked him too and Charity could see why. They would make a good team.

Charity spoke about what it would be like when they arrived. There were the practical arrangements. Joseph would have to sleep in Raph's room and Beth with her but the rooms were close and brother and sister wouldn't be far away from one another.

"And I have to tell you that my father can be a bit dogmatic," Charity explained. "There are some things you can say and some you can't and it's different for boys and girls. The best thing, at least to begin with, is to just keep quiet. If you need anything, ask me or one of my brothers but wait until we're away from Dad and Mum – especially Dad. Got that?"

"Yes, I think so," said Joseph. It all sounded quite daunting.

"And whatever you do, never refer to the Ruling Council... and never complain about your teachers... and never ever talk about Wormcomm. That's really important. The Ruling Council wants to pretend it doesn't exist. And if they say it doesn't exist, it doesn't. And there are ears everywhere, so it's best not to mention any of these 'never evers' even to me, Raph or Luke. Walls have ears."

"Is your dad on the Ruling Council?"

"No. He's only halfway up the social ladder. He wants to climb higher but it's hard. There are lots of men who would do anything to get up it and it's pretty rough for him. The way we are seen to behave as his family could bring him right down. So he has to be really strict with us and Mum. The pressures of the whole thing put him in a bad mood. And he didn't ask for you to come to us. He's scared of what your being around will do to him in the eyes of the powerful, so he's going to be pretty strict with you. The quieter and more compliant you are, the better he will feel. If you get on quietly at school, you will give him points. If you don't, he will lose them."

"Everything sounds impossibly hard."

"It is."

"Has it always been, like, this hard for kids... especially for girls?"

"For a long time. Long before I was born."

"So it's going to be like this forever, then?"

"No. I think that things are going to change. It's, like, in the air, so be patient and don't draw attention to yourselves. The authorities are nervous. A lot of us think change is on its way – things are bound to be different very soon. Your space-village arriving with your own way of doing things will make a big difference. The Ruling Council are on edge and those who disagree with them are getting fired up. That's why they're clamping down – there's even talk of a curfew. No one's sure what's going to happen next. So keep your heads down. Be model pupils. Just put up with stuff... at least for now. OK?"

"OK," said Joseph.

"Beth. You got it?" insisted Charity.

"I'm scared."

"You'll be OK. You've got us."

"But I'm still scared."

"Don't be. At our house, you'll have me, your brother and my brothers. Kid-power... Oh, and Nathan, too."

"Nathan? Who's he?"

"My intended. He chose me because I'm not your meek and mild sort. He does not want a girl who expects him to boss her. He wants a friend."

"Did he have to, like, choose someone?" asked Beth.

"Yes. All guys aged twenty have to get betrothed to girls aged sixteen. Then you have five years to get to know one another before you get married."

"What if it doesn't work out?"

"If the guy really doesn't like his betrothed, he can dump her. He can't once they are married, though. That's what the five years are for... The girl has no say in it, of course. She can't dump her fiancé."

"What happens to the girl if she's 'dumped'?" asked Beth.

"It doesn't happen very often. But if she loses her intended for any reason, she comes up for auction again the next time round. Usually, no one goes for her then because she's second-hand and she's lost status. If a girl's not bid for, then she gets given to an older guy who's on his own. Mostly, someone whose wife has died. The idea is that no woman of childbearing age should be denied children."

"What if she doesn't want to have children?"

"Hard cheese. No choice."

"Will all this apply to the villagers too?" asked Joseph.

"Officially, yes. It would cause a lot of trouble if the system changed. But it depends on you villagers. Three and a half thousand people are a huge number when, altogether, we are only just over thirty-five thousand on Haven."

"Really? We were told that with three generations and the arrivals of the space-villages, there should be twice that number."

"Should be. But you'll see pretty quickly that this place is not thriving. Kids die. Women have miscarriages. Some people just seem not to be able to make babies. And it's getting worse."

"Why?"

"I have my theories. Your parents are to work on a farm and they'll be shocked at the state of it. Nutrition is poor. We haven't maximised the potential of this planet. The food we grow and rear is getting weaker year on year... But enough of the gloom and doom. We're nearly at the house."

"Hold up," said Joseph. "I just want to check my phone. Just to make sure I have a signal?"

"You have a phone?"

"Of course."

"And it's in range of the space-village network?"

"That's what... Yeah. Look, I've got a signal. A pretty good one."

"Look. Just hide it. OK. It might be better if you gave it to me in case they want to know what's in your pockets."

"Are we going to be, like, searched or something?"

"Not like that... but they will still be curious about what you've got on you."

"If I give it to you, what will you do with it?"

"Give it you back when we're upstairs on our own. Trust me. I won't steal it. But how are you going to charge it, anyway?"

"I have a lead in my bag—"

"With a plug that won't fit any power socket in the town."

"Oh. I didn't think about that."

"Look. No one thinks you'll have phones. Keep quiet about it. Lie if you have to. The boys may be able to get you a charger that'll work but you have to hide it and not use it."

"What about Mum and Dad?"

"They'll certainly have no charging facilities... Look, call them now. Tell them you're OK but you shouldn't have phones and they need to hide theirs. OK?"

"OK."

David McPherson's pocket buzzed. "Hi, Dad. It's Joseph."

"Hi, Joseph. How are you?"

"Great. Charity is cool. But she says if I get caught with my phone, it'll get taken away. So I'm going to hide it. And she says you'd better hide yours, too. We can't get any charge, in any case. But Charity says she's sure things will change when all the space-villagers come into the community. They will have to if all the new arrivals are to be properly fed."

"Put Beth on, Joseph. Her mum wants to talk to her."

Joseph handed the phone to his sister.

"Hi, Mum."

"How are you?"

"Hungry. But Charity's nice."

"OK. Be kind to her."

"I will."

After a few moments, Charity began making hang-up signs.

"Oh. Charity's saying we should hang up now."

"Then you must. Love you. Be good."

"I will. Love you, too. Bye."

In the darkness, David McPherson took his wife in his arms. Neither said anything. At least their children were safe.

Charity smiled. "Well done, guys. It'll be fun having you stay at ours. Now remember to be ultra-polite when we arrive. Remember to speak to Dad first, then to Mum and then quietly to my brothers. Answer all their questions but don't ask any yourself. OK? If you need to ask anything, ask me afterwards."

"Got it."

Despite her brother's arm around her, Beth began shaking with more than the night air. Joseph cuddled her. Then Charity separated them, telling them to wait until they were upstairs for any intimacies.

The introductions went OK. Charity had schooled them well. She breathed a silent inner sigh of relief. Her dad had been on edge, but the reality of Joseph and Beth was less threatening than he had imagined.

Upstairs, beds had been arranged for them. Both were hungry; they had had nothing to eat since breakfast on board but they had arrived after the evening meal so they would have to wait until breakfast time in the morning. Charity told them they would survive. The same applied to her. She had been out for the meal so that was that.

As she lay down to sleep listening to Beth's breathing, Charity couldn't help feeling a little bit excited. Things were definitely going to change and if this family was anything to go by, it would definitely be for the better.

37

Sam logged in at the agreed time. Already waiting for him was Tom from Queensland.

"Hi, Sam. What's the weather like there in the old country?"

"Rain, rain, and more rain. Queensland?"

"Dry as your proverbial bone, mate."

"That normal?"

"Yep. Every time there's a drought, the farmers complain like it is worse than ever but, truth is, it's often like this."

"I heard you have to have regular rain to grow pineapples and bananas."

"You do. So there's no growing pineapples or bananas in this part of the state. It's mainly peanuts."

"They tell us that the worst years of the extremes are behind us. According to the statistical records."

"Maybe. But that doesn't stop the farmers calling for a month of prayer."

"Ah. Here's Amy. Look, I'm going to have to log off, Tom. We've got a pre-booked call to outer space."

"Yeah. Tell me about it. I've been displaced."

"Never, Tom. One day maybe we can get you into a call. For now, it's just a pilot thing."

"A private thing, did you say?" Tom laughed.

"That depends... Speak later, mate. Sleep well."

Amy stepped into the frame. "Goodnight, Tom."

"Morning, Amy. Nice girl, Sam. I like the look of her. Mind you look after her. Ciao." He was gone before Sam could protest that Amy was not his girlfriend.

"I think he fancies you."

"He can do what he likes if he's safely 12,000 miles away."
They turned their attention to Wormcomm.
"Earth to Talbot-Theta," called Amy.
Fran appeared on screen, alone.
"Hey there, Fran. How's it with you lot? Venturing further onto your planet yet? Where's Joseph today?"
"Hi, guys. Yeah. We have news. Joseph's outside – on the surface with his family in the local community."
Fran filled them in on the recent agreements with the locals and Joseph's adventure into the unknown.
"Wow. That's good. How's it going?"
"To tell you the truth, we're worried. He phoned to say he and his sister were staying somewhere different from his mum and dad and that he wasn't supposed to use his phone and he couldn't call again. So we haven't heard from him since. That was, like, thirty-six hours ago. Our hours, not yours. They are a bit shorter, I think."
"Not much. That's still a long time."
"I said that if he could phone, then we could patch him into you. But, apparently, the authorities here don't want anyone to talk about Wormcomm. It's forbidden."
"I guess they have security concerns, too," said Sam. "But I'm sure they can get them sorted out."
"It sounds like it's more than that. It feels like there are things going on in Pure Haven town that they don't want us to know. Sometimes, we get that maybe they don't want us here."
"Who?"
"Those in charge of the planet? We don't know... That's the thing; it's like we're here but kept in the dark. They didn't want any of us to get off except for three families who have been forbidden to make contact."
"That does not sound good."
"He says the other families are all in different locations. Mr and Mrs McPherson are living on a farm and Joseph and Beth are with a family in the town. He didn't know much else other than that he couldn't get caught using his phone and that he had no way of recharging it anyway. He finished by asking us to pray for them

all."

"That sounds scary," said Amy.

"Sounds like they don't like you," said Sam.

"I don't think it's like that with most people, especially the young ones – just the leaders. They have this thing called the Ruling Council. I guess they're scared we'd change things too much if we all descended on them at the same time. There are only 35,000 of them and we would increase the population by 10% in one go. They're really strict on some things. Like, it's official that girls – and all females – are definitely second class. They have to do what the men say, and we get the feeling that they are scared our women wouldn't accept that. Well, I wouldn't."

"That's, like, complete rubbish," said Amy. Girls are every bit the equal of boys."

"That may be so, but it's not the way here. It seems that every girl in year 11 has to be paired with a boy four years her senior."

"Has to be?"

"Yes."

"So the dating apps are busy in your year."

"No, it doesn't work like that," Amy explained what she had managed to understand about the Haven betrothal system.

"The girls get no say in it at all?!"

"Their fathers have to see to it that they get a good deal."

"Whoa. Fran. That's, like, super harsh," said Sam. "I thought that kind of thing went out centuries ago"

"Where you are, maybe. But not on Pure Haven."

"What are you going to do? I mean, when you get out of your space-village?" asked Amy.

"If we leave the village. There are a load of us who say we're staying put."

"But the space-village – at least the Alpha hub – is supposed to leave in a few months, isn't it? What then?" asked Sam.

"We all go together. We've lived in our modules, since like, forever. Like the crew, we can just travel around the galaxy for the rest of our lives if we need to. It would be good to explore this planet but not if we can't be who we are."

Amy was concerned. "What about Joseph and his family? They're already outside."

"I know. The Ruling Council says that once they are out there, there's no coming back, but our elders are saying they can come back whenever they want to. We're waiting to see what's going to happen. I'm not going anywhere unless we all go. I'm sixteen, which means if I were 'out there', I would be given a fiancé whom I may not have even met."

"OK, Fran. That sucks. Wish we could do something to help," said Amy, feeling helpless.

"You are. This Wormcomm is just so ace. We might be light-years away but it no longer feels like we're lost in space with just you guys to talk to. Everyone is saying they want a connection on Earth – even the adults. I don't know why they even wanted to leave all those years ago. Can you find more people to link up with? I mean, we only have you two. Don't get me wrong, I'm not saying that—"

"No problem, Fran," said Sam. "The more the merrier. You need as much company as you can get. We'll ask. There are loads of people interested, but they say it's still a pilot scheme... But there *is* something that's just come up. How would you like to link up with someone on Terraspei?"

"Terraspei? Wow! That'll be, like, really, really cool... Are you serious?

"No. It's for real," said Amy. "We've got a connection with two people our age as part of the project. A three-way connection has been suggested. But we know that what you're telling us is, like, not for public transmission, and it would mean your news and stuff being talked about somewhere where we couldn't guarantee—"

"That would be brilliant. Look, we're going to have to say what we want here eventually. I'm not going to abandon my ways – my principles – for the rest of my life just to fit in. Just telling people about things – people listening across the galaxy – that's tops."

"Like us, they wouldn't be able to do anything to help—"

"Just listening, sharing. It's everything. I'm feeling tons better than when we started. I don't know how it works but being able to tell someone helps so much."

"OK. We'll ask about establishing a three-way connection," said Amy. "The girls in Terraspei are called Anna and Elle. Elle's funny. I mean haha funny – guaranteed to cheer you up any day."

"But be patient about that," said Sam. "It's only a suggestion at this stage. It'll depend on our supervisors and, I guess, those on Terraspei, too."

38

Mr Gilbert had been intrigued at Katie's suggestion of a three-way link. And since Sam had already got a regular connection with Tom in Queensland, he could see which way this might go. It would have to be properly monitored and he would suggest Stanton Wick be the responsible body if the pilot scheme was extended. Exams were coming to a conclusion and the young people would have more time to devote to the project.

Amy and Sam gave frequent reports on their experiences with Talbot-Theta and Terraspei. They were pleased with the way the connections were benefiting all concerned and enthusiastic about the possibility of a four-way link with Terraspei, Talbot, Queensland and themselves.

It was just before the end of term that the school was given permission to embark on the requested wider connectivity. On Talbot-Theta, Fran recruited a guy called Pete to sit with her in Joseph's absence. Sam invited Tom to join them.

"So what's happened to the private bit?" he asked.

"It's still private," insisted Sam, "but you're in on the secrets. You can keep a secret?"

"Of course. Why so hush-hush?"

"You'll see. Not everyone in the loop is living in a free country like Oz."

"Ah. Got you, mate."

Fran and Pete found they didn't need permission from Talbot to include Tom. So many were already talking freely and venting their frustrations to their Earth families, so somewhere else on Earth was immaterial. As Fran said, the more people intent on listening, the happier they would all be. It would be different with Terraspei.

However, to her surprise, she was met with enthusiasm from her mother and loads of others on board. Some of them had already begun to think that Terraspei was a possibility if things didn't improve with the negotiations on Haven soon. Links with Terraspei might increase their chances of being accepted as immigrants there if it came to that.

Amy approached Elle and Anna.

"It seems we've got the go-ahead from here for a three-way. How's it your end?"

"They're cool with it," said Elle, "as long as we're sensible. The concern is for the guys on Talbot and Pure Haven."

"Talbot are really keen."

"OK. So let's do it," said Sam.

"Yay!" went Elle.

"Agreed," said Anna, calmly.

So Elle and Anna joined Sam, Tom and Fran on an exclusive three-way link. Nothing was off the table. Because they were unlikely ever to meet, the teenagers felt like they were brothers and sisters rather than friends with all the complications of romantic possibilities. Gender tensions were explored in depth. They asked ultimate questions: how everything fitted together, what life meant, why people did harmful things, what they would do if they ruled the universe and so on. The philosophers of Earth's history would have been proud of them.

"The future's all about connectivity," said Fran.

"Always has been, I guess," said Elle. "If the universe were not joined up, there wouldn't be anything at all, would there? It all fits together in a wonderful order with universal laws of interactivity that make it all work."

"That's, like, real profound," said Tom.

"Sure is," said Sam. "Elle, you're a genius."

"No. No. It just stands to reason."

"So why do the authorities on Pure Haven want to avoid communicating?" asked Fran.

"Because," said Anna, "they understand its power. In order to boss things, they must control everything. They have to call the shots on every level. If people start communicating with each other without it going through them, they risk losing that control, especially if it's with people on other planets."

"If they are trying to stop people from talking to one another, then it's a sure sign they are malevolent," said Amy.

"They have bad intentions," agreed Elle.

"But you've got to shut some people down," said Pete. "What about people who spread lies or lead kids astray? Or share graphic footage with children. Shouldn't they be shut down?"

"That's different," said Tom. "Hate speech is wrong and should be controlled. Films should be censored. So should the Internet and social media. No one ought to be posting stuff about making bombs or persuading kids to kill themselves."

"But who decides?" asked Amy.

"The government," said Anna. "Laws are derived from established moral principles and for keeping people safe."

"But the law should not be used to oppress people and prevent them from being themselves," said Amy.

"If *all* communication is controlled for everyone, then that's not right," said Elle.

"Like stopping people calling up their friends from space-villages," bemoaned Fran.

"Oh, Fran. Have you heard anything at all from Joseph and his family?" asked Sam.

"Nothing. Not a whisper. It's, like, they're in another universe. One without phones or even letters at all, let alone Wormcomm. This is the most wonderful invention out. Tell your scientists that, Elle. We love you, guys."

"Just keep us posted. And if Joseph does connect, tell them we're thinking of them. We're praying for them," said Amy.

"I will. I will."

39

Nathan was as curious about the new kids staying with the Williams as anyone but he didn't want to seem too keen, so he left it a couple of days – the day before Joseph and Beth were due to begin at the school.

"Hello, Nathan. Come in." Charity welcomed her intended with the right form of deference at the door. "Would you like to meet our new space-village children?"

"Delighted."

"They're out back."

In the backyard, Nathan saw two youngsters studying a tree with Raph. Raph was explaining that it was supposed to be an apple tree grown from a pip brought from Earth but it had never had any apples on it. Joseph was saying he thought that his father had told him about some cryogenic cuttings in the store. Maybe a graft could be found for it. They were so focused on the tree, they didn't notice Nathan had joined them.

"Fascinating," said Nathan.

Joseph looked up, startled. He had been overheard by someone. It was the very thing Charity had warned him about but Charity stood beside the tall young man and she looked happy.

"Meet my intended. Nathan, this is Joseph and his sister Beth."

"Hi. Pleased to meet you. Your coming to Pure Haven is the greatest thing. And Charity is so lucky to have the first of you in her house. Tell me all about what it was like living in a space-village."

"It's all right," smiled Charity. "Nat's safe. And we're outside. No walls with ears." She turned to Nathan. "I've warned them about saying too much... and about the "never evers"."

"Right."

"You'll soon learn who you can trust, Joseph. Not many, I grant you, but some. And Nat is one of them."

"It sounds like you're in some sort of gang," said Joseph.

"Something like that. There are those who suck up, those who just don't think – just go along with things, and those who believe things have to change. That's us."

"Do you want things to change, Joseph?" asked Nathan.

"I want things to be like they are in Talbot. A place where girls are equal to boys and people talk about things and vote. Where adults don't scare kids. Where people can select what they want to study post-sixteen and choose their own girlfriends and boyfriends and—"

"Basically, a free society without power struggles and where people look after one another."

"Well, yes. I guess. I hadn't thought about it much before. We just lived like that."

"In a community where goodness and kindness are more important than rigid rules."

"Oh, we have rules. In Talbot, you can't just do anything. There are lots of rules. Rules about being kind to people. Rules to keep you safe. There are lots of rights and wrongs to stop people from hurting themselves and other people. And being honest is important – it wouldn't work if people cheated or lied."

"The Ten Commandments?"

"Yes. We learn what God wants us to do to be good. And there's Jesus' *new* commandment."

"What's that?"

"Love one another as I have loved you," Beth supplied.

"Funny we never seem to hear much about that one here," said Charity. "Despite my name."

"I think it's the most important rule of all," said Joseph. "After all, if you love someone, you will look after them and do all the right things for them."

"I like that. When you think about it, it's not really a commandment at all," said Charity. "Imagine a world where everybody just loves everybody else."

"I think that's what our parents were thinking Pure Haven was going to be like. A place where they could bring up their kids in safety. Where people were not always thinking of themselves."

"If only, Joseph."

"All the same, there's a lot of it about," said Nathan.

"What?" asked Charity.

"Love. If the Ruling Council and all the marshals just disappeared, people wouldn't run around doing bad things. People would look after each other because love would tell them what to do."

"I guess."

"Think about it. Your family would. My family would. All our friends would."

"Because they already do, Nat."

"Exactly. We do the right things *despite* the Ruling Council, not *because* of them. They don't command our hearts."

"Love does that," said Beth.

"Yay! Beth," said Charity. "You say it all. So, whatever the Ruling Council does or says, we've, kinda, won. Love's won."

"That's what Jesus did," said Beth.

"You know you two are already changing things. From the moment we met you, it's been like when Tau has come out from behind the clouds."

"Like right now," said Joseph. "It's beautiful. You have a really beautiful world. A planet is much nicer than a space-village. Even the soil smells nice."

"It was a wild storm. I was worried that it would send you scurrying back to the safety of your village," said Charity.

"You weren't scared, so we weren't either. The noise it made, though. It was loud. We had pictures and videos of these things, of course. But if something's on a screen, you can always turn down the sound."

"But you can't turn down the sound of nature?"

"True. And the sounds under the Taushine are fantastic. Made by things we cannot see."

"Oh, you can see them if you know where to look."

"And the smells. You can't get smells on a screen," said Beth. "I love smelling things on this planet."

"I think we have much to learn here," said Nathan. "We take so much for granted growing up in a place. What are we doing hanging about here? Let's go out to your lovely garden."

"Yes, let's," said Charity. "You know, I had never thought about it being lovely – there is more to nature than food production."

As they wandered around in the garden, discovering different plants and minibeasts, Nathan whispered into Joseph's ear, "I hear you have a phone that connects to the space-village."

Joseph shot Charity a look of panic.

"It's all right, Joseph. You can talk to Nat."

"Yes. But I don't use it. Charity's parents don't know I have it. I can't charge it, anyway. The electricity supply here isn't compatible."

"If you let me have your lead, I'll see what I can do."

"But Charity says not to use it."

"She's right. But there will be opportunities when you can. When you were on board, did you ever talk to anyone on Earth?"

"I had a couple of buddies in a school on Earth. A place called Chew Valley. We set up a chat. It was, like, amazing after growing up in a space-village."

"And would you be able to access ... this 'chat' from your phone?"

"I think so. I have full access to my account from it. They agree on times, though. I would have to find out when they are."

"Just be patient. Things are going to change but it will require you not to rock any boats. Charity tells me you've been brilliant so far."

"I'm learning... I think."

Nathan considered. It wouldn't do to reveal he was better taught on the space-village.

"How good are you at school?"

"OK. I'm best at maths."

"Can you simplify surds?"

"Of course. We did that ages ago."

Charity smiled.

Nathan continued, "I thought so. Listen carefully. You can't afford to be too clever here. Don't get all the answers right at school. Make sure the teachers think you're at least average. Give them the idea you haven't learnt stuff on board, even if you have. Best give them the impression that you aren't that bright."

"OK. It'll be hard not being like... who I am, though."

"Tell me about it," said Charity.

40

The first few days at any new school are a scary experience. But Charity stayed with them right up to the time Joseph and Beth were taken off to their various form rooms. At break time she was pleased to see Joseph surrounded by boys and Beth being led to the girls' yard by kids her own age. Charity need not have worried – they were celebrities. Everyone wanted to know the new kids from the space-village. The questions never stopped.

Were there schools on board? How many teachers did they have? Were they any good? What sort of things did they eat? How did they feed all those people without anyone going hungry?

It became increasingly obvious that the growing teenagers on Pure Haven were especially interested in food. Despite having a whole planet to themselves, there didn't appear to be enough food to go round – at least not enough to stop these kids from getting hungry. Joseph was grateful for the breakfast he had had that morning. It was clear that he was going to have to get used to not having as much as he was used to.

Joseph did his best to answer all the questions but he didn't forget to heed Charity's warning about saying anything that might alarm any adults the kids talked to. One kid talked openly about Wormcomm and he just shrugged as if he didn't understand the question. When they asked about phones, he said yes, they had phones. They were spread all over the ten space-village hubs and they used them to keep in touch after school. And teachers used them to set assignments. All that was true. For years that had been the limit of their phones but now it would be possible to connect from the town, or, indeed Earth, via Wormcomm. But he didn't mention that. He hoped no one could read his mind. When they asked to see his phone, he said he didn't have it on him. He had no use for it and besides, he couldn't charge it. The sigh of disappointment from a whole group of boys was audible – they would have loved to look at a new piece of tech.

Beth found the attention from the girls quite demanding. Charity rescued her at lunchtime and fended off some of the pressure.

"Don't worry. The novelty of having someone new will wear off. Especially when other people come from the space-village."

"Do you think they will? I mean, some of my friends?"

"No idea. I guess you're, like, guinea pigs."

"What are *they*?"

"Oh. It's just an expression. It means they're trying things out with you. Seeing how it works."

"How does it work? I guess they've never had anyone new join from outside."

"Not in this generation."

"Is it working? I mean the experimenting on us?"

"Yes. Just go along with things. If you get bored at school, don't worry. Raph and I will help you learn stuff at home."

"What happens at lunchtime? Do we get to eat?"

"Yes. If we bring stuff from home. Mum won't pack too much though because we have to avoid making other kids jealous."

"Jealous. Of our food?"

"Some kids don't get much. Some don't get any at all for lunch. It doesn't help to have a full box."

"That's awful."

"It is. It depends on your status. We're OK. Dad gets paid enough for us to get food. The high-status girls get to eat in a different building."

"So people don't get jealous of them?"

"That and because they think they are more important than the rest of us. And the boys eat in their yard."

"So I won't ever get to see Joseph at school?"

"Boys and girls don't mix most of the time."

"I miss him. I miss my mum and dad..."

"I'll take you to the farm again as soon as school is out tomorrow. Don't worry."

The following day, a member of the Ruling Council 'descended' on the school without warning. The teachers were all on edge as he sat at the back of lessons. But it wasn't the competence or compliance of the teachers that was being investigated. It was all about watching the performance of Joseph and Beth.

Things were not so hard for Beth. Lessons like needlework and cooking were not about pretending anything but Joseph's STEM and language classes were more of a challenge. He found himself in sets where expectations were far below what he had already achieved – it didn't seem as if they would get to simplifying surds for years.

Citizenship lessons were the hardest, though. In maths, two plus two always added up to four, even if you pretended you didn't know how to work things out but in citizenship they learnt that truth was what the Ruling Council said it was. They claimed it was God's truth – absolute truth, something that was true everywhere in the universe. So, truth beyond question. But he knew that some of the things that were meant to be true were definitely not. They told lies about what people did on Earth and even on board space-villages but he did not dare tell them they were wrong. And one big obvious lie was that girls were not capable of doing maths and science. Did they really believe that? Did they know it was a lie and were just pretending to themselves it was the truth? He could not be sure. A lot of people seemed to believe it.

One thing was certain: if a kid argued with his teachers, he got beaten with a stick that had been brought from Earth in some earlier space-village. The teacher was proud of it, and not slow to use it. It became apparent that kids were being beaten all the time, even for making mistakes by accident. He didn't want to be beaten, but could he live with the lies all his life? One day, he told himself, *I will tell them they are wrong and I won't care what they do to me. But not yet.* Charity and Raph had told him his time would come. Things were going to change but they asked him to be patient for now. They were right. The teachers couldn't beat all three and a half thousand people in Talbot ready and waiting to tell the truth as they saw it.

On that inspection day, the teachers were relieved that the visiting member of the Ruling Council went home satisfied that Joseph and Beth were no threat.

41

After school, Charity waited for both Joseph and Beth and led them out of the gate in the opposite direction from the way they had arrived. They dodged a few kids determined to get a look at the newbies and met Nathan at the end of the street. At the sight of him, the attention melted away.

"Hi, my charming intended."

"Hi, guys."

"Like me, Nat has ideas about farming and that's why we are attached to the farm. When we get there, we'll show you our project, but – like everything else – best not talk about it to anyone."

"Like I would say anything to anyone anymore. It's all, like, be dumb, be thick," said Joseph with a tired expression.

"Yep. But, like we said, it's bound to change. So hang on in there for now."

"Guess you guys have been hanging on in there for years. That, like, sucks."

"Tell us about it. But with you space-villagers here, we're getting... excited," said Charity. "Just to talk as we are is brilliant, and to discover that you're not like the Ruling Council. We were afraid you'd all be like them but you're not."

Nathan grimaced. "My intended, Charity, you will soon learn, is impetuous and gets herself into trouble all the time," laughed Nathan. "And while I like that, I have to remind her not to get into too much trouble. It's all right her telling you to be careful but just don't go following her example."

Charity giggled. "I can't wait for your people on board to make things better. But I guess I will just have to wait a little longer."

"And keep it cool. OK?" said Nathan.

"OK, intended." And she stuck her tongue out at him.

"You can see why I like this young firebrand. But you two, seriously, sit on your personalities for a bit."

Half an hour later, the farm came into view. The recent storm had left muddy puddles all around the entrances to the house and barn. It looked even more untidy to the eyes of someone who had lived 'indoors' in a space-village for all of their lives.

Mud was a new thing. But it took only a few minutes from her first encounter with it for Beth's face to light up with joy. Mud was a wonderful thing. It's hard to describe the reaction of anyone who has only ever seen mud in pictures and videos. It was not just the feel of it, but its scent. It was good but as they got nearer the farm, its smell became decidedly pungent.

Beth screwed up her nose. She wasn't so sure about this farmyard mud. "*This* mud smells bad."

"This? This is a good healthy farmyard fragrance," laughed Charity. "It's the town that can smell bad... sometimes dangerously so."

"Do they have a sewage system here on this farm?" asked Joseph.

Charity smiled. "They have a long drop – an earth closet. It is very deep and the smells aren't noticeable – well, not over those of the sheep and the damp hay, that is. Ah, look, there is your dad coming out of the outhouse right now."

And there was their father, still hitching his trousers trying to get comfortable. They weren't his trousers but a pair too big for him that the farmer had lent him to do some of the dirtier jobs. He ran over to his children.

"How's it all going, guys? How's school?"

"It's OK," said Beth. "I have to learn to sew."

"That's very good. And what about you, Joseph?"

"I thought it would be hard not knowing everybody but we're like, celebrities and everyone wants to know what it's like on board a space-village." He glanced around – only Charity and Nathan were in earshot. "We have to be very careful not to tell them too much in case the authorities think we're dangerous. Charity, Raph and Nathan have told us to keep a low profile."

"You're a wise lad. It hasn't taken us long to gather that even here. But it's not been hard looking ignorant because we are. Come inside. Your mum has been missing you."

Charity and Nathan and the farmer and his wife stood gazing at the lovely family scenes as they cuddled like they had been apart for weeks rather than just two nights. Charity touched Nathan's hand. This was the kind of family she wanted. Nathan looked down at her and smiled and her heart warmed. This family may have been on a steep learning curve on the surface of a planet but they had so much to teach them on Pure Haven – if they would be permitted to.

After they had inspected their parents' sleeping quarters and Beth had said how nice her bed was in Charity's room, Joseph asked if he could see what she and Nathan were doing that was so hush-hush.

"Follow me," said Nathan. He led them through the barn into a large back room with a bolted door. Inside it was a museum of plants of all kinds.

"We've been collecting samples of every native plant we can find; anything that grows in the open or under trees."

There were carefully pressed plants beside some drawings with a written description. "Charity's artistic," said Nathan. He was proud of his intended. "She's begun recording their seeds or fruit as well as the plant itself. Before Charity came along, I could only collect them but now we are doing a proper inventory."

"The next stage," said Charity, "is to analyse each one of these to discover the properties they have – which are nutritious, which poisonous, which we can use medicinally."

"Hasn't anyone done any of this before?" asked Joseph.

"No," said Nathan. "The colony has put all its efforts into cultivating seeds from Earth. Some have done well, others not. Some of the Earth plants need to be pollinated by hand. There are few insects yet. A few have been introduced – especially after the last space-village fifteen years ago – but there is not enough for them to eat. The native plants largely depend on wind-blown pollination."

"There aren't enough of the introduced species to ensure we have a properly balanced diet with all the vitamins we need," added Charity. "But instead of tapping the local resources, they have put all their effort into getting better yields of wheat, barley and oats," said Charity.

"And sheep?"

"And sheep. But, to be fair, beyond our rudimentary research, no one has the technology to test these local plants short of people eating them – and that is far too great a risk."

"And even if people didn't die in agony, it would take years to know if they had any long-term threats or were any good at all," added Nathan. "The farmer here just wants me to get his seeds to grow better and I do that. Look, over there," and he showed them a corner with louvres through which the sun shone. "I'm trying to grow wheat in different soils and with different amounts of light and watering to see which works best. That's what he – and the Ruling Council – are really interested in."

"These are stronger on this side," observed Joseph.

"They are. It's the soil. Not too heavy and well drained seems to be the answer. Next spring the farm will plant further up the slope. We are already clearing the land of the native plants."

"What we would love is for your dad... and your mum, I guess... to bring us the tech from the space-village to do some testing on the native flora."

"Are they going back to fetch it?" asked Beth, looking for a reason to visit 'home'.

"If they can persuade the Ruling Council," said Nathan.

"Which has no idea what we're doing here," reminded Charity.

"Because they wouldn't like it?" asked Joseph, half rhetorically.

"Because they can't control it themselves. And it would be too risky for them to let a young middle-rank man – let alone a teenage girl – meddle with anything that might change the way we do things on Haven."

42

Elle was really excited. It was as if Earth was just next door. The stars and planets out there might be hard to see with the naked eye – the planets impossible, even with the large telescope – but now it was so, like, wow, amazing – you could actually talk to people on them. On your own computer! How cool was that? They were no longer being just a few people on a small world orbiting Epsilon Eridani.

"Hi, Sam. How's it going on Mother Earth?" she asked when they next logged in.

"It's OK. It's been windy and the rain has been lashing down. And it gets dark so early this time of year."

"On your part of the planet?"

"Sure. They're having the usual heat waves further south. And Tom still hasn't seen any rain in Australia."

"The planet's too hot. Global warming."

"Yeah, but we think it's cooling down a bit now. We're turning the corner. It's taken hundreds of years but the carbon capture programmes are working. Nobody wants to go back to the old way of exploiting the Earth. With today's tech, we don't need to."

"And you've given up on wars."

"The shooting and bombing kind? Yeah, mostly. If you don't like anybody these days, you just try to undermine their computer systems. No need to drop bombs. Nowadays, you just make sure your enemy's health systems, food distribution and so on break down. The poorer countries can have their whole economic stability wrecked, so we still have refugees and starving people."

"And that's progress?"

"Kinda, if you think about the mass destructions of the past.

Guns are not being made on an industrial scale anymore. Missile stocks are no longer being maintained. Mainly because the kind of people who made those kinds of weapons now get more out of exploiting communities rather than destroying them. We still get the evil types running things and that can be devastating for a lot of people. You can have your freedoms taken away without you having a chance – it can happen before you know it's coming."

"That's scary."

"But the positive news is that, somehow, good always seems to manage to win. 90% of people are good, kind and honest. When someone gets hurt – like if your house burns down because of the fires, someone will take you in. We have learnt that we need to work together on Earth – we're still calling out the bad guys for what they are. They haven't disappeared but neither have the good guys."

"You're winning. The good guys are winning?"

"Sort of, I guess. The bad keeps popping up. There'll always be bad guys but they will never destroy truth," said Amy.

"We have to warn you," said Sam, "I'm being serious. Earth's bombs may not affect you so far away. You can forget *Star Wars* with fighter space vehicles, phasers and torpedoes, nuclear bombs and all that. All that's fiction. But, with Wormcomm, Earth's evil online assaults definitely can do damage. You have to be careful. The government here is worried for you. We got a visit the other day from MI5 to make sure we were legit. We have to be positively vetted."

"How great is the risk?" asked Anna.

"Oh, you can be sure that evil minds are already planning how they can use Wormcomm to exploit the innocent. But be assured, our government defence ministry has sent all the latest online security stuff to your planet, so you can set up firewalls against the insidious malware that will inevitably come your way."

"You wouldn't believe the security that has been put in around us here," added Amy. "All these government guys are monitoring everything. We're pretty lucky to be the ones trialling this. Loads of schools would love to get involved but at the moment it's only us.

Lucky Stanton Wick."

"Are they – your government people – listening in to everything that we're saying?" Elle felt embarrassed. She may have been, like, kinda flirting with Tom while all the time being listened to. Creepy.

"Pretty much." Sam laughed. "The AI does the monitoring – only calls in humans when needed if it thinks things are getting dangerous. Don't worry. I doubt we're doing or saying anything that will trigger any alert. It's more about what might happen alongside our chat, anyway."

"Like what?" asked Anna.

"Like malware uploading without us knowing – attaching itself to our connection."

"Now you are scaring me," said Elle.

"But it's clean, Elle. If it weren't, the bots would have raised the alarm good and proper with all that's happening around us, Sam reassured her. "We're good... Ah, here is Space-Village Talbot. Hi guys."

"Hi everyone." It was Fran.

"Hi, Fran," bubbled Elle. "How're things on Talbot?"

"Nothing's changed on board. We're doing school and everything like before we landed. But it's not the same. It isn't right without Joseph and Beth. There's a gap. They've kinda just vanished. It feels strange."

With all the negativity, Elle's bubble began losing a bit of its fizz. First the warning about malevolent software from Earth and now the worries from Pure Haven.

"So, how's it with you, Elle?" asked Fran.

"We're so lucky here on Terraspei. Everything's good. I'm getting more opportunities than ever to visit the observatory. It's definitely the way I want to go in my studies."

"You cheer us all up, Elle. Your planet sounds like fun."

"I never thought of it as fun before. But to have all that I have and do what I want to do is fun. Fun is not just about parties and dancing, is it?"

"You do dancing?"

"Well, not seriously. Just like when we have a fling."

"Like, on a date?" asked Sam.

"Date? Oh, no. Everyone goes. You don't have to have a partner. Look, don't take me down that route. There's too much of 'When are you going to get a boyfriend?' from the old folk already, without you chiming in. I've no time for boys at the moment. Don't worry, Sam. Nothing wrong with boys in general; I just don't need a relationship, thank you very much."

"I completely get that," said Fran. "It's a bit like that here."

"We're chilled about it in the Chew Valley," said Sam. "If you want my view on it, it's, like, if it happens, fine. But it's a waste of time going out there trying to find someone. I don't do dating like some guys. One day, I want to leave this valley and head off somewhere else – meet new people. But I guess it's different for you in your smaller communities. Nowhere really to go?"

"Precisely," said Elle.

"But not really for us," said Fran. "I mean there are all these guys out there – just beyond a fence – and we've no idea what they are like. It feels like they could be monsters just looking for fresh breeding stock. With a bit of luck, they're all already spoken for. But left single, that would definitely not be allowed."

"Oh, Fran. That's awful," said Amy.

"And that's why it's so great to talk to you guys."

"We wish we could do something to help," said Elle.

"You have. You are... by just being there and caring. And you can pray."

"Of course," said Elle.

"I'll have a go too," said Sam. "Can't say I've done that much praying before, though."

"God'll be pleased to hear from you, then," laughed Elle. It would take more than a bit of sad news to burst all of her bubbles.

<h1 align="center">43</h1>

A week passed on Pure Haven and it felt like an age to Joseph and Beth. But they were rapidly getting to know how things worked.

At the weekend, Nathan called round. The family had been used to him coming and had begun to like him and Charity's mum, especially, was pleased for her daughter. He had been a good choice – or, rather, an option because her husband hadn't had much say in it.

"Hi, Joseph. You still got that phone of yours?" asked Nathan.

"Yeah. I've stashed it."

"I've made an adapter for your lead. I think this will work. It won't blow your phone at any rate so long as you don't plug it into the mains. Have you got a battery pack?"

"Whoa. Thanks, Nathan. No. I haven't got one of those."

"We'll find you one... Just be discreet."

"I will."

"Tell me how it goes."

The following day, Charity handed Joseph a little black box.

"It's old and doesn't hold much charge. I haven't used it in an age but it still works. You'll need to keep plugging it in but I think it'll be enough."

"Thanks, Charity. Should I try it tonight when it's dark so no one sees?"

"No. Don't use it around the house. Save it till you're outside in the country."

"No worries. I'm getting the hang of things. It's so sad. It shouldn't be like this."

"It shouldn't but it's been this way a long time. We're the first generation on Haven to take any steps at all towards revolution. Mum hates the way it is but like everyone her age, has just had to learn to put up with it. She tries to teach me to do the same. She's scared – especially for me. Dad isn't bad – really he isn't. He wants the best for us and so insists on everything that he thinks will make us better off... but mostly just keep us safe. As you've heard, like, a million times, it doesn't do to have too high a profile."

"Nathan's different. He's going to make things happen."

"He is. And he's not the only one. The Ruling Council has reason to be nervous. That's why life is so dangerous. And why they don't want you newcomers upsetting things."

"They don't want us to stay?"

"Yes and no. What they want is all the resources you bring. Stuff for making electronics – they haven't located any lithium on the planet yet – and your up-to-date tech: replicators, hydroponics... loads of stuff. This planet is desperate for all you've got in those modules."

"But they don't want the people?"

"Oh, they do. We really need fresh genes. And your skills in engineering and food production. What they don't want is your ideas – your culture."

"But three and a half thousand people who have lived together for twenty years – we're going to be different."

"Different? Like, free to become who you are – allow your nature to come through without being squashed or moulded, morphed into something alien?"

"No one in Talbot would try to do that in a million years."

"So with all three thousand plus of you joining the community... I can't wait for that."

"They might not choose to stay. At the moment, I don't think anyone wants to disembark. They're probably deciding right now to leave."

"And leaving you behind?"

"If I get my phone working, I can talk to them. They could try and call us in, I guess."

"They might call you to return?"

"I'll try and persuade them to stay. I'll tell them about you and Nathan."

"No. No names! Anyone might be listening in."

"No. I won't use names – just say there are some lovely people living here."

The battery pack worked. On his way to the farm, Joseph stepped off the path and called up Fran.

"Hey, Fran. It's Joseph."

"Hey, Joseph. Wow. I was beginning to think you'd, like, completely vanished."

"No. Still here. But, look, I can't talk openly. I have to hide my phone. I can't talk much. It isn't safe."

"How? Why can't you come back and visit?"

"Same reason you're not allowed out. You're a bad influence."

"Tell everyone we're OK. How's it going with Wormcomm?"

"Brilliant. We're even talking to Terraspei now. We've set up a three-way link. It's brilliant. It's like... a much better connection than this."

"Fran, will you talk to the elders and ask them? I've got some young people here – safe people – who want to join the Wormcomm link; they could use my phone."

"What? Join the Wormcomm group?"

"Yes. Maybe just mostly with text messages."

"I will."

"Actually, I think texting's a good idea for everything. Text me anytime and I can pick them up when no one's looking."

"Yeah. I'll do that. I'll tell you what people say about Wormcomm."

"OK. I have to go. I'll get back in touch. And don't worry about us. We're OK. Beth is fine – even if she hates the food here."

"OK. Everyone will be pleased that you phoned."

"Bye, Fran."

"Bye, Joseph."

In the woods on the way back, Joseph retrieved his phone from the lining of his coat, where he'd hidden it. There was a text from Fran. The elders and parents aboard thought that all communications should be by text until things changed. And he was not to get caught with his phone because that might jeopardise some of the delicate diplomacy that was taking place. Plus, it was vital that he didn't get it confiscated. They needed to keep in touch. Joseph wondered what he would say if he were asked a direct question about owning a phone. He would have to deny it. This regime was teaching him to lie. That was another way of testing whether something was good or bad. If it made you lie, it was bad, he thought. If it was safe to be truthful, then it was most likely good.

A couple of evenings later, Nathan swung by. Joseph told him about his conversations with Fran and about how they were now talking to Terraspei, too. Nathan and Charity's expressions were priceless. This was even more than they could have dreamed.

"You mean, you can get to meet people on Earth AND Terraspei?" enthused Charity.

"Yeah. Apparently, the Wormcomm link is crisper than between here and Talbot. If we can get a decent signal to Talbot, I'm sure it would work. Fran is asking if it's OK, though. The village elders will have to approve because they are the ones responsible for keeping everyone safe."

"Rulers, again," sighed Charity.

"No. It isn't like that. They are there to keep people safe. That's all."

"He's right, Charity," said Nathan. "And they are wise. Tell them you're talking to us – needn't give names just yet – and say we'd like to send a message to both Earth and Terraspei. Tell them that some young people on Haven wish to join the conversations but conditions are not right just yet."

"Haven?"

"Yes. Drop the 'Pure'. 'Pure' is a lie. What happens among the elite here has nothing to do with purity... but don't tell them that... yet."

Joseph was seeing a boldness in Nathan he hadn't witnessed before. He was gaining the confidence of a revolutionary.

44

The farm, it turned out, was not totally without access to electricity – unlike some places in the town and most of the other farms. Someone in the past had built a leat that turned a precarious watermill connected to an even older-looking generator which still worked. It seems that the water supply was pretty dependable – one of the reasons, perhaps, why the farm had been sited where it was.

The McPhersons settled in remarkably quickly – especially when the farmer found them willing helpers. It didn't take long for Joseph's mum to get the wife to talk when the men were elsewhere.

"Your husband seems to allow you your opinion on things," she said, bluntly.

"We're a team."

"That's not a word you'd often use around here. Around here you'll quickly learn. It won't take long. He'll soon be like the rest of them."

"Like what?"

"Oh. Making all the decisions. Telling you what to do."

"But you and your husband are a team. On a farm, I guess you have to be."

"He's the general and I'm a private. If he could, he would even decide what we're having for dinner each day."

"If he could?"

"I can't cook what's not there. What's in is what we eat."

"I wouldn't have thought a farm was a place where you'd be short of food."

"Don't you believe it. We have quotas set by the Ruling Council to fill. Sometimes they take everything if there isn't

194

enough... often there isn't enough. And it's getting harder. Yields are down. Every year, it gets harder."

"It's tough work."

"Very. They sent a couple of kids on a weekend to help. Nathan – he's been coming since he was fifteen. He's a bright one. And now he's brought along Charity, his intended. I think she's brighter than she lets on – but keep that to yourself. Nathan has some ideas about getting native stuff to grow and eat. Not that it is much past the experimental stage... Probably won't work but you've got to hand it to the guy."

"So what can I help you with? Would you like me to do some cleaning? You never get a chance with all you have to do in the kitchen and outdoors."

"Sweeping out the living room isn't on my husband's list of allocated jobs, so I don't get round to doing it often. I don't know how he thinks it gets clean – just by itself, probably. Have a go if you want."

Faith McPherson discovered an old straw broom and a rusty thing with a handle that could be used as a dustpan. Maybe it was meant to be one – it wasn't obvious from it's design. On board, all the cleaning was done with vacuum cleaners and mostly by Dave, who enjoyed doing it. Using a broom made of soft stems of some local bush was a novelty. She wasn't prepared for the dust, which was thick behind the woody sofa chairs padded with straw cushions. She resolved to change the straw, which was already disintegrating.

By the middle of the day when the men came in, she had only finished half the room but the contrast between what she had done and what she still had to do was like a before and after picture.

The farmer stepped in and grunted. Dave McPherson whispered a wow and kissed his wife. He wanted to say something but couldn't, of course. He didn't need to. His smile said it all.

Two days later, Faith McPherson had been through the whole house with the exception of their hosts' bedroom and the business end of the kitchen. Her hostess expressed her thanks.

"You're making yourself indispensable," she grumbled.

"A working farm needs more than two people. Maybe when the space-villagers start to come into the community, you will get a lot more help in all sorts of ways."

"Well, it looks as if you're here until they get round to building more houses – or until you give up on us and get back into your space-village and head off back to Earth."

"I don't think that will happen."

"Won't it? You might not have any choice in the matter. It'll depend on the Ruling Council and they don't want husbands who treat their wives as equal partners in a team."

Faith McPherson thought about it. Men had begun by being the dominant gender on board when they had set off but it had changed over the years. And the young people were definitely far more equal than their parents. They had just grown up together. She couldn't imagine her son ever thinking girls were second to boys. They weren't. They did equally well at anything kids had to do on board.

Dave McPherson had been busy too. He took his wife to what looked like a pile of woody spars but it turned out to be a covering for a vehicle.

"An old-fashioned agricultural tractor-bike!"

"Yeah. We have several of a more recent model stored aboard the village. Extra-powerful electric quad bikes built to tow a trailer or farm implement. There's a large battery over here, which seems like it's meant to fit."

"It looks like a heap of junk. Do you think it's working?"

"It's probably shot."

"We could try powering it up now by using the watermill. That way we would know if it's any good before we put a lot of effort into repairing the bike."

"If we can get it working, I thought that we could build a

garage for it using these solar panels I've found for a roof. We could do with more room, anyway."

"Good idea. But how are we going to mend this machine? We'd need spanners at least."

"No problem. I've discovered a whole box of tools under those piles of dead beetles."

"Mr McPherson, you are a marvel."

"No. Just stuck here with nothing to do and looking for a hobby." They laughed. Somehow, she felt, we're going to get through this.

45

Within two weeks, Dave McPherson had already got some seeds growing in the barn. With a bit of heat and light, he persuaded some wheat grains to germinate in a makeshift hydroponics solution. Nathan was impressed.

"That's pretty cool, Mr McPherson. How do you make that fluid? How did you do that? How do you know what solution to give them?"

"Without my testing kit, it's a sheer guess, I'm afraid."

"An educated guess."

"Well, yes. The thing is, you need a basic mixture of nitrogen, phosphorus and potassium and then, over a longer period, for the greatest success, a selection of other elements and compounds according to what you're growing. It depends on what you've already got in your water."

"How can you know that? I mean, what's in the water here? It looks pretty clean."

"You're supposed to use a testing kit, which I don't have. So, in my case, it's what it tastes like. Another way is looking at what is left in the bottom of a pan when boiled dry."

"Oh, I see. Like salt or lime scale."

"You've got it. After that, adding nitrogen is key. You nearly always have to add that."

"Where do you get that?"

"Urea is the easiest one."

"Pee?"

"Exactly. Pee is also good for phosphorus and potassium. So, this solution has creek water, which I've strained through some leaf mould, dashes of pee and some crushed beetle juice."

"Betelgeuse? Like in the red giant star?"

"That would be something. No, beetle juice as in some squashed beetle-looking insects that run around the corners of this barn. I've no idea how much but I guess they will have a variety of proteins and trace elements that the plants need."

"Well, it seems to be working. What can I do to help?"

"Persuade your Ruling Council to let me go back to my space-village and collect my testing kit."

"Sorry. No one persuades the Ruling Council to do anything. Anyone who tries is likely to be severely disciplined."

"I know. Only joking. But, really, it's no joke, is it? Don't our rulers know the writing's on the wall for their colony unless they start trying to work with the natural resources of this planet and accept all the scientific expertise that's offered?"

"No. They don't. I don't know what they think in private but most of them seem to be in total denial of any decline, despite all the evidence."

"That's ridiculous."

"Of course, it is. But it makes sense if the most important thing for them is to keep their power, exercising full control over everything – every little thing."

"Micromanage. Because they like being in charge."

"And because they honestly believe they're God's gift – they are called to rule."

MacPherson lowered his voice. "... and because they're scared of anybody being better or cleverer at anything."

"That too."

"Hence we keep a low profile... By the way, I've been spending my time tidying up this barn and guess what I've found?"

"What?"

"Among other things, an old set of solar panels. Come and see?"

They walked out the back of the barn and there, among a pile of what looked like metal and plastic junk, were some ancient solar panels. Most of them were unbroken and set in white flaky but intact aluminium frames.

"Must have been discarded when the water power did all that was needed," said Nathan.

"I see no reason why they shouldn't still work if connected up the right way... and then there is this." He led Nathan to a corner of the yard behind another heap of rubbish and tugged at a piece of plastic sheeting, revealing a tractor-bike crusted in dust and sticky goo.

Nathan gasped in amazement. "I haven't been allowed to touch one of these before. They are the preserve of an elite group of mechanics whose status is kept high and who only take on their own as apprentices... Not that it has ever really appealed. It only serves to keep the Ruling Council and their enforcers mobile."

"Probably why whoever owned this on the farm hid it away. I guess it could be decades old," said Dave.

"It was definitely made on Earth, so that would be at least thirty-five years – the time the last space-village left."

"It could have been in use for a few years after that, though."

"Even if we could clean it up, it's not going to do anything without a working battery," observed Nathan.

"Correct. I expected the battery to be well and truly shot. But I'm getting used to surprises on this planet, so I tried it."

"You mean, tried to power it up? No chance."

"I knew I wouldn't get it working – it would take a lot of cleaning up even if nothing was wrong with it – but the battery has an LED and if that gave a flicker, it would give an indication of life. So I tried it."

"And?" said Nathan, disbelieving.

"It's as dead as a doornail. But it seems we've got a lot of useful junk here because I've also found a trickle charger. It was under a pile of dead beetles." He heaved a heavy box-like device onto the ground between them. It's ancient but electricity is electricity. We could plug this in for a day and see if it lights anything up."

"I wouldn't have known what that thing was if you hadn't told me."

"We use them aboard. Making batteries last is crucial. There are more modern ones but it is clear what the charging voltage is, so I know it'll be safe if it works. It also has an LED indicator – a low-charge detection light. If that comes on, at least the charger is working."

"So what are we waiting for?"

"These beetles leave a sticky mess everywhere but that's good news because it has protected most of this stuff from the air. Underneath the goo, it seems to be in pretty good condition. Give me a hand lifting this outside. There is always a risk of fire with these things."

"That would be dangerous on board a space-village, I guess."

"Very. We contain all batteries in a CO_2 environment."

"Oxygen-free."

"The carbon dioxide is kept at positive pressure. You can't be too careful if you're light-years adrift in outer space."

While Nathan got to cleaning up the terminals on the charger, Dave rummaged around in the toolbox and found a spanner or two. It took a bit of tugging but eventually between them, they managed to shift some of the bolts on the tractor-bike.

"Best remember where each of these goes, so we can reassemble it when we're done," said Dave.

"Here, put them in this empty box." Nathan knocked a lot of dust and a few live beetles out of an upturned box, the original contents of which had long since disappeared. There was something really satisfying about working together constructively. Dave applied himself to the bike while Nathan scraped away at the charger, cleaning off the sticky deposit. After a good hour, it seemed to be working – at least they got a low charge indicator light when they attached it to the battery. However, there was no light on the battery of any colour.

"So far, so good," smiled Dave. "At least we know the trickle charger is working. I reckon we should leave it at least a day – it could take a while. One has to be patient when breathing life back into a battery. With lithium-ion batteries you never know, so we shouldn't leave it unattended. Any risk of it raining again today?"

"I can't be sure but it doesn't feel like rain." Nathan looked around the yard, which was looking a little more ordered. "It seems like we've made a good start."

Suddenly, Dave felt tired. The initial boost of being able to show Nathan what he had discovered had waned and the lack of proper food and sleep took over.

"I don't want to give you false hope, lad. It's probably too far gone," he muttered. "But it was worth a try. Better stick around for a bit... keep an eye on it. I'll see if I can rustle up some tea."

Dave wandered off to the house. Nathan felt excited. Dave was a wonderful gift. *I reckon we should clean up the rest of the tractor-bike, whatever. Even if this battery doesn't work, we might just happen on a spare one.*

Dave reappeared with Faith, carrying two mugs of what passed for tea. It was a brew of local leaves which Dave was trialling. It tasted nothing like tea but was better than just hot water.

"So far," said Faith, "Dave hasn't managed to poison us. But I do miss my Assam blend."

"Amazing," said Nat. "Welcome to the future!"

"Future?"

"Things are changing. Look at all this. Change is already happening..."

"Don't be too sure," said Dave. "Talbot will lose patience if it goes on too long... but for now, we might as well finish the job."

Faith smiled. "Actually, Dave, you're having fun, aren't you? Like a child playing with his toys."

"I guess. But we've a really good grown-up toy here, wouldn't you say?" patting the tractor-bike.

The tractor-bike cleaned up pretty well. In some ways, the layers of straw dust and beetle juice had kept it safe. There was hardly any rust and the oil that had been used on the moving parts had lasted. Between them, they had soon dismantled it, scraped, scrubbed and wiped each part clean, and then carefully reassembled it.

"That looks almost presentable," said Dave.

"As good as any I have seen," agreed Nathan. "Look, the battery LED! It's showing a dim red. Coming back from the dead."

"So it is! It'll take at least another day for any real charge to register but, who knows, that red light might just turn green in a couple of days."

That, thought Nathan, *might be a sign. The breakthrough has begun. The green light to turn our community around is coming. Slowly but surely.*

46

Multi-year assemblies in Stanton Wick were a rare occurrence. The school was too big for more than one year to meet together on a regular basis. But that day, Sam and his small group of Wormcomm users – nicknamed the 'interplanetary wormers' – had been invited to share their experiences with the whole of years 10 and 11. Even some of those in years 12 and 13 managed to sneak in at the back of the upstairs gallery along with teachers from all departments with free periods.

The headteacher addressed the assembly.

"I am extremely pleased to report that our school is among very few participating in this interplanetary experiment. When I was your age, I never believed it possible to have a two-way conversation with colonies on planets over ten light-years away. Nothing could travel faster than the speed of light but I was wrong, as these young people have proved.

"The government made their choice of this school precisely because we do not enter into this blind. We are fully aware of the impact that this will make on people isolated from each other for centuries – especially those small colonies numbered in thousands rather than billions. Great care has been taken to ensure that the vast quantities of spurious online trash that pervades our digital environment are prevented from arriving in these places. They do not need to endure a tsunami of lies from Earth.

"Up till recently, Wormcomm has been limited to direct communications by the scientific community. Now they are trusting a few young people in a few pilot schools. It is well-established that young people are among the most enthusiastic about expanding their horizons and so the UN, in their wisdom, thought it best that a few very lucky young persons be included at the earliest possible stage.

"So it's an amazing privilege to introduce our international wormers - trailblazers in communication, Sam Brooks and Amy Huck."

The hall was filled with rapturous applause.

The head smiled at them and then sat down. It was their turn. How should they start? They expected questions and hadn't anticipated a speech. The two looked at each other and then Amy got to her feet.

"Er, thank you, Mr Gilbert. You make this sound like something very special. I guess it is. But it isn't really. I mean, we *know* we're talking to people, like, billions of miles away, but it doesn't feel like that. I mean we get better reception through Wormcomm than I do on my phone from downstairs in our dining room... Not, err, that my mum and dad let me use my phone at the dining table. But that's not what..."

She hadn't meant to say that. No doubt she'd pay for it later from kids that would mock her and her family's ways. She continued. "Wormcomm is like talking to friends anywhere. For example, we have this friend, Elle, on Terraspei who's into space stuff - watching stars and the like and then there's her friend, Anna. Oh, and we are also in contact with guys inside a space-village that has just landed on Pure Haven. They've joined our group, too." Amy looked at Sam. "Er, Sam wants to say something."

Sam caught his breath. *Do I? This is like...* He breathed in. *You can do this, Sam.* He stood up and cleared his throat.

"Yeah, that's right. On the space-village, there's Fran. We began with Joseph but he's left the space-village and is out in the community of Pure Haven, so we no longer get to talk to him. We follow what they do day by day. They are all at school like us and all of them are keen on hearing from us on Earth. They really care about how things are here. Worried about us."

Mr Gilbert stood up and Sam sank back into his chair. "May I ask a question? Can I ask, what do you talk about most?"

"Well, all sorts of stuff. The usual," said Amy.

There was a ripple of laughter. The students knew exactly what she meant. Everyone, except most adults, knew what young people talked about – what 'the usual' was.

"The usual?" pressed the head.

"Well, kinda, like what we talk about with our friends here in school," answered Amy.

"About your lessons?"

"Yeah. Sometimes."

"Teachers?"

Amy went a shade of red and Sam came to her rescue.

"Only the good things, sir."

The hall broke into more laughter.

And so the assembly continued. Some of the teachers asked intelligent questions about the technicalities and the pursuit of their subject areas on Terraspei and Talbot. Amy and Sam fielded them as best they could.

One teacher asked about communications with Pure Haven.

"You say you have frequent exchanges with Space-Village Talbot, which, if I have heard you correctly, is currently parked on Pure Haven. Do you have any direct contact with the people outside of the space-village in the community?"

"No, Miss."

"Is there a reason for that?"

"They are not included in the pilot scheme, Miss," replied Sam.

"Why not?"

"Sorry. You will have to ask the people in Cambridge that, Miss."

Amy was impressed at the way Sam had dealt with the question. They knew the answer but it wasn't for them to get into the problems on that planet in so public a manner.

They were aware that some kids were getting bored and the two lucky interplanetary wormers understood that once the wonders of the tech had been absorbed, most of the kids were not really interested in the people at the other end. They might be billions of miles out in space but they weren't aliens, so they were just ordinary. What they were doing was no different from last term when Mr Wu from China came to tell them about what went on in Shanghai. In fact, what he had to say was more interesting because he was good at telling stories. The centuries-old Chinese culture had some fascinating angles to explore. But neither Sam nor Amy had much experience at telling stories and, besides, the kids on Terraspei and on board Talbot had grown up talking English and went to school studying the same things. They even sat the same exams. What was left? *Ah, food,* thought Sam. And he told them about some of the local foodstuffs on Terraspei and the hydroponics decks on Talbot and then it was time to call it a day.

"So, we're chatting online," Sam concluded. "It might seem amazing that the people are light-years away. But, actually, it's no different from, like, chatting with your relatives around the world – same difference."

Nothing, however, seemed to dent Mr Gilbert's pride at being the head of the first school in Britain to house interplanetary wormers.

After the assembly, sitting outside in the park watching a group of kids playing football, Amy asked Sam. "Do you reckon that was OK?"

"Like we made it sound like it was pretty boring, you mean?"

"Well, yeah. I guess."

"If we hadn't, we'd not be sitting out here without anyone wanting to know more."

"And that's good because we don't *want* to talk about what is *actually* happening on Haven."

"Right. We can't talk about that."

"No one says what they chat about with their friends anyway. I mean, if they asked me what me and Leona chat about, it might be interesting but it's private."

"Ooh. What *do* you and Leona chat about that's so interesting?"

"It's *private.*"

"Ah. Like, who you fancy among the boys?"

"You wish. It's you boys who talk like that. Comparing girls' body parts and... stuff."

"How do you know what boys talk about?"

"Like... like... If what they post on their phones is anything to go by. Let's... let's just get back to the subject. What are we going to say to Fran and Pete on Pure Haven?"

"Listen. Provide a listening ear," said Sam. "There's nothing else we can do. *That's* when eleven light-years feels like a really long way. There's just no chance we could ever actually get there. Even if we hopped on a space-village today, we'd be thirty-six before we arrived..." He tailed off because he caught sight of Tanya, lurking.

"Hiya, Lovebirds."

"Tanya. What are you doing here? You're not at school anymore."

"You may not have noticed but you are *outside* the school right now. So, tell me, what is it like talking to people on the other side of the universe?"

"Like talking to VR friends anywhere. Pretty boring really." Sam just wanted her to vanish. But she didn't. What was it with her?

"All sorts of things," said Amy. "It depends."

"On what?"

"On what they're good at. Interested in. Same as here."

"Like getting taken on by a modelling agency?" Oh, so that was it. She wanted to make sure he knew and wanted to show off.

"Haven't come across that one," said Sam. "So, I guess, that's, like, you."

"How did you guess?"

"Where do you go for that?"

"Nowhere. They just send me clothes – for free – and you get someone to take pictures as you model them."

"Sounds exciting," said Sam, trying not to sound like what he was actually thinking, which was 'how excruciatingly boring'.

Tanya gave him her withering look. "It might sound boring to you. But it's a lot more exciting than talking about the weather to some kid on another planet." And with that, she sashayed off.

"She'll be back," said Amy.

"Why? What's it with her?"

"She'll find another reason to approach you. Like when she's discovered being a model isn't so fulfilling. What she really wants is you."

"Whaaat! No. You've got that wrong. Where did you get that from? I mean, who—"

"It's obvious. You boys are hopeless at picking up the signs."

"I guess... but why me?"

"Because, actually, compared to a lot of people, you're well-liked and not bad-looking. And you've just stood up in front of everyone else in your year, which gives you some minor celebrity status. So you're a good catch. And you're a good listener. Added to the fact she actually *likes* you."

"Help."

"Don't worry. She'll get the message... eventually."

"And listening? I do listening?"

"Yeah, you do listening. That's, like, more important than it sounds. Like on Haven, just telling somebody who's interested and cares, especially if it's not their problem, is really helpful. I don't know how that works but it does. You're good at that."

"Am I? Never realised."

"There's a lot that's good about you that you don't realise. You were very diplomatic in there, for example."

Sam hesitated, taking it all in. "Thanks."

After a minute of silence. Amy continued. "Even if we were on Haven, there is nothing we could do more than those who are already there, is there? There's three and a half thousand just sitting around in the space-village."

"So we just listen, wherever we are."

"That way we know we're not alone. Somebody cares whether or not they are near enough to give you a hug."

"And as for giving hugs, Tanya Payne is on the other side of the universe as far as I am concerned."

"Absolutely."

"She doesn't lack guys who fancy her."

"Maybe. But they don't have your qualities."

"Yeah... Thanks. You know, Amy, you're quite clever. Wise, I mean. You know that?"

She giggled. "Yep." *But why are you boys so thick sometimes when it comes to reading hearts?*

47

Three weeks had now passed without any seeming development in the negotiations to begin the disembarkation from the space-village. Commander Pritchard was becoming impatient.

"It's always been the understanding that it would take time for the transfer of people out of the village but this lack of progress is worrying," he told the village elders in their weekly meeting.

"We agree," said one of them, who was feeling equally frustrated. "We have been travelling twenty-plus years only to be made to feel unwelcome."

"What is the Ruling Council telling you?"

"To be honest, nothing. They come up with excuses even to talk."

"What are the three families you have out there reporting? How are they getting on?"

"Badly. Well, that's the impression we have got. They cannot call in because, for the most part, their phones are dead; they claim they have no means of charging them. At least two of the families are living without any electricity at all. One of the McPherson youngsters with a working phone says he has been warned by the local kids not to be seen using it. It seems they have a very closed and carefully ordered society that the people at the top of the tree do not want disrupted. We get the impression that they would wish us gone. However, things are not good on the planet. In fact, they are on the cusp of a dangerous slide. Inbreeding of stock is a serious problem. One suspects that is also true of the people. We can address that and so we are useful. Plus they would want our more developed tech – not to mention all the rest of the things we have in the cargo holds."

The commander looked glum. "Is there any danger of violence? Do we need to be ready for an assault?"

"I don't think so. There are only a few ways of entering the modules. None if we seal the hatches."

"But they can be damaged. Setting a fire beneath a module wouldn't be a good idea."

"They would have to come with a mob but I suppose that could be done."

"At the first sign of trouble," suggested the Theta Module captain, "we can start up the engines ready for takeoff."

"That will definitely keep them away," smiled the elder. "They won't be able to approach within a hundred metres. But I doubt it would come to that. And, besides, the three families in the community. What about them?"

"That is a pity. They could easily become hostages... if they are not already," mumbled the Commander.

"When we establish contact, we should call them in," said an elder. "As far as we know, they are still free to move about. Tell his friends that if the young Ferguson lad phones, they are to call him and his family to return to the village."

48

*I*t was on the first day of the fourth week that things began to happen. It started quite early in the morning in the queue at a bakery. Bread had been on ration for a year. The rations were barely adequate but even then there often wasn't enough flour to meet the demand.

That particular morning, the Ruling Council had called a meeting of men from the more elite families in the Town Hall. These privileged few never went short – along with their rations, they had other ways of procuring the food they wanted. They could call in favours to ensure they got far more than their fair share. Everyone knew how it worked, of course, but no one could argue with it. The power lines were strictly drawn.

The queue outside the bakery was made up of women. Women meeting together was discouraged by the Council – they were much harder to control *en masse* – but they couldn't do much about a bread queue. For one risky moment, they forgot to be careful.

Just as the baker was opening his doors, a tractor-bike fitted with panniers drew up and a single young rider with an air of superiority – in truth he was more than intimidated by so many women – pushed his way in front of the queue. He had an order for a large number of loaves for the elite men's meeting about to begin. The men had already breakfasted but they needed the bread for their mid-morning break, it seemed.

The brave baker refused to fulfil the order; he claimed he was afraid of the women.

"Sorry, son. Not today. I have barely enough for these families' rations. There will be trouble if they go hungry."

213

"That's your problem, not mine," said the young man. He couldn't afford to take no for an answer – he would be in deep water if he returned without the Council's bread. He and the baker got into a loud argument, which the ladies followed word by word. In the end, the young man pushed the baker backwards, leapt over the counter, took up a basket and began filling it with loaves before the baker could get back to his feet. At the head of the queue was a large lady who was not afraid of this young imp. She was not going to let this youngster escape with all their bread.

"Put the bread down," she barked. "That belongs to our kids. I'm not going to see my children go hungry one more day."

The guy tried ignoring her but she barred his way. Then other women took courage and joined in, preventing him from getting through to his transport. At the back of the queue, a young woman, hardly older than a girl, turned her attention to the tractor-bike and began trying to push it over. She wasn't anywhere near strong enough – it had a very low centre of gravity – but she was quickly joined by others and soon the bike was on its side. With its wheels in the air, it looked a sad sight. The young man panicked. He turned his attention to his bike; the baker pulled the basket out of his hand and began distributing the loaves to the women.

"Take 'em, ladies. Settle up tomorrow. Go!"

By the time the young man had managed to get his tractor-bike back on its wheels, the women had dispersed and the baker had retreated into his shop, put up a 'sold out' sign and barred the door.

Within the hour, a marshal of the law – a man who belonged to what Charity called the Ruling Council's dog pack – was banging on the bakery door.

The baker denied all knowledge of the event, saying he had seen a young man who had somehow managed to turn over his tractor-bike but he had been too busy to help him.

The truth, however, was not to be covered up. Women were beginning to see that together, they had power. The 'dog pack' was intent on trying to discover which women had led the 'riot'.

No one seemed to know, or who had led the turning over of the tractor-bike.

"You did what?" Nathan couldn't believe what his intended was telling him. "They're bound to find out. They won't hesitate if they think you have led the rest. They've already got husbands worrying about their jobs because their wives were involved. If they find those who incited the riot, they'll be down on them hard."

"I didn't incite it; that boy did. He pushed the baker over and stole our bread."

"You know that won't wash. You didn't have to upend his bike."

"No. But it was fun, though."

"Oh, Charry. What are we going to do?"

"While I can, I'm going to tell my story to the universe. I'm going to call up on Joseph's phone and ask to get patched through on Wormcomm."

Nathan stood looking at her. Temporarily shocked. But then it all made sense. Charity's freedom was limited and she was going to make the most of it.

"Well, I guess you've got nothing to lose."

"I haven't. Look after my family for me. I'm sorry; it could have been good being married to you." She cuddled him. "Things are going to change - bound to. They've already begun. I'll go down in history. Just imagine."

"When they change, we'll get you back."

"It depends. The people that disappear seem to melt right away. I doubt I'll be any different... But now, to action. Raph might know where Joseph hides his phone."

Twenty minutes later, Raph appeared home from his part-time work. He had been dismissed early. Something was up.

"Guess you heard the Ruling Council is on the warpath."

"They are. And your sister here is for it," sighed Nathan.

"Why? What have you done?"

"No time to explain. Do you know where Joseph hides his phone?"

"Yeah. Do you want me to get it for you?"

"Yes. Now. There's no time to lose."

Raph found the phone and Charity called up Space-Village Talbot immediately. She explained to the woman who answered what was happening and why she had possibly only a few minutes before she was arrested.

"Is there any chance I can get onto a Wormcomm call?" she asked. "I want to tell Earth and Terraspei what's happening here while I can. The more we have praying for us and even putting pressure on the powers-that-be here, the shorter the terror will last."

Within a very short time, the phone beeped and a voice explained that he was the commander of the village. They had already decided to recall their families but they had been hard to contact. Remarkably, he agreed to her request without argument. He promised to call Joseph's phone as soon as they made contact.

"We need to get Beth and Joseph back to the village," said Raph.

"Yes," agreed Nathan. "Get around to Beth's school and take her to the farm. We'll go pick up Joseph and join you there."

"Let's hope we have time."

"No point in worrying about it," said Charity. "Just act."

"'Just Act' should be your nickname," he laughed. "I knew I was getting someone special when I asked for you but wasn't aware of just how special."

"Well, you do now."

"And, guess what, I like it. Short but very sweet."

"And you know, I think I might actually get around to loving you!"

"Act. Now!" shouted Raph. "No time for the sloppy stuff. This is all getting too much like a twentieth-century Hollywood blockbuster."

Ten minutes after they had all left, a marshal of the law came knocking on the door of the Williams house. He had not anticipated anyone at home and was quite content to wait. He would call back when Mr Williams returned from work.

Raph met Beth at the school gate and propelled her onto the woodland path that led to the farm. Nathan and Charity impatiently waited for Joseph, hiding behind some bushes on the country side of the gate. They began wondering if they had missed him when, all on his own, he emerged. Nathan called and he saw them and made his way towards them.

"What kept you?"

"Detention."

"What for?"

"Knowing too much. The maths teacher got irate when I tackled problems I wasn't supposed to know how to do. I didn't know they hadn't got that far in the book. Anyway, what's with you coming to collect me?"

Charity explained.

"Whoa. You did what? That's, like, so cool. They'll be out to get you now, though."

"Yep. Right now we've got to get back to Talbot. They're expecting you."

"Beth?"

"Raph's collecting her and taking her directly to the farm."

Just as they reached the farm, Joseph's phone rang in Charity's bag. Charity answered it.

"That's my phone," protested Joseph.

"Yes, and I'm using it... Yeah. This is Charity Williams... Yeah, we've got Joseph here... and Beth. We're at the farm now... OK, I'm listening. I'll put it on speakerphone so my fiancé can hear this."

"Right, listen carefully." A woman with a distinct Space-Village Talbot accent spoke slowly. Our contacts on Wormcomm are willing to talk to you. They know the situation. They understand how things are here but you can't do it on a phone. It must be on a direct line. There is a Wormcomm hub in your town. Apparently, it's working but not monitored. Have you got a laptop with a camera and SIM card of any kind?"

"It's got a camera but not a SIM card that I'm aware of. It's got Bluetooth but—"

"That'll work. Take this phone and put it beside your laptop. We can then programme your computer with the connectivity you will need."

"But they'll be aware of what I'm doing."

"Unlikely, unless they suddenly decide to try and open it. Up to now, they seem to have been avoiding their potential."

"The laptop is at home. The dog pack – the marshals are likely to call anytime."

"It's up to you. If I were you, I would try and brave it out. Where can you go? If you run, they'll find you. You'll have a better chance by pleading innocent."

"She's right," said Nathan.

"I guess. At least we've got this family heading back to safety."

"We can't leave you," protested Joseph.

"Sweet of you but no alternative," said Nathan. "It's Charity's problem. Brilliant as she is. You would only risk making the problem worse away from the village."

"How?"

"They might use us as hostages, son," replied his father. "Charity, Nathan, Raph, we are very grateful indeed for what you've done for us and this place. We pray that it may continue. For now, we'll say goodbye and hope it won't be long before we all get this sorted out and we can take our rightful place on this planet as its latest immigrants."

49

Before they left the farm, Dave suggested they take the now beautifully restored tractor-bike. It had taken a week but the battery seemed to be holding its charge. The previous day, he had test-driven it out and around the fields. The battery had held out well and he had had it on charge again for the past few hours. It was good to go.

Along with the battery, Dave McPherson had tried to recharge the farmer and his wife with a bit of hope but with poorer results. They were so conditioned to resist change that they just zoned out. They had no opinion about Charity and Nathan taking the tractor-bike. Nathan wanted it near to the Williams so that they had wheels if they needed them. The news that the McPherson's were going back to the space-village was clearly a relief to the farmer and his wife. They were not at all disappointed to lose them, despite the fact that Faith McPherson had bottomed most of the house and Dave had transformed the barn and farm. They had little interest in the experiments. They could now sink back into some kind of obscurity.

Nathan drove the bike with Charity in the trailer through the forest and parked it in a hollow behind the houses where people dumped their garden waste. They piled a heap of pruning debris on top of it until it was hidden. It would be easy to remove again when they needed it.

Getting back home, it was clear something had happened. Charity's dad was waiting for them.

"Where have you been?" he demanded.

"At the farm where Joseph and Beth's family lives."

"That's what I told them." He was clearly relieved.

"Told who?"

"The law. We've had a visit from a marshal. It appears there was a riot in town and someone upturned a tractor-bike."

Charity hated lying to her father but she knew better than to bare all.

"What?"

"They think it was you."

"Me?"

"I asked them how my daughter could possibly have turned over a tractor-bike. Tough as she is, she's not heavily built. They said you had help. I told them it couldn't be you because you'd have been at the farm."

"I was."

"Good. But watch out, they're on the warpath. From what I can make out, a lot of women were involved. Something to do with bread. The baker claims the guy made up the story to excuse turning over the bike himself."

"And men are not wanting to believe that," put in her mother. "Mr Hall's wife is accused of starting the riot by putting her large frame in the way of the young man."

"I'm sure she wouldn't have done that deliberately even if she was there. You know how big she is. Mrs Hall would find it hard to dodge out of anyone's way."

"Whatever's happened, the Ruling Council is angry. So just be sensible for once, Charity, and be a compliant young girl. I'm sure, Nathan, I can rely on you to keep her from doing anything hotheaded."

"No problem. She never argues with me."

"Good."

"I'd better go now," said Nathan. "If there is trouble, my parents will be worried if I delay."

"That's what I like to hear. A person who is sensitive to their parents' feelings."

Charity accompanied her intended onto the porch and saw him off.

"'She never argues with me'," she parroted, in imitation of Nathan's last remark.

"You don't."

"Only because you never boss me."

He smiled. "I didn't tell them that bit."

Charity giggled and Nathan took her into his arms.

"It looks like most people have clammed up. No man wants to dob his wife in. So, for the moment, you may have survived."

"Amazing."

"Seriously, though, Charity... if they find you online to Planet Earth..."

"I know. But the die is cast. They're expecting me. I'm not going to turn down this opportunity. What happened today is a reminder that we're not going to survive on this planet unless things change. Some way or another, I'm going to be either disappeared or the Ruling Council will fall – even if the space-villagers desert us. No one's going to survive anyway; we'll all starve to death under this present regime."

"I know. I'm not arguing with you. Just take care, OK?"

"I will. And I think I do love you, despite making up my mind that I was never going to love anyone. That's not a good thing. I wanted to be fancy-free... And I can't help getting anxious about your safety; you could get into trouble looking after me."

"You don't have to worry about me; I can look after myself. Just do your thing."

"My thing is getting a connection to Wormcomm."

"Do it." He smiled and kissed her as he took his leave.

Charity called the number on Talbot and explained she had her computer open and connected to the phone by Bluetooth. It took a few minutes but then she found a screen that she had never seen before asking her to sign in. She spoke to the woman who gave her a code and told her to choose a password that only she would know. "Share it with no one and don't write it down anywhere," she instructed. She asked about the McPherson's.

"Joseph and Beth and their mum and dad, are they with you?"

The operator spoke to someone and reassured them they were all safely back aboard. Charity breathed a sigh of relief but also of anxiety. Now that every one of their community was back, Talbot could depart at any time they wished. If that happened, Haven was doomed. However, she now had her Wormcomm established, and it wasn't dependent on her being in phone range of the modules.

She logged on and composed as strong a password as she thought she could memorise. She wrote it down on a scrap of paper and committed it to memory. Then she swallowed the paper.

Almost without any delay, she found herself with a choice of hubs to call up. There were three on Earth, one on Terraspei and one on Space-Village Talbot. Who should she call first? There was something drawing her to Terraspei - 'land of hope'. She clicked on Terraspei University. Instantly, she was presented with a screen depicting the university main building. It was amazing. It was a vast edifice that was at least five storeys high like nothing on her own planet. This place had been established at the same time as her own colony but it looked much more developed. There must be dozens of departments in that uni. On Haven, they had the Institute and that was it.

On the page, she had a further choice of contacts. She looked down them. They were mostly technical or academic but towards the bottom, she saw a link that was labelled 'Observatory young people's chatline'. She clicked on it, and there was Elle.

"Hi," said Charity.

"Oh, hi. You've caught me struggling with my maths. These surds are, like, absurd."

"I know the feeling."

"Where's Sam?"

"Sam? There's no Sam here. Are you on Terraspei?"

"Yeah. Who are you?"

"My name's Charity Williams and I'm calling you from Haven... er, Planet Pure Haven."

50

"Wow! Like, wow!" exclaimed Elle. "Like, I thought you guys weren't allowed to use Wormcomm."

"We aren't. Things are happening here and I've got this chance. Tell me about Terraspei."

"Sure. I mean, what do you want to know?"

"Everything. What's it like being sixteen where you are? What it's like being a girl? What do you study? Are you allowed to study what you like?..."

"OK. Yes to the last one. We have to do maths, a science and a language but after that, we can choose what we're good at, and what we find interesting. I'm into science. I want to be an astrophysicist. We've got an observatory a few kilometres out of town."

"Amazing. So you can choose the same as the boys, like on Earth."

"Yes. Gender doesn't come into it. People are people. It doesn't matter what sex you are. Whether you're male or female. I mean, there are even some people who are gender fluid. They start off as male or female but then change if that's the way their brains take them. So you can't make any rules for things being different for girls or boys."

"Amazing. I keep saying that, don't I? I wish it were like that here."

"From what I gather from Space-Village Talbot, that's why they've banned you from using Wormcomm, I guess. Stop you getting ideas."

"That's the plan but believe me, it doesn't work like that. They can try and make us be obedient females absorbed in our needlework and child-rearing but something inside just screams no. No one taught me to be revolutionary. I just am. And it's not just me. Most of us teenage girls are, and a good chunk of the boys, too."

"If I lived where you live, I'd be in trouble for sure."

"You're called Bubbles, right?"

"Who told you that?"

"Joseph. The guy who we were looking after from the space-village."

"Yeah. That's what they call me because I'm supposed to be like a fizzy drink. Say, how is Joseph? We haven't seen him for weeks?"

"He's fine. He's got on remarkably well in school, considering. But he's back aboard now."

"Look, 'Charity' - that means, like, 'love', doesn't it?"

"Yeah, 1 Corinthians chapter 13 in the old English translation. We've all got Bible names here."

"Great. So, look, why don't you join us tomorrow when Sam, Amy and their gang from Earth and Fran and maybe Joseph again from Space-Village Talbot meet up? I don't know how your days work on Haven but that'll be twenty-two and a quarter Earth hours from now. I have a clock here that runs at Earth time."

"That's easy to work out; it'll be just getting dark here then but we'll have had our evening meal and I can be alone in my room."

"Over and out till tomorrow, then. Bye."

"Bye. Don't let me keep you from your surds. Bye."

And then Elle was gone. What a girl. Full of *joie de vivre*. No one bubbled like that on Haven. Life was too serious a business.

Charity made a note of the link and saved it on her computer.

Twenty-two Earth hours later, Charity logged back into Wormcomm. She had collected Nathan and Leah to join her. A screen appeared saying they were letting the host know they were there. After a few moments, Elle appeared on the screen munching on some sort of cake. It made Charity feel hungry.

"Hi, Charity. You're early."

"I guess. Didn't want to be late. I've got my friends with me. This is Leah Donaldson." Leah smiled a hi and waved. "And this is my inten... boyfriend. He's called Nat."

"Oh hi, Nat. Is that short for Nathan? Another Bible name?"

"Yeah. All our names are."

"Nathan was the one to tell King David he'd been a naughty boy," explained Charity.

"Yeah. I know the story. I guess no one gets called Bathsheba, the woman in the story?"

"Amazingly, yes. There is one. But as far as I know, her intended is not called David."

"And, I guess, doesn't bathe outdoors with guys spying on her from their rooftops," added Elle.

Charity laughed. This girl was aptly named Bubbles. "Do you make everyone laugh all the time, Bubbles?"

"Most of the time. Can't help it... Ah, here's Earth, Sam and Amy. Hi. Meet Charity, Leah and Nat from Haven."

"Haven? As in Planet Pure Haven?! I didn't think..." began Amy.

"Yeah. Hi," said Charity. "Where there's a will, there's a way. I got the help of the space-village here. Please to meet you guys."

"Wow, that's wonderful..."

A fourth window popped up on their screens.

"Hi from Talbot-Theta. Can you see us? We can see you."

"Hi, Fran. Welcome," said Elle.

"Hi. Great to see you all... and you must be Charity and Nat. Joseph has been telling us all about you."

"We are. And this is Leah."

"Hi."

"Ah, here he is – the very man. Joseph, we've got your friends, Charity, Leah and Nathan on screen."

"Hi everyone," said Joseph, breathless. "Overslept. How are you all? Are you safe?"

"For now," said Charity. "They no longer think it was me that turned over the tractor-bike."

"Great. It was, though, wasn't it?"

"Careful," said Nathan. "You're forgetting yourself!"

"Yeah. Sorry. Walls have ears."

"The tractor-bike won't matter a jot if they catch us on Wormcomm," sighed Charity. "If we get caught, it'll definitely mean being banished."

"Yeah, I know," said Joseph. "You're always looking over your shoulder. Do keep safe. Accessing Wormcomm would be deadly if they catch you, considering no one's allowed even to suggest it exists."

Terraspei and Earth were glued to their screens – fascinated by a conversation between two parties on the same planet, both threatened in different ways by powerful overlords.

"That sounds really terrible," said Elle. "I just can't imagine."

"We feel so useless here," said Sam. "It's like you're next door but when you realise we're eleven-plus light-years away by standard radio waves and twenty-four years travelling even with the fastest transport, it's like, impossible to imagine. We can't do anything to help you."

"You've no idea just how much having friends somewhere means to us – wherever they may be in the universe. Someone to talk to about what it feels like to be living here on Haven. We daren't say anything about what's on our hearts here; you can never be sure it won't get back to our rulers. Your listening and being interested gives us *hope*. You're proof that human society doesn't have to be like it is here. There can be – *there are!* - places where people are free and justice is based on love. We've got that here inside many families – only not in the imposed regime run by the self-appointed Ruling Council."

"It must be dreadful knowing you might be punished just for sharing something they don't like," said Elle.

"Some of us handle it better than others," said Nathan.

Charity became defiant. "I believe it's only a matter of time before our corrupt, lying regime collapses. And thanks to Joseph and Fran and their people, that change is not far off."

"And the fact that if things don't change, we're all going to slowly starve," added Nathan.

"Oh, that's terrible!" Elle was visibly upset. "What can we do? I wish I could give you a piece of my cake."

"You can pray," said Nathan. "And I've tested it. Prayer works."

"You got it. I promise."

"And from us, too," said Sam. Truth to tell, he hadn't bent the Lord's ear much before but he would now. God seemed to be closer when things got bad. Maybe He was.

Leah began, "Tell us about things on—"

BANG! It was the Williams' front door. Mr Williams was storming up the stairs.

"Charity! We have to leave. NOW." She didn't expect her father home at this time of day.

"O... kay. Coming." Charity sighed. "Sorry, guys, we're going to have to go." But before she finished signing off, her father burst into her room.

"Charity. Right NOW!"

"What...? You can't just—"

"If you don't want to spend the rest of your life in the wilderness or wherever it is they send you, *now* is the time to leave. They are on their way."

"Who—"

"NOW, Charity. For goodness sake, do as you are told for once in your life. You can argue with me later. You, too, Nathan and Leah. You've all gone too far this time."

"Yes, sir. Come on, Charry."

"All right... Just let me—"

"NOW!"

The other wormers, still listening and watching on their screens on Earth, Terraspei and Talbot were, of course, watching all this. Elle saw the urgency on Charity's dad's face, not just in his words. "Go, Charity. Go. I will pray for you. Do as your dad says."

"OK. Bye, Elle. Catch up later—"

"Go!"

"Leave everything. Back door," barked Mr Williams.

"But they'll see who I've been talking to."

"THEY ALREADY KNOW!"

Her dad pulled at her arm and then she saw the total panic in his face. Nathan leapt to his feet. "The tractor-bike."

"You've got a tractor-bike? Where?"

"In among the garden waste over by those trees. It's got a trailer."

"That might just be the thing that saves us."

51

"What happened to them?" Elle demanded.

"I don't know," said Sam. "I think that man was Charity's dad. Something awful's happening."

Joseph and Fran were still on the screen but they wore alarmed expressions.

"I... I think the Ruling Council is coming for them," whispered Joseph. "It's dangerous out there..."

Dave McPherson poking his head into the shot. "You guys are going to have to end this call. Sorry, but the line is not secure. We'll let you know what's happening as soon as it is safe to do so." And then the Talbot-Theta connection dropped, leaving the Terraspei and Earth participants wondering what to do next.

"I think we should talk to our school head," said Sam. "There are people here who might need to know."

"And us, too," said Elle. "Can we make a date for the same time, tomorrow – Earth-time."

"I'll ask. Can't promise."

"Charity and her friends seemed pretty sensible," said Amy.

"Like they were going to get themselves somewhere safe?"

"Yeah. Maybe. Hope so... I think if anyone on Earth can do anything... it's kinda urgent," said Sam.

"Yeah. Get onto your headteacher and get the ball rolling – see if there is anything they can do... I'll do the same here."

"We'll talk tomorrow. Bye for now." Sam waved and he and Amy were gone and Elle was alone. She wished Anna had been with her; she must make sure she was the next day. It was a peculiar thing to feel so lonely, so isolated on a little planet billions of miles away from the action. On her screen was a picture of Charity's empty room. Emptiness. All of a sudden, the universe seemed to have just shrunk. There was nothing left but the familiar walls of her own room on a tranquil planet where nothing dramatic ever seemed to happen or even threatened to disrupt the calm. What was happening there on Haven was like on another world – it *was* on another world, six light-years away. She drew back her curtain and stared into the night sky. *I feel so helpless.*

In Harptree, Sam and Amy agreed that Sam should contact the school and let Mr Gilbert know what had just happened. Amy was about to leave for a camping weekend and had to get home to pack. Sam tried to contact someone at the school but with no success. Was he overthinking the urgency of this? He texted Amy. He wanted her opinion on what to do. She didn't text back and he tried to call her. Her voicemail kicked in.

"Hi, Amy. I've been trying to contact the school. It's out. Should we try to find Mr Gilbert at home?"

He waited. She didn't get back to him.

On Theta, the McPherson's were in immediate contact with the bridge. Dave reported that the Williams family was probably fleeing towards them. Their home, however, was on the other side of the town from the spacedrome fields. They would have to pass the houses clustered around the town hall and main church.

"There are two other possibilities," explained Dave. "Either they go on foot, which will mean trying to hide somewhere in the brush, or they will take the refurbished tractor-bike and trailer. If it were up to me, I would favour speed over stealth. If the marshals are already on their way and find them gone, they'll know they'll be heading here. All they'll have to do is put more guards on the perimeter and wait. No. My guess is that they are on the tractor-bike. We must be ready for them."

"Agreed," said the commander. "I'll issue orders to get ready for takeoff. That will keep them at bay. But we'll leave the ramp down on Theta for your fugitives to embark."

"Thank you, Commander."

"You may well thank me. I came to deliver three and a half thousand people onto the surface of this planet and, if this goes to plan, it looks as if I'll be leaving with more than I arrived with."

"To the spacedrome?" Nathan confirmed with Charity's father.

"Yes. It's our only chance of safety. If they see us coming, they might take us on board."

Leaving the house, Charity saw the whole family already assembled. They all followed Nathan swiftly across the open ground and into the hollow.

"Give me a hand," he called, and he began to lift off the pruning debris, revealing the newly refurbished tractor-bike and trailer.

"Wow!" said Luke. "Cool."

As soon as it was free of the debris, the young people and Mrs Williams piled into the trailer and, with Mr Williams standing on the tow bar and clinging to the back of his seat, Nathan drove out over the scrub.

"Keep out of sight of the road, son."

At that moment, Charity's pocket began to vibrate. It was amazing that she felt it in among all the drama. It was Joseph's phone. She read:

"Get to us. The commander will take you aboard."
"You sure?" she texted.
"Completely. He knows everything."
"On our way."

Just then, through the trees, Charity glimpsed two tractor-bikes racing along the main road to, presumably, their house. They would soon find them gone and might guess where they were headed.

"Did you see that?" she yelled.

"That was close. Too close," replied her father.

Two marshals on tractor-bikes drew up outside the Williams' house. All seemed still. The door was shut and there was no sign of life around the house.

"We've missed them."

"They were quick. They were definitely here. Control was monitoring them on some kind of electronic connection."

"Wormcomm, was it?"

The other stared at his colleague and gave a meaningful glare. "What's that?" he said, acerbically.

"Nothing..." He had temporarily forgotten that Wormcomm didn't officially exist. "They're not at home."

"Well, don't stand there knocking politely. Get this door open."

"Yes, sir." He prepared to shoulder charge the door while his colleague tried the doorknob. It was not locked.

"Sometimes brains are stronger than force," he mocked.

Inside, there was plenty of evidence of a speedy departure. There was a pan still hot on the stove, washing up in the sink and a pantry door stood ajar.

"Why don't you make yourself useful and go and look in that room while I do this one?" commanded the marshal to his dull-witted partner.

"OK. Your call." He received another glare.

In the bedroom, he found several half-eaten biscuits and half-full glasses of some kind of yellow liquid, which indicated that there had been at least three people in the room. On the desk stood a monitor and the computer was still running. The screen showed a picture of an oddly-dressed girl staring out of what looked like a window of some description. The girl moved.

"Hello," said the marshal, "I've seen most of the films in the TV archives but I haven't seen this one before."

"Oh, hi. Who are you?" The man looked like someone you wouldn't want to meet.

"You're not... live, are you? Can you see me?"

Instinctively, Elle tapped exit.

The marshal staggered backwards. The TV had seemed to see

him. Who was this girl and where was she? She was dressed in strange clothing. Quite attractive, too. His mate entered the room.

"There's a girl in the computer. She's live." He indicated the screen. It was blank.

"What the hell are you talking about? Why they have put me with such a thickhead, I'll never know."

"They've gone now."

"Obviously." He turned on his phone. "Sir, sorry to say we've missed them. Left in a hurry by the look of things..." The phone squeaked an order. "Yes, sir. Right away."

"Get on your bike if you know how to drive it. We're to head towards the spacedrome."

"Why?"

"Because that's where they're headed, idiot."

Elle felt she needed to tell someone and called up the uni hub and got through to the duty officer.

"Interesting. You have actually been talking to someone on Haven?"

"Yes." Charity explained. She finished with, "?And then this adult guy with a silly hat was staring at me, so I severed the connection."

"Wise. Very wise."

"I think Charity is in danger."

"Leave this with us. Keep your phone on just in case anyone wants to speak to you."

"Right. OK."

Elle called Anna and reported on what had happened.

"Can't leave you a moment, Elle," she laughed. "The minute I turn my back, there is an interplanetary crisis."

"Just hope you can be by my side tomorrow."

The next day, Saturday morning, Sam still hadn't heard anything from Amy. She'd probably be somewhere away from any signal.

Could it wait till Monday? No. It couldn't wait, he decided. He needed to talk to someone; someone should hear this, listen to what was happening or what they feared was happening 11.9 light-years away. Even if there was nothing to be done, Charity and her friends would be glad that someone cared. He was playing football that afternoon and was due to catch the bus. He would try Amy again when he was on board.

Sam headed for the bus stop. On, no. There, waiting for the bus, was Tanya Payne. *For goodness sake!*

"Hiya," she said, brightly.

"Hi."

"You look like you're lost in another world."?

"That's because I am. Look, Tanya, I don't want to talk – got too much on my mind."

Tanya looked fazed – for about two seconds. "Tell me about it."

"I can't."

She gave him one of her withering looks. He didn't wither.

"Try me."

"OK. Something terrible is happening on Haven."

"One of your mates on some exoplanet?"

"Yes. And I need to tell someone about it."

"You can tell me."

"Someone who might be able to do something about it. Like Mr Gilbert."

"The headteacher?"

"The very man."

"He en't 'ere."

What is with this girl? "I know that. It's the weekend."

"I mean, he's in Cambridge."

"Cambridge? How do you know?"

"Me dad said. He tried contacting him to ask if I could repeat year 11."

"I thought you had a job? Modelling."

"Oh, that. Give it up. Got bored."

"So he's not around, then."

"Not until Tuesday. Why so keen? Apparently, he and Miss Brankhurst have gone to Cambridge to talk about your Wormcomm."

"How'd you know about that?"

"Dad heard when he demanded to speak to him about me...? and me brother."

"You're brother?"

"Got suspended, hasn't he?"

"That's bad. How? I mean, what's he done?"?

"Nothing. Apart from giving old Brankarse some lip. She had it in for him from the start. Told him he'd better behave because she'd had enough of me when I was in her class. She told him off for doing something he didn't do and he gave her lip."?

"That's not fair." Sam recalled sitting outside the head's office with this girl for something he hadn't done.

"Too right. Anyway, Dad's got to wait till Tuesday."?

Tuesday!

The bus came. They got on. Leech Tanya sat beside him for the whole journey to Wells. She talked about what she was doing with her life, what was not working - modelling - and what was - working in a coffee shop. As the bus drew into Wells bus station, she stood to get off. No sour look, just a smile and with a "Thanks for listening," she was gone.

Sam tried Amy again. She hadn't replied to his text. He got voicemail again.

Cambridge, he thought. *That'll be the place where the hub is located. Maybe I can get the contact details.* After a few searches on Google, he came up with a number. He called it. He was answered by a pleasant voice. He explained who he was and asked if he could speak to Mr Gilbert. Something was happening on Pure Haven. The woman said they would ring him back. After ten minutes, as he was approaching the football grounds, his phone buzzed and he found himself speaking to none other than the director of the Wormcomm project himself.

52

"Charity," her mother was clearly angry, shouting above the noise of the tractor-bike hurtling through the scrub on the outskirts of the town, "you realise that you have your father to thank for coming for you. If it was up to me, I would have seen Raphael and Luke safe and not risked us all."

"How do you mean?" Charity had come round to the danger at last but could not yet understand why everything was kicking off at that precise moment.

"They were just waiting for you to be online with your off-planet friends so they could have incontrovertible evidence to prove you to be a liability, a loose cannon, a dangerous subversive."

"Dangerous? A subversive? But I only—"

"Have an opinion that is contrary to what you should have. It's one thing disagreeing with the powers-that-be quietly to yourself; it's quite another to broadcast them across the universe," said her mum.

"But..."

"According to some of the girls," said Raph, "you believe the Ruling Council to be 'monsters', their policies to be 'bullshit' and their interpretation of the Bible to be 'self-serving'."

"But I never... Oh. When?"

"At school. Walls have ears."

Her father turned and saw his daughter – a mixture of horror and guilt. "Yep. Both you and your beloved have made our job even harder."

"Harder?"

Her mum yelled in her ear. "There's a lot you don't know. Your father and his colleagues were on the cusp of bringing the Ruling Council to account but, no, you had to draw attention to us with your hot-headed pranks. With a little more time we might have taken a few keepsakes, at least."

It was at that point that Charity felt virtually naked. She had only the casual clothes she had on. No luggage, no handbag, no ID, not even a brush for her hair. All she had in her pocket was a used hanky and Joseph's phone. Her own phone was still on her desk with her computer open to anyone who wanted to examine them. But it wasn't just her – no one had anything. Leah was in tears. At least Charity had her family and Nathan but Leah was running away from all her loved ones. There had not been time to even give them a call. And it was all her fault... How had she been so unaware of her own father's involvement in some kind of resistance? Her respect for him trebled in that bouncing trailer. *Oh, Charry. You've been so full of yourself and your own self-righteousness that you could have blown the only real chance this planet had. And now we're fleeing for our freedom and ready to desert everyone here and it's all my fault..."*

Nathan was going as fast as he could but the going was slow off-road. They had passed most of the town centre, though.

"Get onto the road now, son. They'll know where we're headed by now. No hiding, just speed." Nathan drove them over a rough pile of dirt that lined the track and then the going was much smoother. Just another two kilometres to go.

Charity was silent for two minutes, which was a long time for her. Then she said, "We could be onboard the space-village for years."

Her father shouted. "If the village leaves, the revolution will have to go ahead without us."

Leah sobbed. Charity took her hand. "It'll be OK," she wanted to say but it wouldn't, would it? She said, "Sorry," and began to weep herself.

As they rounded the final bend with the sight of Space-Village Talbot ahead of them, Charity spotted their pursuers less than a couple of hundred metres behind. They were gaining on them.

Although they, too, were on tractor-bikes, theirs were unencumbered by a trailer full of people.

The gate to the spacedrome was, of course, both locked and guarded. Nathan yelled, "Hold tight!" As he drew level with the perimeter, he turned the wheel to the right and swung off the track. They plunged down a slope straight towards the paling fence. To Mr Williams' surprise, although apparently not to Nathan's, a section of the fence collapsed as they struck it. They rode over the palings, almost catapulting Leah out of the trailer but Raph grabbed at her and she fell back onto its floor.

"Aaow!" she yelled. Her elbow began to bleed and she clutched her head. "Oooow!"

"Nearly there," yelled Nathan as he swung the tractor-bike around towards the only module with its ramp still down – Talbot-Theta. The ramp may have been down but the craft was making an ominous sound and billows of dust began to spread across the field.

"It's ready to take off," yelled Dad.

Nathan got as close as he dared and then brought the bike to a stop. Their pursuers had followed them through the broken fence and were hurtling towards them and more guards were running across the field from the gate.

"Up the ramp," yelled Mr Williams. His wife leapt from the trailer but landed awkwardly.

"Oh, no! My ankle. Go! Leave me."

Without a word, her husband just swept her up into his arms and ran towards the waiting ramp, pursued by Luke. Raph and Charity had jumped down but a screaming Leah was struggling to get over the side of the trailer. "I think it's broken," she cried, clutching her damaged arm with her good one. Charity was too short to help her over. Raph got back into the trailer to lift her but their pursuers were almost upon them. Nathan rushed round to Raph's aid and together they got Leah out of the trailer and Charity steadied her onto her feet.

"Go! Run!" shouted Nathan. Raph took Leah around the waist and propelled her towards the ramp where his dad was waiting for them.

Then the marshals were upon them. The first one made a grab for Charity but she dodged him and Nathan swung an arm, connecting with his jaw.

"Run, Charity. Go, go!"

Charity hesitated but only for a second. The second marshal was coming for her and she took off towards the base of the ramp, easily outrunning the stocky man. Nathan grabbed him from behind and pulled him backwards as Charity's dad caught his daughter and pulled her up. On the ramp, villagers were urging them into the craft.

Nathan ran. A third marshal made a grab for him. He dodged sideways but the first two were back on their feet and the three of them overwhelmed him. Only twenty metres from the base of the ramp, they made sure of his capture.

"Nat!" yelled Charity but the ramp had begun to fold up and the hatch to close. There was nothing they could do to rescue him.

The last Charity saw of her Nathan was him being dragged back to the perimeter of the field away from the module as its motors roared into life. The air was filled with great clouds of dust and Haven grass clippings, taking both Nathan and his guards from her sight.

Charity was distraught. Her grief on top of all the adrenaline was unbearable. Her father put his arm around her shoulders but she threw it off – her mum stopped him from saying anything. He turned his attention to Leah, who was sobbing loudly, clutching her arm, with blood dripping down her face.

Joseph and his parents hurried towards them.

"Let us get you to sick bay," said Faith McPherson. "And you too, Mrs Williams. That ankle doesn't look good."

"Silly of me. Less haste, more speed."

"Welcome aboard. I'm Faith, Joseph and Beth's mum."

"You were at the farm?"

Faith nodded.

"What about Nathan?" pleaded Charity.

Before anyone could answer, a klaxon sounded and a

disembodied voice implored them to take seats and fasten safety belts. Everything was beginning to shudder. Charity found herself led to a seat from which she could just see through a large window. From the perimeter of the spaceport, she saw a line of tractor-bikes and marshals but no sign of Nathan.

Then the shuddering stopped and the dust cloud lessened. They'd stopped – they were going to rescue him. Charity's heart jumped for joy. But it wasn't to be. The lack of vibration only signalled that they were becoming airborne. The ground was receding beneath them and Nathan was down there somewhere, captured by the Ruling Council, who would have no hesitation in dealing with him.

53

As the adrenaline receded, Charity watched the ground disappear beneath a blanket of cloud and sank into a deep depression. She blamed herself entirely for the whole escapade. What *she* had done had led to this. She was the dangerous one. It was she who had defied the authorities and said what she thought without thinking that her conversations could be all too easily intercepted. It was she who had led Leah into danger. Betty had declined, saying it was all too risky and had refused to join them but Leah had been persuadable and now she was going to be isolated from her family, perhaps forever. And, above all, it was she who had landed her beloved Nat into the worst trouble of anyone. All the care he had taken to keep his profile low, denying himself the study he deserved - none of that mattered now.

"Nathan," she mumbled. She wasn't speaking to anyone but herself but her father read his daughter's mind, and her heart.

"He knows nothing," he whispered.

"What?"

"He knows nothing of the plans. He won't put the revolution into jeopardy."

"What plans? A plot?"

"The movement to remove the Ruling Council and replace it with a democratically elected authority."

"You didn't say—"

"Charity, do you honestly think anyone could have entrusted anything to you? And, besides, only those who need to know, know. That way the secrets stay secret and fewer people are in danger of being charged with treason."

"Nathan...?"

"Like I said. He knows nothing."

"What will they do to him?"

"Banish him probably. I doubt they'll do more." Charity sobbed. "But there is a chance the revolution will happen soon. Not as soon as we had hoped, though. Now that the space-village has left, the Ruling Council has regained the upper hand."

"My fault, again, I suppose."

"You could say that, Charity." She snivelled. "But I will say this. I would rather have a daughter who stands up for what she believes in than one without any gumption. And it's a hundred times better to be gloriously transparent than cunning and deceitful. You're a good person."

"But I've fouled it all up."

"No. Not all of it. It'll still happen. And you'll learn tact with age; what counts is where your heart is."

"Nathan."

"Is he more important than what you believe in? He wouldn't want it to be. I guess that at this moment he is overjoyed you got away and that he helped you to safety."

The module went completely silent. The red lights turned to green. They unbuckled and Leah and Dorcas were taken off to the sick bay.

"Are we really going to Earth?" Charity asked her father.

"If we're going anywhere, I understand it'll be Terraspei. They're not sufficiently equipped for twenty-three years but can manage the shorter journey of just twelve. I shall speak to the commander or whoever it is who makes those decisions. Maybe they can hold station in orbit for a few days. See what transpires below. In the meantime, you, Raph and Luke must make friends on board. And don't give anyone a hard time. Right?"

"If you say so."

"Not just because I say so, Charity, but because it is the right thing to do."

Joseph and Beth approached. They were anxious to show their friends the quarters that had been found for them.

"Mum and Dad have found beds for you all and Leah when she recovers," explained Joseph.

"An old lady has volunteered to give up her cabin so your mum and dad can be close by," explained Beth.

"That is more than kind," said Charity.

"You took us into your home. Now it is our turn to take you into ours."

54

The rumour mill – the most reliable source of true information – relayed the story. The Williams family had fled aboard the Space-Village before it had taken off. People said they were heading for Terraspei. It was also rumoured that Nathan Rogerson had been instrumental in helping them escape and had been taken into custody.

Leah's parents began to worry when she wasn't home for tea. She had told someone she was going around her friend's. They thought it was Betty's. But when they checked, Betty said it wasn't to her house but Charity's.

"They were going to do some connecting on Charity's computer," she said, "but I was worried that it might be, like, dangerous and said to count me out."

"So Leah was at the Williams' when they fled?" said Mr Donaldson, now apprised of the situation.

"Yeah. I guess," said Betty.

"And now if they are all aboard the space-village, you think that is where she is?"

"If she hasn't been arrested, almost certainly. She was with Charity."

"How dare they abduct our daughter?"

"She may have been scared of being arrested. If it were me, I'd not hang around to find out. Charity had a phone she could call up the space-village on. Maybe that's still around."

"W...What! She was phoning the village. How on Haven... I can see now why she was in so much trouble... and our Leah being part of it? I can't believe it."

"If you don't mind me saying, I think she's safer on board than

244

we are down here."

"But on her way to Terraspei," sobbed Mrs Donaldson.

"And there she will be free and have a better life."

"Now, Betty," urged Mr Donaldson, "you say nothing. Absolutely nothing to anyone about this. You understand?"

"One hundred percent. I only said what I said about Leah to you because you're her mum and dad."

"Good."

"What are you going to do when Leah doesn't show at school?"

"We'll face that when it happens. But you have no idea where she might be, remember?"

"As I said, Mr Donaldson, you can count on me one hundred percent."

The following day, the Ruling Council issued a statement. A spokesman said that Space-Village Talbot had decided that Pure Haven was not for them. Despite entreaties to stay and become part of the community, their elders had felt the place was not to their liking. According to the Ruling Council, this was an illegitimate act – the supplies and equipment stored in the holds of the modules had been amassed and dispatched by their supporters on Earth twenty-three years before for the whole of the existing community. It belonged to Pure Haven and the villagers were engaged in blatant theft. All possible measures would be taken to get the space-village back and put the elders on trial.

The Ruling Council claimed no responsibility for the action of the village elders. Their excuse was that they had become too accustomed to the confinement of the village and had decided to make a return trip. This wasn't entirely unfounded. It had long since been known that transitioning from a space-village onto a planet was a daunting step. What the Ruling Council failed to refer to was that there had also been a sizeable number of people who perceived integration into the ways of Pure Haven too difficult. The women in particular were very unsettled and families were frightened for their daughters but, of course, no mention was made of that.

No mention was made by the Council of the capture of Nathan Rogerson, either. Nor were the Williams family or Leah Donaldson referred to in the statement.

A week passed and still no official mention was made of anybody escaping on board Space-Village Talbot, which had now disappeared over the horizon. Leah was absent from school, of course, and rumours quickly spread because their classmates had seen her leave with Charity. The Ruling Council, however, was playing it cool – treating the whole space-village fiasco as history. Talbot had gone and that was an end of it. The entire Williams family, Nathan Rogerson and Leah Donaldson were among many before them who had just vanished. People were led to conclude that they had been banished into the wilderness like others before them. It was a subject that no one discussed – no one dared to commiserate with the Donaldson family.

Betty Jenkins suffered perhaps more than any of them. Now, she had absolutely no one to talk to at all.

55

Parked in a Haven-stationary orbit on the opposite side of the planet from the settlement, the elders and residents of Space-Village Talbot were getting a detailed description of the history of the colony from Jonah and Dorcas Williams. They outlined how the original idea of a perfect society based on love and generosity had, in their opinion, degenerated into an authoritarian regime. As the resources diminished, self-appointed ruling councillors had imposed a status-ridden regime in which they and their families were kept comfortable. Any suggestion that would involve sharing power with people outside of their circle was dismissed. The elite knew best.

"They rule by fear," Jonah explained to a group of elders. "Anyone who breaks the rules is just 'disappeared'. We are in terror of waking up one day and seeing our children gone. They made it so families are forced to constrain their children, especially the girls."

"Why should that be?" asked one young father. "Why especially the girls?"

"I think they are scared of them," said Dorcas. "My theory is that women pose a threat because we generally put our children before status. The Ruling Council justify their actions by using verses from the Bible to claim women are the second sex. But you can see from the stories of Jesus and the early Christians it wasn't like that among the first followers of Jesus. Women sometimes even took a leading role."

"Jonah, is that your opinion, too?"

"It is very hard for fathers. Children are taught at school the rights and wrongs and a father cannot be seen to behave so

247

differently without risk of losing status, income and even their home. Fathers are made responsible for training their children. Anyone who allows privileges to his daughters is in danger of being disciplined and having any status he has accrued removed."

"That puts you in an impossible position," reflected the young father.

"Without status," said Jonah, "you are far less likely to be able to feed your family. Status is everything – it represents survival. Charity, here, doesn't take kindly to being constrained; we had to be very strict with her. We didn't like doing it but she scared us. We felt she was too hot-headed..."

"And so it proved," mumbled Charity. "I didn't realise... But the more you held me down, the worse I became."

"That was becoming obvious. We were on the point of thinking we were going to have to tell you more about the plans for the revolution when Nathan came onto the scene and we didn't want to bring him into the plot. If it all went wrong, it would have been worse for both of you if the authorities found out... Plus we were determined to share the plans with only those who needed to know. With Nathan also at risk, we decided we would wait."

"Your young man?" asked one of the elders. "Is he the brave lad who was arrested getting you all safely to the ramp?"

"Yes." Charity snivelled. "Nat. Oh, Nat." She broke down. So much had been her fault. If she had been less rebellious, she would have been trusted. "If only I had been less stupidly arrogant..."

Her mother reassured her. "To be honest, Charry, Nathan encouraged you, didn't he?"

"I guess."

"And he wouldn't have chosen you if you had been like everyone else," put in Raph. "He bid for you because you flouted the rules."

"Without him, we would all have been captured," said her father. "Charity, you must be proud of him."

"But what will they do to him?"

"Banish him. They won't hurt him. He will feel free to talk – answer all their questions – because he knows you're safe. They won't need to torture him. And he knows nothing of the plans."

"But where will they send him? Where do banished people go?"

The intercom sounded an announcement from the bridge of Alpha. The modules were aligned and the gangs were ready to reconnect.

"We are holding station behind the planet," said an elder. "If they cannot see us on our way, they'll guess where we are. In your opinion, would your 'plotters' prefer the authorities to know we are waiting or see us leaving?"

"If they think we're really gone, the Ruling Council might relax and be less vigilant," said Jonah. "The revolution does not depend on the space-village. A new regime will know they can always call us back."

"I'll ask the commander. If your revolution is a success, we'll return."

"That's wonderful," exclaimed Charity, almost hugging him but restraining herself in time.

He smiled. These were good people. "Pleased to oblige."

With the modules safely reconnected, the new arrivals were shown around the village. There was so much of it. Leah didn't join them – she was still in sick bay on Theta being examined by a doctor.

"I definitely think you've damaged the bone. Now that the gangs are reconnected, I'm going to send you to the infirmary on Beta. They can scan you there and we'll know the best way forward."

"It hurts... a lot."

"I know. I'm going to administer a local anaesthetic."

"I don't like needles but—"

"Needles? You're a hundred years out of date. They gave up using needles on Earth long before my parents were even born."

"On Haven it used to be like that, I think. But they have gone back to using needles. Pretty blunt ones, too. Are you a real doctor?"

"Now what would a real doctor look like?"

"A man."

"Ah. I see the problem. I'm fully qualified and this new Wormcomm is helping me to get right up to date. There are ten doctors on Talbot; five are men and five are women. And we have ten more in training. Now, let's kill this pain and get you to Beta."

She passed a small device that hummed lightly over Leah's elbow. The pain eased and she instantly relaxed.

When they arrived at the infirmary, Leah gasped. She had never seen anything like it. It was gleaming with all kinds of machines.

"Are all these for healing? Healing machines?"

The doctor smiled. "They are rather out-of-date now but were state of the art when we left Earth. With Wormcomm, however, we have already managed to begin recalibrating them. And our medical engineer is studying the blueprints for a new design."

"Will this machine make me better?"

"This one is just for diagnosing the extent of your injuries. There is a treatment suit in the next bay."

"There is nothing like this on Haven."

"There would have been if your Ruling Council had accepted us. Beta and Gamma were to remain with all the technology and stores sufficient to last us until the next space-villages arrived. Two are on the point of departure from Earth as we speak. Our intention was to open a new medical school on the planet and train young people to be a new generation of doctors."

"Including girls."

"Of course. Would you like to become a doctor?"

"You mean a real doctor?" Leah was amazed at the possibility. "I... I wouldn't be clever enough."

"That's to be seen. Your talents will emerge as soon as we can get you into study. Now, lie here and keep still. Allow the diagbot to do its job." A strange but pleasant-looking machine wheeled itself forward.

"It's singing."

"Music helps you to relax and allows it to work efficiently."

"It's alive?"

"It's empathetic. It senses your feelings but it's not alive like we are. It remains an it."

Across the room, a screen lit up with the diagbot's findings. The doctor cast her eye over them. "The bone in your elbow is chipped. And you have a scalp wound above your right ear. Those can be easily mended. And it shows that you haven't eaten for twenty-four hours as well as revealing deficiencies in your system that indicate you have been short of several vitamins and minerals for some time."

"I haven't eaten today. We ran away instead."

"Quite. And before that?"

"We eat when Dad gets home. So last night."

"No breakfast or midday meal?"

"We have breakfast on Sundays. And only old people eat in the middle of the day."

"I would say, young lady, that you are on the cusp of malnutrition."

"The harvest was poor last season."

"I don't doubt it. So it's next door for the treatment. It won't take more than ten minutes and then it'll be just being gentle with your elbow for a month."

"Treatment?"

"Another machine. But I'll be supervising it. It'll repair the bone and you won't need any more anaesthetic. It'll feel sore for a day or two but then you'll feel 'right as rain', as they say... ah, rain... I do miss the rain. We've got everything we need here but no weather."

"Rain is vital for the crops."

"Indeed. The planet needs us and we need the planet."

"Are we going back, then?"

"That all depends on your council, doesn't it?"

Leah shuddered and began to cry. The idea of the Ruling Council allowing change was unimaginable. "I miss my family."

The doctor walked her into the treatment room. The machine

didn't touch her but filled her arm with a warm soothing sensation that complemented the gentle music it sang.

"I like the music," said Leah after the bot backed away and went silent.

"Music heals. Now, what I am prescribing for you is a balanced intake of food consumed in the traditional manner together with vitamin and mineral supplements."

"I'm tired."

"I know. We'll see you're reunited with your friends and given a comfortable bed."

56

On Terraspei, Elle and Anna were instructed by the uni hub not to use Wormcomm again until they got official clearance.

On Earth, Sam and Amy were getting similar instructions. They were not to try and get online to Wormcomm. "Leave this to us," the director at Cambridge had said. Sam and Amy wondered what could be done and if anyone connected with the project could do anything constructive. It was all happening so far away.

On Talbot, Joseph and Fran were also being told to keep off of Wormcomm until further notice.

"The Ruling Council on the planet will be monitoring everything," the comms officer warned. "They have already hacked into Charity's computer at least once. That's how they knew where to go."

"So we can't call up our friends on other planets, even?"

"Not for the moment. Not until we assess the situation with the hub on Haven. They may have been monitoring you but we're monitoring them. They are keeping quiet but we know their microportal is being kept alive."

"Our friends on Earth and Terraspei will worry about us."

"I suspect that if they reported anything to anyone, their hubs will be telling them the same thing. They and you will all have to be patient."

A shadow passed across Joseph's face. "Leah's, like, fretting for her family. They don't know she's here."

"I'm sure they'll have guessed that. But be assured Earth, Terraspei and ourselves are in contact on encrypted channels. Anything that can be done will be. And as for what happens with our negotiations with people on the planet, you can trust your elders and our commander."

After her conversations with the Donaldsons about the circumstances of Leah's sudden absence, Betty spoke to no one. No one doubted what had happened but no one talked about any of it. All except her brother, who was gloating in her grief. He became unbearable, accusing her of being the one responsible for her friends having to flee.

"It's all your fault. They'll all have been banished by now."

"You don't know that."

"Oh. I do." He tapped his nose. "They've all been apprehended but I'm not going to let on to you where I got that from, am I? You can't be trusted."

"It's not true. They're on the space-village."

"Says who? Do you know that? If someone's saying that, you'd best report it so they can be dealt with."

"You're mean and horrid."

"They could come for you being friends with those kinds of people but, don't worry, you're not worth it."

With Charry and Leah gone, Betty didn't have a friend anywhere.

At school, her classmates gave her a wide berth because being associated with Charity Williams made her an untouchable – not that anyone was in the habit of talking to her anyway. At home, her father was savage in his wrath. Talk of his daughter being connected with the Williams, who had been 'disappeared', made him furious. He had just been elevated to the lower ranks of the elite and he was not going to allow his daughter to bring him down. Betty's best strategy was to keep out of his sight.

She took to wandering outside in the strengthening spring Taushine. Anything to get herself outside of the house. Her father didn't seem to care she was not at home and even if she missed a meal, no one seemed to ask where she had been. She had been seen about, just ambling in the scrub that surrounded the edge of the town, looking at the things that grew there. If it increased the speculation that she was off her mind, then all to the good. She was harmlessly mad and her family could pass her off as unrepresentative of the rest of them. Her brother told everyone lies about her. He made up stories of quirky things and odd behaviour and laughed about it.

Betty began to think that even if the stories her family told about her were untrue, they were probably right to say she was quirky.

Betty didn't quite acknowledge to herself that her wanderings outside the house would deliberately take her near the now silent Williams' dwelling. It had once been a centre of activity filled with Charry's energy. Just to see the place reminded her that, wherever she was now, Charry had had time for her and, even if she never met her again, she had been befriended by a very special person. Charry didn't give her friendship to people lightly. And it wasn't just Charry; her brother Raph too had been really nice to her.

Around four or five days after the crisis, Betty noticed the back door was slightly open. Had they returned? She hurried to the door and knocked but all seemed silent within. She pushed at it lightly and it opened wider. She looked into the kitchen and immediately she could see that the place had been looted. Stepping inside, she saw open cupboards and the pantry door ajar. It seemed like it was food that they had been after. Most of the utensils and tableware had not been touched – they hadn't owned anything grand enough. She ventured further into the house. The robbers had gone for the linen – sheets, towels and even a few of the better clothes were missing. The furniture appeared to remain but was bare.

Betty headed for Charity's room. She felt as if she was stepping onto holy ground. Charry had been full of life, straightforward, honest and caring. Maybe she could still find traces of her there. But the room had been violated – her bed had been stripped, the pillows were missing and her wardrobe had been ransacked. Hardly anything that spoke of Charry's character remained. Her desk had been tipped over but her files were still there. They were strewn about – files of maths and science notes that told Charry's story. At least they remained. Betty righted the desk, picked up the papers and put them carefully and neatly back in their folders.

Then another find. Under the bed lay Charry's laptop, open and on its side. Whoever had been in had not been interested in computers. Betty pulled it out and set it back on the desk. She was about to close the lid when it turned on; her touch had woken it up. It opened on a page inviting her to log on to none other than Wormcomm. *Charry must have been chatting on Wormcomm when she had to flee. I wonder... should I?* Betty hesitated for about five seconds. *Go for it. Charry would. I have nothing to lose. I don't care if they banish me – I'm kind of banished already.*

The charge was low; she needed to find the lead and searched further under the bed. She found Charry's phone and pocketed it. She would give it back to her when she met her again, which she surely would. At last, she came across the lead at the back of one of the drawers and plugged it in. The house still had power.

She found Charry's stool. Righted it and sat at her desk. Her friend was feeling closer. In her actions, Betty was sort of bringing her back. She checked the on-screen menu. 'Earth', 'Terraspei', 'Talbot'. She double-clicked on 'Talbot'. Almost immediately she was presented with the face of Izzy in comms.

"Space-Village Talbot," she said. "To whom am I speaking?"

Betty may have been ham-fisted at many things but was gifted at saying things clearly and succinctly. She explained who she was and where she was.

"Hold this line," said Izzy. "I will put you through to the commander."

As soon as Commander Pritchard had been apprised of the connection, he ordered Izzy to call up the McPhersons and Williams.

"Hello," he began, "I'm Commander Pritchard of Space-Village Talbot. What is your business?"

"I'm Charity William's friend, Betty. I'm on her computer. I just wanted to ask if she was OK."

"She is safely here aboard. Your Ruling Council knows that."

"They haven't told us anything. Everyone's just vanished."

"Well, Betty, the news is good. Perhaps you can tell us exactly what the situation is in your township."

Betty answered all his questions as truthfully as she could. Then the commander smiled and said he had someone who would like to talk to her, and there, on her laptop, was the smiling face of her friend Charity Williams.

57

etty's tears flowed as Charity chuntered on about the events of the escape. She listened as her friend poured out her love and despair for her lost boyfriend. There was something Betty could do. She could go around to Nathan's family, assure them Charity was OK and find out more to tell her. She could visit the Donaldsons and tell them their daughter was safe and cared for. She could even take them Charry's laptop and see if they wanted to risk talking to her over Wormcomm.

Charity told her to be careful, though. If Wormcomm had been monitored before on her laptop, it could be again.

"I don't care," Betty said. "They can do whatever they like to me. I am happy now. My father has rejected me. He's been made a member of the elite and he wants rid of me. To be banished would be better than being placed in the secure detention for the insane."

"Aw, Betty. That's awful."

"While I can, I'll do anything I can to help you and—"

"Just a minute, Betty, did you say your father has been promoted to the elite?"

"Yeah. Ridiculous as it may sound."

"Hold on."

Unbeknown to Betty, Jonah Williams had been listening to everything. He didn't want to appear on screen in case it was being monitored but he had a question for Betty. He mouthed it to her.

"I have a question," continued Charity. "If your dad is now part of the elite, has he been called to the Town Hall yet to be formally inducted?"

"No. Not yet. Apparently, they have a meeting tomorrow morning. I'm not supposed to know about it. It's to be kept secret but he is so delighted in his good fortune that he told my brother loudly and I overheard. They are all gathering tomorrow morning. It will be his first meeting and they've got some sort of initiation thing lined up for him."

"Wait up, Betty." Charity's dad was signalling that he had an idea. "Er..." Charry looked at her dad. "Betty, would you like to be totally brave and do something for us?"

"Anything. I don't care what it is. I'm not feeling scared of anyone."

"OK. This afternoon, would you go to the bakery – you know, the one where I, with the help of a few others, turned over the tractor-bike?"

"Yes."

"Knock on the door and ask to speak to the baker himself. No one else."

"Yes."

"And tell him the elite have a secret meeting at the Town Hall tomorrow morning. As far as you are aware, they will all be there."

"Yes. No problem. Is that all?"

"Tell no one but the baker you have spoken to me."

"Got it. No one else. Not even under the pain of death." And she meant it.

"I hope it doesn't come to that, Betty."

"You know what, Charry, I don't care. I feel free. I reckon, literally, like I'm the most privileged girl in the whole of Haven!"

"Do you know what, Betty? You probably are. Now you'd better get away from the house. Take my laptop with you."

"I will."

"Stay safe."

"I'll try."

"Bye. Love you."

"Love you back, Charry."

Betty couldn't remember anyone telling her they loved her

before, not ever.

Picking up Charry's backpack off the floor, Betty shut the laptop and put it and its lead safely inside it out of sight. No one would even begin to suspect Charry's battered backpack was not hers.

She contemplated going home first but thought the quicker the errand was done, the better; there was no telling when the authorities would catch up with her.

The baker was on the point of going to bed. Normally, he was the first to rise in the early hours, ensuring that the colony had fresh bread for breakfast.

When she arrived, she found all was quiet and still. The baker opened his door to Betty's gentle knock and was surprised to see a young sixteen-year-old girl. Girls were not in the habit of coming to the bakery, even when the shop was open.

"Can I help you?"

"May I speak to the baker, please?"

"I am he." He looked the part. His clothes seemed to be covered in a light dusting of flour.

"I have a message for you."

"From whom?"

"That doesn't matter. I have to tell you that the elite are holding a secret meeting in the Town Hall tomorrow morning."

"The elite. Will they all be there?"

"I think so. My father has just been elevated to elite status. It will be his first time."

"So if it includes him, it will include them all."

"That's the impression I got."

"Thank you. I won't ask your name. Better that I don't know it."

"Is that OK?"

"That is perfectly fine. You have done a good thing. You can be proud of yourself." He gave her a meaningful wink and her heart leapt. "Wait here." He went onto the rear of the shop and returned with a freshly-baked bread bun. "Just for you. Don't be seen eating it."

"Oo, thanks"

"Now off you go. Stay safe."

After she had gone, the baker took out his phone and texted a very select group of people a simple message:

Bright day tomorrow.

Among those included was a large lady who was often at the head of the bread queue. He could trust her to pass on the message that there would be no bread tomorrow. Then he went to bed; he could have a lie-in tomorrow morning.

58

Emboldened by their raid on William's house, their capture of Nathan and the departure of the space-village, the Ruling Council felt relieved. Most of them were delighted to see the back of it, despite the fact that they had been robbed of their rightful resources. They had been greedy for the supplies and facilities on board but they had disagreed among themselves about the course of action to take. Now the modules had gone, however, and they were united again. The rioting outside the bakery had left them with metaphorical egg on their faces but now that the disrupting immigrants had gone, they believed the time was ripe for the re-establishing of their authority.

They now felt free to call a full meeting of the elite in the Town Hall but, just to be on the safe side, they insisted on it being kept a secret. But because of what Betty had done, it was a secret no more.

Unbeknownst to them, a meeting of this nature was exactly what the plotters were waiting for. All the people of influence would be together in one building, including the chief of the marshals. The operation had been dubbed: 'Bright day'. Now the wheels were in motion. All it needed was the council to send for bread. Which is precisely what they did.

The elite wanted to make a point. They deliberately dispatched the same rider as before to collect the same number of loaves from the same baker. It was to be a statement of authority. They would show beyond doubt who was boss.

The young marshal pulled up his bike outside the bakery as before. He was relieved to see there was no queue that morning. This was going to be easy. The baker greeted him, however, with open palms.

"Sorry, lad. There is no bread."

The young man began to panic. "What do you mean, no bread? There will be no riot today; I can call a troop of marshals. And, in any case, there's no queue. Here's the order." He placed a list of the bread required, written on valuable paper, into the baker's hand.

"Sorry. As I said, no bread. No flour, no bread."

The young marshal couldn't return empty-handed a second time.

"Yes, there is. Where is it?"

"No flour, no bread. If you would like to place an order for tomorrow..."

He pushed the baker aside and stormed into the bakehouse. The ovens were cold. The baker hadn't been lying.

He panicked. "Where can I get bread?"

"The families have been asking that for months. It's worse for me. With no bread to bake, I have no job. Why don't you go and see your bosses in the Town Hall and ask them where I can get flour? Then I would be more than happy to bake them bread."

"You're being impertinent."

"Only truthful. If you and your families are hungry, I suggest that you and your marshal friends out there go and ask those in charge of this town."

The young marshal stomped out of the shop. There was clearly no bread; there had been none baked that morning. He called his colleagues. It hadn't occurred to him to check the bakery cellar, where several sacks of flour were stacked.

A sergeant arrived with a few men.

"What's to do here?" complained the sergeant. "There's no trouble. Back to your beds, lads."

"No, don't leave me. I can't go back to the Town Hall without any bread. They'll kill me," protested the young marshal.

"The Town Hall? Bread?"

"It's the same as last time when we had the riots. The Ruling Council wants to make a point... but there's no bread. I don't know what to do."

"Are you sure?"

"He's not lying. The ovens are cold. What are we going to do?"

The sergeant and his men stood around shuffling their feet, thinking of ways to tell the Ruling Council the news they didn't want to hear.

"The space-villagers," said one, "they've deserted us. Without them, it's only a matter of time before our kids starve. We all know the score with the village gone."

"The village is just holding off. They'll be back," said another.

"No. I watched it last night. They came into view; they were moving away. Then they went into full drive and quickly moved out of sight."

"I saw it, too," said a third. "They went in the direction of Terraspei."

"We've got to get them back."

"How?"

"The Ruling Council has done this. It's them that has scared them off."

That was bold. It was on the cusp of treason. They fell silent – not even any shuffling of feet. The truth had been uttered but it was forbidden to speak against the Ruling Council. The truth was that no one wanted the villagers to leave except the councillors.

Eventually one spoke. "One thing's for sure. We can't give the Council any bread. They won't like that."

"They'll get angry with us. I don't like the way this is going to end."

"We need to stick together," said the sergeant in charge. "It's OK, young man, we'll not let them do anything to you. Let's bring them the bad news."

Watching from his shop, the baker sent a text to several people:

'Bright day. Imminent.'

His large female customer activated a chain of calls among the wives of hungry families without bread – the same ones who had spread the news to keep away from the bakery that morning.

Inside the Town Hall, the chief of the marshals received the text. He was expecting this. They were ready to act. 'Bright day' was the message he wanted to get. He hadn't known until an hour before, when he had been summoned to the Town Hall but the baker had known. Good work. He relayed the signal.

Bright day. Imminent.'

His co-conspirators would drop everything and make for the Town Hall. The baker would ensure the women did their part. With a bit of luck, they might even accomplish this before Space-Village Talbot was not that much farther away.

On arriving outside the Town Hall, the sergeant sent the young marshal in with his news that there would be no bread... again.

He wasn't gone long before he ran back out of the building pursued by a tirade of loud vitriolic words, a fuming councillor and the chief of the marshals.

The chief spoke calmly to the councillor. "Let me handle this. Go back inside. I'll see we get the bread."

The councillor's temper eased. Seeing the marshals in number, he felt reassured that due authority would be restored.

As soon as he had retreated, the chief ordered the young marshal to park his tractor-bike up against the rear doors of the Town Hall.

"But, sir, they open outwards," protested the sergeant. "It would prevent them from opening."

"Precisely. Do as I say."

A broad smile appeared on the sergeant's face. "Do it, lad. You've had your orders."

"Yes, sir." He got back on his tractor-bike and drove it around to the rear of the building.

"I think we can settle this business of the space-village returning," smiled the chief.

It didn't take long for women to start to appear on the streets. Tentatively at first but when it became clear they would outnumber the marshals, more and more joined the throng. Soon they began to pour into the area in front of the Town Hall.

Inside, panic was mounting. The marshals didn't seem to be doing anything to disperse the mob. Women were a problem; they needed to be controlled. They sent out a spokesman – a junior elite – to speak to the chief.

The sergeant barred his way. "Sorry, mate. You're going to have to stay inside with your friends until this situation is sorted."

"He's right," said the chief. "I fear the only way we can get these people to disperse is if you agree to contact the space-village and bring it back."

"The village has gone. The villagers would not agree to our terms." He was seething at the chief's insubordination.

"They will come back on their terms."

"Unthinkable."

The women were getting more and more restless.

"What else can we do? This town will be ungovernable. The discontent is too far gone. If it has to be on their terms, then so be it."

"But they are ill-disciplined thieves and a lot worse."

"Whatever. They hold the solution to the future of this planet. Whatsoever they demand, you accept."

"But—"

"We want freedom to choose who governs us," yelled the large woman who had spoken out during the first riot.

"Call the space-villagers back," shouted another. "We like the way they treat their women. Let *them* decide how this place is run."

"Call them back! Call them back!" chanted a strident woman amidst the growing tide of people. Soon the chant was taken up by the whole crowd. "Call them back! Call them back!"

Alarmed, the councillor retreated back inside the building. Some of the Ruling Council were now trying, unsuccessfully, to get out of the back door.

Soon men began joining the crowd and for a fleeting moment, the sergeant half expected them to try and pull their women away but instead, they took up the chant, too. They even deployed themselves to prevent councillors from escaping from the windows.

"Keep them inside until they give in," commanded a large mechanic.

Finally, as if by magic, more marshals began arriving from different directions and ploughed their way through the mob to the front doors.

"Let me back inside. I'll handle this," said the chief.

"They're angry, sir. Very angry," said the sergeant.

"No doubt, Sergeant. But they are also terrified and wondering how they will get out of this. We don't want violence, Sergeant."

"Absolutely not, sir. All the people want is to see the space-village back."

"Me, too, Sergeant."

The door was prised open enough to allow the chief in. The chanting continued.

59

It didn't take the ruling councillors long. They feared for their lives, despite the reassurance of the chief of the marshals that his men would ensure there wouldn't be any violence. But he was also of the opinion that they would become beyond thirsty and hungry before they would be allowed to leave the building.

"We're not going to allow Space-Village Talbot back on their terms. The traditions of this colony are paramount. We have a pure culture that should never be tarnished," said one.

"I'm sure you will be permitted to maintain your culture – live your lives as you and your families choose," said the chief. "But you cannot deny that it is in the overwhelming interests of the ordinary people of Haven – Pure Haven – that the space-village returns."

"They are demanding elections. We don't do that. And they allow their females to exercise power that should only be accorded to men."

"Maybe but if we can't give the women the bread they need for their families, you can see what happens."

"This is a conspiracy."

"Call it what you will, can I tell the mob out there that you agree to recall the space-village?"

"Not on their terms."

"Then, I fear. We will all die of thirst before they disperse."

"Force them to."

"My marshals will not use violence unless it is in defence of the person, sir. We will keep you safe but we will not apply force to disperse them."

"This is insubordination, chief. We will have you removed from office."

"You may do as you wish, sir, when this emergency is over. For now, I suggest you take my advice and placate this mob."

"And recall the space-village on their terms?"

"Whatever it takes to bring them back and share their blessings with us."

"*Their* blessings. They are *ours*."

"But they have them, so we need them back whatever it takes."

Ten minutes later, the chief texted the baker.

Fire up your ovens. Bright day achieved.

Then he called his men to open the front doors.

"We are to escort the Ruling Councillors' delegation to the Institute," he told his men. He raised his hand. The mob fell silent.

"Your Ruling Council has graciously agreed to contact Space-Village Talbot and negotiate their return. They have promised not to conclude the negotiations until the return is assured.

"And now I have it on good authority that the bakery is firing up its ovens and your bread will be available."

The mob cheered.

"Now, please allow the members of the Ruling Council through to the Institute, from where they can contact Talbot. There is to be no violence."

The marshals formed a path through the crowd and began to escort the leading members of the Ruling Council to the communication centre in the Institute. The angry mob hurled abuse at them – abuse that had been stored up in their hearts over decades, held back only by fear. They crowded in but the large woman and her friends called for calm. "Let them through to do as they have promised."

The call came through to Alpha.

"It's the planet's Ruling Council, Commander," reported Comms Officer Izzy. "They want to negotiate. Persuade us to return... on our terms, they say."

"It took longer than I thought," said Commander Pritchard. "They know the villagers' terms. Put them through... and call the elders together."

The commander expected a negotiated return but what he heard amazed him. The conditions the Ruling Councillors accepted were even more radical than they had been before. They not only agreed to there being an election but also asked the elders of Space-Village Talbot to organise it.

The elders desired that a vote would be given to everyone of the age of sixteen and over, irrespective of gender, status or how long they had been on the planet; it included all the villagers. Questions pertaining to education and opportunities for girls would be left to the newly elected council to decide, although they hoped proper note would be taken of the traditions and founding principles of the Pure Haven colony.

There was no further discussion. The practical details could be ironed out as Space-Village Talbot sped back to the spacedrome.

60

People lined the streets as the first hundred people from the Space-Village made their way over the four kilometres into the heart of the town. Among them were the Williams family and Leah, who was bouncing with health and joy at the prospect of being reunited with her family – if not with the boy she had been promised to. She had her speech ready if he tried to hold her to the former arrangements.

On the perimeter of the town, the chief of the marshals greeted them. He fell in beside Jonah Williams.

"You were right. It was only a matter of time. The stupid Ruling Council played into our hands."

"They really had no idea so many were conspiring against them?"

"Apparently not. They were too taken up with the shenanigans of your Charity and her determination to access Wormcomm."

"So she was not a dangerous loose cannon then?"

"Quite the opposite. She provided the perfect smokescreen."

The long ears of Charity heard her name.

"You talking about me?"

"Just saying you caused the Ruling Council a lot of work."

"Their fault. When do I get to vote?"

"As soon as the elders get it organised. Now, why don't you show a few people around town before they have to return to their village quarters before it gets dark?"

"We're going to Leah's."

"Of course. And don't forget to apologise."

"What for?"

"What for? For getting their daughter aboard a space-village on its way to Terraspei," he smiled.

"She's much healthier for her trip. All the food."

"Maybe. But just put yourself into the shoes of her mum and dad."

"Yeah. Got you. We were never going to go all the way to Terraspei, were we?"

"If the conspiracy had been compromised, yes."

"But it wasn't. Nathan knew nothing... Oh, Nat. Where do they banish people to?"

"Leave that to me, young lady," said the chief. I think I know who to ask.

"People just disappeared. Sometimes you wonder whether they were killed."

"No. I don't think that was the case. But I suspect that the experience could be life-threatening. Leave it to me. You can wait a few days, I hope?"

"Your mission now, Charity," said her father, "is to get Leah reunited with her parents."

They hadn't gone far when Betty came running up to them.

"Betty!" They hugged. "You did brilliantly."

"I know. I didn't know I was delivering such important information. I had no idea."

"Well, we could not say too much in case you were being monitored."

"I know. And if I had known how important my message was, I might have panicked and screwed it up."

"No, you wouldn't. Those things are your strength."

"Thanks... Oh, this is yours." Betty passed Charity her backpack containing her computer and handed over her phone.

"Oh wow! That makes me feel like—"

"Less naked," laughed Leah.

With the new arrivals, the colony now consisted of nearly forty thousand people, four-fifths of whom were sixteen or over. No one seemed to have a list of them all. At least, the councillors didn't admit to one. There had been no need.

It was decided to trust the honesty of the people. On the first dry day, tables were erected outside the Town Hall. There were ten of them, each of them labelled with letters of the alphabet. People joined queues according to their surnames. An official was appointed to take their names and issue them with a scrap of paper on which they could write the name of any one person on the planet who they thought would make a good candidate for election.

After three days the names were collected and assembled into piles. The top fifty were then consulted. If they were willing, their candidacy was published. Some declined the opportunity to stand.

Charity was amazed to discover she had been nominated by ten people. She was in the top hundred of the nominations but, to her immense relief, was not in the top fifty. All she wanted was the opportunity to study – and get her Nathan back. Betty revealed that she had nominated her and so had other school friends.

"We need people like you in charge," she told her.

"Thanks. But I don't want to be on a council. I just want to be able to do science at school."

"Maybe for now. You're a natural leader."

"I prefer being a rebel."

Betty laughed. She was right. Charity would always be a rebel. But Charity didn't laugh with her.

"Why so sad?"

"How can you ask that?"

"Oh. Sorry. Nathan. I should have been more, like, tactful... aware."

"That's OK. It's not your fault. How's it going with your fiancé?"

"Dumped him already – within hours of the announcement that you were coming back. The old idiot didn't know what to say. He said he loved me. As if. He knew he only got me because no one bid for me. One thing's for certain, things have changed – he can't do anything about it."

"I'm pleased for you, Betty. I really am. I didn't want to be allocated a fiancé but it turned out I liked him.

"And now he's gone."

The fifty names were put before the public and thirty of them were elected. The new council was in place after just two weeks. They consisted of both men and women – the youngest being only twenty – and included three people from the Talbot, two of whom had served as elders. There were no members of the former Ruling Council, although no one had prevented them from standing. The first thing the newly elected did before appointing an executive was to rename themselves the 'Haven Assembly'. The term 'Ruling Council' had too many bad connotations.

The process had been smooth and remarkably fast but not for Charity. When would the chief come back to her about Nathan? Weeks had passed but Charity had heard nothing about Nathan from him. Had he forgotten? She resolved to get the question of the banished on the agenda of the new council.

That evening, while she was on her computer at Leah's, Charity received a call from Fran and Joseph. They had now been given clearance to call up their friends on Earth and Terraspei. Would Charity and Leah like to join them?

The experience of the space-village had changed Leah. She seemed to Charity to have grown up, to have grown into being less of a kid. When she got home, she found herself caring for her parents, who had found her disappearance even more distressing than she had. She was reassuring them every morning. And like Betty, she had no hesitation in ending her betrothal. It didn't surprise her that he was relieved; his heart had always been for the girl he had put first at the Annual Betrothal Festival and she had had no compunction in ditching the son of a former member of the Ruling Council to take up with him.

"Wormcomm? Go for it. Count me in," said Leah. "Without the subterfuge, it feels almost normal."

"Sounds cool."

"Oh. I'll have to call home and tell Mum what I'm doing. She needs to know when I'm online."

"That's a new one. Tell your mum."

"We're not keeping secrets anymore. We've had enough of that."

"That's good," said Leah. "The old ways made everyone secretive – even inside families. If we can't be open and able to trust each other even at home, then there's something wrong with things. It's amazing how it's changed here with the space-villagers. If they hadn't come here, we'd be doomed."

"I know. And Wormcomm has made all the difference, too. The more connections we have the richer we all are."

"It's about listening to people. Everyone's got something to say about how the worlds work."

"Hiya, Elle."

"Charity! Leah! You're back."

"Yep, back on planet Haven and back online."

"You've been for a round trip into space, I gather."

"Indeed. If things hadn't been sorted, we would be meeting you in person in twelve Earth years."

"You would have been welcome."

"Thanks. Actually, that was the best bit of it. Your place sounds really good. But things are going the right way on Haven now. We're going to set about exploring the possibilities of getting food from the local plants. Talbot has got a fantastic analyser that can detail the composition of every plant that grows here. It will assess its nutritional value and indicate any possible poison it may contain in an instant."

"Yes. We do the same here. We have been doing it for at least eighty years."

"Not on Haven."

"What's wrong with people?"

"It's all about power and control, I guess. If you want to boss things, you only permit the things you can understand and think you can manage to your advantage. But, in the end, you can't control nature. If you interfere with it beyond where it wants to go, you destroy it."

"Climate change on Earth. Great example. Restore the conditions in which things evolved and it recovers – so long as you don't let it go too far."

The screen opened a new window displaying a smiling Sam.

"I heard that. It's true. I can't imagine what it must have felt like when climate change was threatening everything. Some people even decided not to have children because they didn't feel they could inflict a broken Earth on them."

"While others, like my ancestors, took to the skies," said Elle.

Charity and Leah explained blow by blow what had taken place on Haven since their last catastrophic meeting.

"So where's Nathan?"

"He didn't make it," snivelled Charity. "He got us all to the space-village but was captured and we haven't seen him since."

"He's alive, though?"

"We don't know. The longer it goes without finding him, the more likely it is that he isn't."

"Can you go out and look for him?"

"We've no idea where to start. The chief of the marshals says he's onto it. He says he's trying to find the old guard enforcers but they've gone to ground. Someone will know but no one's owning up to it yet."

"Something else for prayer," ventured Sam.

"I appreciate that, guys."

61

"*I* have new bosses now," said the chief to one of the leading former ruling councillors. "And I am charged by them to find those whom you banished."

"If you had done the job you were appointed to do, you would not have new bosses. You're nothing short of a traitor. When we have re-established ourselves, you can count on being properly dealt with."

"I'll face that when that happens. For now, there is a Haven Assembly that wishes me to find the lost."

"'Haven Assembly'," mocked the former councillor. "Appropriately, they seem to have dropped the 'Pure'."

"And you're pure?"

"Yes."

"That's a matter of opinion."

"Don't put yourself into the place of God."

"And God says you're right and pure?"

"It will all be revealed at the coming of the Lord on the last day."

"On that, we agree. For now, I want to know where the banished are. I trust they haven't been summarily dispatched."

"Of course not. But as for their whereabouts, I cannot help. I didn't deal with that side of things."

"So who did?"

"I really have no idea."

"OK. I'll interview each member of the former oligarchy one at a time."

"Oligarchy?"

"Sorry, that was a tad judgemental. Ruling Council. And as the members are all 'pure', I expect them to tell me the truth."

"Truth? You've no idea what that is."

"As I understand it, truth is of God and God is love and compassion and all about setting people free to be who He has created them to be. So it says in Scripture."

The former councillor wasn't in the mood for arguing about the Scriptures. He wanted this man gone.

"The truth is I do not know where your banished are."

"I believe you. You might, however, point me in the direction of someone who would know."

A day later, the chief was organising a search party out to the west. It transpired that people had been transported to the western wilderness, there to survive or perish 'as the Spirit deemed fit'.

They had been blindfolded and driven in a trailer for several hours – as far as the driver could go, leaving time to return home in daylight. There, the banished were left in the bush with nothing but a loaf of bread and a litre of water. What happened after that was left to God – or fate. No one knew what happened to them. None of them had been seen since, although one driver, when pressed, reluctantly reported seeing smoke on the horizon.

The chief called together a search party of selected men. Out there in the wilderness life could become tough.

"We'll begin a search half a day's journey away. We're looking for any sign of human beings: tracks, clothes, water bottles, bones."

"You don't expect to find anyone alive, Chief?"

"If I dropped you off with a single loaf and one litre of water, how long would you survive?"

"There are green things they could eat. And creeks. It's not really a wilderness in the desert sense. It's no different from what our ancestors encountered when they first arrived on Pure Haven."

"Except that they had a space-village around for a year or so to get them established."

"How long will we be gone for, sir?"

"Pack enough provisions for seven days. You'll need tents and a solar battery charger."

"Yes, sir."

Four tractor-bikes with two trailers and six officers set off due west. They held out little hope but after three days they caught sight of smoke to the north. On the fourth day, they found an old campsite with a blackened heap of burnt brush.

"If they have the capacity to light a fire, they have the ability to cook," said the leader. "We may well find someone alive."

On the fifth day, they found increasing signs of human activity: a burnt log, a whittled stick, a footprint in some dried mud and a cairn – a heap of stones placed, presumably, as a waymarker. As they approached a forest of Haven oaks, what they saw astonished them.

"Are they houses?" said the search leader.

"No. Can't be."

"They are, you know. Look, through those tall trunks there are at least three wooden houses with turf roofs."

"And gardens. A proper settlement."

Getting closer, they saw more and more houses. It was a sizeable village.

"How are we going to do this? They could kill us."

"Keep down."

But it was too late. They had been seen by some children playing among the trees. The children fled screaming back to the houses. As the search party watched, adults gathered them up and disappeared into the forest. They vanished, camouflaged by strange robes the colour of the trees themselves.

The marshals entered the village and stood silent in the 'main street'. Everyone seemed to have left.

"What now, sir?"

"Wait. Do nothing. Don't approach the houses but be on your guard."

After what seemed like an age, a single man with a long white beard dressed in rough cloth to his knees emerged from one of the houses. He carried nothing.

"We come in peace, old man," said the marshal leader.

"You come from the Ruling Council. While they rule, there is no peace."

"The Ruling Council is no more. We now have an elected Haven Assembly. They have dispatched us to find the banished and invite you back."

"Why? Why should we return to the town? Here we are free. We do not need your ways. You are not welcome here. If you mean peace, you will leave us be."

"We have no plan to take away anyone's freedom. You seem to have a good place here – even children. If any of you wish to return, you may but if you wish to stay here in the wilderness, that is your choice."

"I have been here three decades. This is where I belong."

"Of course. But in particular, I am looking for a recently banished boy." He showed a picture of Nathan on his phone. "Have you seen him?"

"Who wants to know?"

"His fiancée, Charity Williams, and his family. He was among the last to be banished by the former regime."

"Wait here. No one is to move if you want to return to your loved ones."

The man ambled back to one of the houses but he soon returned.

"We don't trust you. The girl you mention is no longer on this planet. What do you want of us? Do you plan to banish us a second time? No one has sought to return and cause trouble. We have already been banished."

"If you have heard that this girl has left the planet, then you must have found her boy. She is no longer in space. The space-village has returned and the Ruling Council has been overthrown; things have changed in the town. I promise you, no one wants to disturb you, least of all banish you a second time. The young lady is desperate to find her beau and I promise you, she and her family are back home and she misses him."

On hearing this, Nathan stepped forward out of the shadows.

As soon as the marshals were in range of the settlement, they phoned ahead and a crowd had gathered to meet them. At the front of them was Charity with her family, the Rogersons and the relatives of the others.

"I won't believe it until I see him," said Charity in tears. Her mother hugged her close.

"Best not have too high hopes. He's not going to be in good condition, is he?"

"I don't care. If he's alive, I'm going to get him straight into the hospital on Beta with all their marvellous machines."

The crowd parted to allow the tractor-bikes through. They hadn't even stopped before Nathan leapt from one of the trailers and gathered Charity and his family in his arms. The people applauded. Nathan smelt of the wilderness – a smell that Charity would henceforth greet with joy.

62

"**S**o tell us again... from the beginning," demanded Charity.

"OK. So I was thrown into a horrible room in the white house – you know, the closely guarded building at the back of the Institute."

"Behind the high fence. We always knew that was a bad place."

"They wanted to know what I knew about a conspiracy. 'What conspiracy?' I said. I knew nothing of any conspiracy. They wanted to know who was involved. Of course I hadn't any idea and it was obvious I didn't.

"So then they quizzed me about Wormcomm. At first, I protested innocence but it soon became clear they had been monitoring your attempts to connect, so I confessed that we knew all about Wormcomm. Everyone did. No one talked about it because it was off-limits.

"They said some horrible things about you – horrible words you didn't deserve – but I knew you were safe off the planet, so I told them everything. Leah and your family were all safe. I told them you wanted to study science and I wanted to find ways of using local plants for food. We weren't interested in revolution – just getting them to listen to ways of making things better. At that point, they lost interest and ordered me to be banished. Then they left me locked in a room with no windows. It was pitch black and there was no way out, so I just sat and prayed for you and everyone."

"What about food?"

"They gave me nothing to eat or drink. And, before you ask, I just had to pee in the corner and, judging by the smell, I wasn't the first to do that. No one came if I called; I don't think there was anyone there. I began to wonder whether they would just leave me to die. That was rather scary..."

"Anyway, at what turned out to be first light, a couple of marshals turned up, blindfolded me, led me out and put me into a trailer behind a tractor-bike. I could hear another bike start up alongside ours and we pulled out after them. I had no idea where we were going only that it was not along any road. At what felt like midday, they stopped. Tau was at its zenith; it was almost hot but I knew it would be cold at night. They took off the blindfold and gave me two loaves of bread and two litre bottles water. Double rations, they said. They were not unkind. One of them told me to follow the smoke. Then they drove off and left me.

"In the distance, away to the north with Tau at my back, I spotted what looked like a bit of a forest. Under the trees, I thought I would survive longer; I might even find a creek of some kind. What I was going to eat, I didn't know but if I could find some of the leaves we had been working on, I could at least put them to the test.

"Before Tau set, I reached what turned out to be a forest of Haven oaks. I had consumed most of one of the loaves of bread – they hadn't given me anything in the white house, so I hadn't eaten for twenty-four hours before that.

"Then, to my surprise, I saw a woman. I thought my eyes were deceiving me at first. Robed in a long shift, she partially blended into the background. But then she called me.

"Within minutes, I found myself in among wooden houses built from the forest trees. Bark walls, turf roofs and even bark floors. I was welcomed like a long-lost son, although I knew no one. There were people of all ages – they're onto their fourth generation now, many of them born there in the so-called wilderness. But there's no wilderness about it – they have developed everything from scratch but it's a stable community.

"In the twenty days I was there, I learnt so much. They use local plants for food, medicines, rope and cloth. They weave robes, make shoes and hats – you name it, they have it. They catch multicellular creatures from the swamps which border on animal rather than vegetable, which probably provide protein – they must get protein in abundance from somewhere because their children are healthy and strong. They have no metal tools except for a few they managed to shape out of belt buckles but they make better paper and ink than here in Haven town. They all read and write. In short, they have done everything our Ruling Council has failed to do to adapt to the planet. It seems that the people who get banished are often quite intelligent because they pose the greatest threat, so they are not short of intellectual high-flyers."

"You sound to have had a whale of a time. Going back?"

"It was a good time but no. I missed the things electricity can give, the textbooks and the potential benefits of Wormcomm."

"Is that all?"

"I guess there is the little matter of a girl I fancy, too."

"So you're not breaking up with me, then?"

"Why should I do that?"

"The list of called-off engagements is as long as your arm because it has all been arranged over our heads."

"Correct. You had no say. Allow me to put that right," he sank on one knee. "Charity Susanna Williams, will you do me the honour of becoming my fiancée?"

"OK. If you insist. Now, get up you daft thing. It's time to stop teasing one another and plan what we're going to do with ourselves in these new times.... Oops, here's my dad and Raph and Luke."

Her dad and brothers joined them.

"What would you like to do? Now that you can choose?" asked Nathan, pointedly.

"I want to finish school – study science and maths like the boys. What about you?"

"I would like to work on all the possibilities of adapting to this planet. We have so much material to work on with the generations of discoveries made by the settlement of the banished. They call it 'Ham Village', you know – home village."

"I guess a few would like to stay there?" suggested Dad.

"A few of the recently banished are coming back I think but most will want to stay where they are. We can trade things and help them install a generator – they already use wind and watermills, so it wouldn't be difficult to set it up. We certainly need to build a road so we and they can come and go and share our knowledge. I would like to persuade them to found a branch of the Institute dedicated to horticulture there."

"On board Talbot they have a machine that can analyse every plant in minutes. We must collect samples of their food plants to look at," said Charity.

Nathan nodded. "With the Ham Village experience and the space-village technology, I think we have a very bright future ahead of us. All we lacked was good government."

"Good governance is key," said Mr Williams. "The elected assembly has put in the new constitution that every official utterance purporting to be fact has to be verified by an independent interplanetary panel of experts. No more making up truths that favour the few."

"Like males are more intellectually capable than females," scoffed Charity.

"It was proved centuries ago that that is complete nonsense," said Raph.

"But that made no difference to the Ruling Council because it didn't suit them," said Nathan. "They brought us all up to believe it and a lot of those we went to school with still do. We need to guard against that happening again with our generation."

"But things are different now," said Charity. "We have Wormcomm to put us in touch with the whole universe. It will be harder to get people to believe lies."

"Wormcomm is brilliant but what worries me is that it also gives opportunities to corrupt people from outside. It might make it harder for our former Ruling Council but easier for evil off-planet predators bent on leading young and vulnerable people astray."

"It will." This was Jonah Williams. "Every new technology can be used for good or evil. And some are bound to try and exploit it.

But you have to believe that, in the end, the good will overcome the bad. If it didn't, humanity would have destroyed itself millions of years ago."

"I can't work out whether you're a pessimist or an optimist, Dad?"

"Both. I'm a realist. Each generation will meet the challenges when they arise, and defeat them. For the moment, the good has triumphed here on Haven and my children are fortunate to be young enough to enjoy it. It's time for them to spread their wings and to have fun."

"Yay! Life has to be fun, at least some of the time," declared Luke.

<h1 style="text-align:center">63</h1>

The Stanton Wick whizz kids looked positively down-in-the-mouth. The final exam was done. The next few days for them were going to be especially trying. Maths and Shakespeare were a pushover compared with preparing for and attending the Summer Ball.

First, there was the tricky and unpleasant issue of finding a partner, and then having to dress up in a way that would make them feel stupid. Some would have been tempted to duck out of it if it weren't for the risk of being totally isolated for the whole of the summer break.

Sam Brooks, however, was quite different. Somehow, having sisters, he'd been surrounded by girls all through his teenage years and he had got used to their ways. He had not been interested in dating any of them. He wasn't alone; more than three-quarters of the girls in his year had had no time for romantic attachments either. It was just a matter of securing a willing partner for the beginning of the evening. Sam had been pleased that Amy Huck asked him if he would partner her. If she hadn't, he would have asked his sister to ask someone.

As was the custom, on the night of the ball, Sam, driven in the family car by his proud mother, called for Amy.

Amy came to the door in a stunning dress. It was midnight blue with silver sequins which Sam's brain kept trying to form into stellar constellations but soon got distracted by the curves beneath. Curved spacetime. He wondered whether Einstein had got his idea from taking a girl to a ball.

"Don't forget to get her back before midnight," said Amy's

father admiring his made-up daughter now almost as tall as him. Sam hadn't made any arrangement with his mother to collect them; he hadn't thought about getting home.

"No problem, Mr Huck. I think the ball ends at eleven. I'll bring her straight home." Was that a slight look of disappointment on Amy's face?

On arrival at the ball, they spotted none other than Tanya Payne on the arm of a large guy. She was dolled up, of course, but actually – strangely – looked quite cute.

"How did she get in here?" whispered Sam. "She left last year. I just don't seem to get away from her."

"Guess she was invited by the guy who she's with."

"Oh, no. He's our right wing-back."

"Who?"

"He plays for our football team. He's good."

"Well, he looks as if he's good with her."

"Amazing. They must have met in Tanya's coffee shop in Wells. I hope they're happy."

"They look it. She hasn't given you a second glance."

"Free at last."

"Free? That depends."

"Oh? On what? I've no idea what you're talking about."

She took his arm and led him to where neither Tanya nor anyone else could see them, leaned into him and gave him a light kiss on the cheek. Sam was forced to admit that there was chemistry involved when being kissed by a beautiful girl in midnight blue – chemistry of a variety that didn't require a Bunsen burner or even a laboratory. Or it may have been just because it was Amy...

An especially exciting thing about the ball was the giant screen that had been erected at the end of the hall.

Mr Gilbert was so full of pride for being the head of the pilot school for the Wormcomm connection and 'interplanetary worming' had been made the theme of the ball, so Sam and Amy and their off-planet friends were to be the kings and queens of the night. On the screen would be projected live pictures from Terraspei and Haven. All the members of the link would be in attendance and they had all dressed in their finest for the occasion, the first ever interplanetary high school ball.

Elle, Anna and their band were there from Terraspei. And Mrs Bannister and Mrs Patel turned up with their husbands to represent the staff along with their headteacher.

And, literally, having a ball on Haven were Charity, Nathan, Joseph and Beth. Zac and Leah were there looking snazzy in matching outfits and Raph had a glowing Betty on his arm.

Towards the middle of the evening when the music gave way to allow the partaking of tables of food, Elle went, "Hi Raph. Introduce me to your girl."

"Yeah. This is Betty, my girlfriend."

"Your girlfriend? Not just like for the ball?"

"No. She's my for real girlfriend." Betty was grinning from ear to ear.

"I didn't think it worked like that on Haven. I thought the boy had to wait till he was twenty and there was some, like, bidding process."

"There used to be. But not anymore. Betty was betrothed to some old guy but with the old regime gone, she told him where to go and I asked her out. Our dads had no say in it. All the former status stuff has gone and all Dad wants is for his kids to be happy. And Mum, too."

"Well, congratulations!"

"Thanks," said Betty.

Just then, the screen flickered and a full-face picture of Commander Pritchard appeared. "Allow me to crash the party," he said. "I just want to remind you that your wonderful shenanigans are being broadcast across the entire universe and all of us on Space-Village Talbot-Alpha are having a ball watching you. May you be blessed on Haven, Earth and Terraspei. See you guys on Earth in twenty-two years! Keep working at improving the specs. Have fun! Goodnight." And then he was gone and the music started up again.

As Charity held onto her Nathan during a slow waltz, she reflected that wherever you are in the universe – tiny planet or space-village, at the beginning of your life or at the end, and ready to move on into a new dimension – everyone is on a journey of discovery. The story never ends.

ACKNOWLEDGEMENTS

Without many wonderful and inspiring people, including teenagers and young people, this book would not have been written. I have received a lot of advice and direction in putting together this story. I am grateful for everyone's patience and encouragement.

Particular thanks go to authors John Lynch and Nigel Messenger for their guidance. David Clarke, Sian Rees, Mary Cookson, and Anne Hewett, all experienced in working with teenagers over many years, have been especially helpful. Also to Molly, Katie, and Anya, who have devoted time to reading through the draft manuscript despite being caught up in exams and other demands of teenage life.

Anna Hewett-Rakthanee began reading and illustrating my work when she was just fourteen. Now at eighteen, she is studying illustration at university and has designed the cover for *Breakthrough*. She is also one of my encouraging beta readers.

David Stubbs has given me some mathematical lessons for what has turned out to be more of a science fiction novel than when I first conceived it. Thank you, David. I hope I have got it mostly right. However, the emphasis is on the fiction rather than careful science, so readers with STEM expertise must forgive the liberties I take with scientific method and accuracy.

As always, I am indebted to my wife, Tina, for her advice, editing, proofreading, and for bringing me copious cups of tea!

And, last but not least, my thanks to God who both listens and empowers.

Trevor Stubbs
August 2025

The FLIP! trilogy

Most people think that life for kids is kinda predictable. But imagine if everything just flipped! Literally.

Whether you like it or not, you find yourself sucked into a spooky grey existence before being dumped back into the world looking like a complete idiot.

And it goes on happening - "the fifth"?...

Cut off from everything they know, will the forces of darkness overcome them?

Trevor Stubbs

... and what are all the daises for?

TABITHA

Millheaton has no claim to fame, being just another West Yorkshire Victorian mill town long past its glory days. On the edge of the town lies a large 1930s council estate, the home of Tabitha, a thirteen-year-old only child of an estranged black father and a white mother. As she grows into her teenage years, her nemesis, Gareth (Griff) Green continues to bully her, but now, as their hormones kick in, things take on new dimensions. How is Tabitha going to cope with it all, and where is Griff's toxic obsession with her going to take them?

9 781915 288134